'And now, ladies and gentlemen, it is my great pleasure to present to you that brilliant, courageous and beautiful young dancer who twice nightly risks her life to give you the most sensational dance of the century! Ladies and gentlemen: Susan Gellert in the Kiss of Death!'

The lights flashed up and in the middle of the stage stood a blonde girl in a G-string with a six-foot cobra draped around her neck. The neck in question being insured for one million dollars . . .

Also by James Hadley Chase

AN ACE UP MY SLEEVE
JUST ANOTHER SUCKER
I WOULD RATHER STAY POOR
LAY HER AMONG THE LILIES

and published by Corgi Books

James Hadley Chase

Double Shuffle

CORGI BOOKS
A DIVISION OF TRANSWORLD PUBLISHERS LTD

DOUBLE SHUFFLE

A CORGI BOOK 0 552 09550 8

Originally published in Great Britain
by Robert Hale & Co. Ltd.

PRINTING HISTORY

Robert Hale edition published 1953
Corgi edition published 1974

This book is set in 10-on-11½ pt. Plantin

Corgi Books are published by Transworld
Publishers Ltd.,
Cavendish House, 57–59 Uxbridge Road,
Ealing, London W.5.
Made and printed in Great Britain by
Cox & Wyman Ltd., London, Reading and Fakenham

Double Shuffle

CHAPTER ONE

I

Maddux's hard, gritty voice barked out of the intercomm. on my desk and woke me with a start that nearly broke my neck.

'I want you, Harmas.'

I hurriedly snatched my feet off my desk and knocked over the telephone as I pawed frantically for the key on the intercomm.

'I'm on my way,' I said, trying to sound less like a Zombie than I felt. 'Be right with you.'

The box grunted and went dead.

Besides being the head of the Claim Department and my boss, Maddux was the smartest assessor in the business, and that means something in this dog-eat-dog insurance racket. I had the misfortune to be one of his investigators. My particular job was to check up on any applicant our agents brought in who Maddux thought was shady, and as he was suspicious of his own shadow, I was kept pretty busy.

As I pushed open the door leading to his outer office I wondered what I was walking into. For the past week there had been an insurance convention at the City Hall, and agents and their sales managers from all over the world had gathered to talk over business, discuss future policy, get to know each other and see how much whisky they could soak up. As our agents had been attending the convention, I had had a nice quiet rest. But I had a feeling my rest was over. When Maddux sent for me it meant only one thing – work.

Patty Shaw, Maddux's blonde secretary, was rattling the typewriter keys furiously as I entered. I paused to admire her. Anyone who could work as hard as she did and still look cute fascinated me. She glanced up without stopping her incessant pounding to give me a bright smile.

'You may not believe it,' I said, bending over her desk to read what she was typing, 'but he sent for me. Do I go in or do I wait?'

'Get in there or there'll be trouble. If I don't finish this. . . .' She rolled her blue eyes and began to pound the typewriter keys again.

I rapped on Maddux's door. He bawled for me to come in.

As usual, he was partly submerged by a mass of papers strewn over his desk. His thinning grey hair was rumpled and his red face was screwed up into a scowl. He wasn't a tall man, but he looked tall at his desk. He had a torso of a prize-fighter and the legs of a midget. Whenever anyone wanted to take his photograph for publicity purposes he always had them take him at his desk.

'Sit down,' Maddux snapped, waving an ink-stained hand to an armchair. 'I have a job for you.' He pushed aside the papers before him. Most of them fell on the floor. Neither of us made a move to pick them up. That was Patty's job. She spent a good half-hour every night clearing up Maddux's office after he had gone home. 'What the hell have you been doing all this week? Nothing much, I bet.'

I sat down.

'I can always keep myself employed,' I said airily. 'What's cooking now?'

Maddux scowled at me, opened a box of cigarettes, took one and pushed the box over to me.

'Maybe you remember I spent a week in New York about three months ago,' he said, as he reached for the desk lighter. 'You may also remember the old man himself took over my desk.'

'Sure,' I said. 'I missed you.'

'Never mind that,' Maddux said, his scowl becoming ferocious. 'I know how much work you did that week; about as much as you've done this week.'

'Every machine has to have a rest,' I said mildly, 'but why resurrect the past?'

'While I was away,' Maddux said, 'a policy was accepted by this company I wouldn't have touched with a twenty-foot pole. The old man didn't see anything wrong with it, and that fool, Goodyear, who sold the policy, couldn't see anything wrong with it either. But that's to be expected. All our agents can think about is making commission.'

That was unfair; Alan Goodyear was our best salesman, but the trouble was he was earning nearly as much as Maddux in commissions alone, and that infuriated Maddux.

'What's wrong with the policy?'

Maddux ran his fingers through his rumpled hair and let out a snort that lifted some more papers off his desk to the floor.

'It's not a proper policy. That's the first thing, and a company of our standing has no business to issue an improper policy.' He banged the desk with his clenched fist. 'This policy was specially drafted to meet the requirements of the applicant. Did you ever hear of such a thing? We spend thousands of good dollars every year employing lawyers to draft fool-proof blank contracts, and then we have to write one ourselves.'

'Would it be an idea to start at the beginning?' I asked. 'That is if you want me to know what you're talking about.'

'Yeah, we'll start at the beginning,' he said, 'and for Pete's sake, listen.'

'While I was in New York last June,' he went on, 'Goodyear went down to Hollywood about Joyce Sherman's fire and theft policy – Joyce Sherman, the movie actress.'

Considering Joyce Sherman was about as well known as Joan Bennett, I didn't have to be told who she was, but then, Maddux never believed anyone except himself knew anything about anyone.

'After Goodyear had fixed the renewal,' Maddux continued, 'he went into a bar, presumably to celebrate. That's an example of how our agents waste the company's time, but never mind that.' He flicked ash on to a pile of unread policies in his In-tray and went on, 'According to him, he got into conversation with a guy who calls himself Brad Denny, a small-time theatrical agent. The conversation got round to accident policies, and Denny told Goodyear a girl he represented was interested in taking out a personal accident policy. That alone should have made Goodyear suspicious. Accident policies, as you know, have to be sold, they don't get asked for, but when someone starts talking about an accident policy for someone else, then every alarm bell in the box starts ringing. But being the kind of dumb-cluck he is, Goodyear thought nothing of it except it was another slice of commission heading his way to help pay for that smart new car of his. He made a date at the Court Hotel that night to meet the girl. And that's another thing,' Maddux went on, shaking a blunt finger at me. 'Even I know the Court Hotel is a rent-a-room-for-an-hour-and-no-questions-asked joint, and I've only been to Hollywood once in my life, and then I only stayed there four hours.'

I leered at him admiringly.

'Well, you didn't waste any time from the sound of it,' I said.

'Pay attention!' Maddux barked, glaring at me. 'An agent who knows his business wouldn't deal with an applicant who lived at the Court Hotel. The trouble with Goodyear is he puts his commission first, without considering I have to clear up his messes.'

I made grunting noises. Goodyear was a friend of mine.

'He met the girl. Her name's Susan Gellert,' Maddux went on. 'She was interested in a personal accident policy for a hundred thousand dollars. Apparently she is in show business, and is, at the moment, perfecting a new act. Part of the build-up of this act is to use the accident policy for publicity purposes. Why the press should be impressed by some ham actress having a hundred-thousand-dollar accident policy I don't know, and Goodyear didn't bother to ask.' He pulled savagely at his thick nose, went on, 'If I'd been there I'd have asked fast enough. According to her the policy is only to be used for publicity purposes. She pointed out that neither Denny nor she has any money, and unless the premium was low they would have to give up the idea. That's when Goodyear should have walked out on them, but he didn't. He quoted them the premium for a complete coverage, and they nearly dropped in their tracks.' He broke off to demand, 'How are you liking this?'

'Sounds okay to me so far,' I said. 'Personally, I can see the possibilities of using a hundred-thousand-dollar policy for publicity purposes. The local papers would go for it, but then, maybe I'm not as suspicious as you.'

'Yeah,' Maddux said bitterly, 'you're like Goodyear. You never look farther than the end of your nose.'

I let that one drift, asked, 'So what happened?'

'The girl and Denny put up a proposition. They pointed out that they were not interested in insuring the girl's life so far as a claim was concerned. The policy was to be the means of getting the girl's name into the papers. They suggested we shouldn't be liable for any of the recognized risks, and these risks should be enumerated in the policy. In this way, they argued, the premium could be slashed to nothing, and they still had a document they could show pressmen if their story was doubted.' He paused to scrabble among the remaining papers on his desk. Finally, he found what he was looking for. 'This is the policy,' he said, tapping the document. 'Between the three of them, they concocted a list of recognized risks of death, and these risks are set out in this policy.' He raised his head to glare at me. 'You're following me, aren't you? If this girl happens to die from any one of the causes set down here, we are not liable, but if she happens to die from any other cause not set down here, we are. Do you get it?'

'Yeah. Did Goodyear draw up the list?'

'The three of them did. I'll read you the risks. Listen carefully: it's quite a list.' He began to read from the policy. 'The person insured by this policy has no claim on the company if she dies by shooting, knifing, poison, fire or drowning: by any form of accident connected with public transport, aircraft or automobiles; bicycles, motor-cycles or any kind of vehicle that runs on wheels; by suicide or illness; by falling from high places or by objects falling on her; by suffocation, asphyxiation, scalding or any kind of head injury; by accidents connected with domestic or wild animals, insects or reptiles; by faulty electric wiring or by any kind of machinery.' He tossed the policy down on the desk and wiped his handkerchief over his red, shiny face. 'How do you like it now?'

'All right. What are you beefing about?'

He pushed back his chair to give himself more room in which to wave his arms.

'With those risks eliminated she gets coverage of a hundred thousand dollars for fifteen dollars a year!'

'We're robbing her,' I said, and grinned. 'Goodyear's covered all the risks.'

'Think so?' Maddux leaned forward. 'All right, we'll go into that in a minute. Let me finish the story. Goodyear talked the proposition over with the old man. If I'd been there I'd have tossed it out so quick Goodyear wouldn't have known what had hit him. For fifteen dollars a year we stick our neck out to be soaked for a hundred thousand. It doesn't make sense. When I pointed that out to the old man, he said we were here to give service, and we couldn't always expect to be on the receiving end.' He snorted violently. 'But wait and see what happens if that girl dies and a claim is made. He'll scream blue murder and try to blame me.' He picked up the policy and shook it at me. 'It states here in black and white that we will pay a hundred thousand if this girl dies from any other cause except the causes set out in the policy. *Any other cause!* Isn't that a perfect set-up for some smart crook to gyp us?'

'Is it?' I asked a little impatiently. 'It seems to me Goodyear's covered every risk. And besides, aren't you overlooking the fact that his girl has arranged the policy herself? Do you imagine's she's planning to die in some extraordinary way so her estate can benefit to the tune of a hundred thousand? I don't believe it.'

Maddux sat back. For a long moment he said nothing, but stared fixedly at me.

'I know,' he said at last. 'Yesterday I thought the same way. But I've changed my mind. I've been lunching this afternoon at the convention.'

'What's that got to do with it?'

'Plenty. I got talking to Andrews of the General Liability. I mentioned this Gellert girl in the course of conversation. He tells me his company has accepted a policy on exactly the same terms as the one we've accepted and for the same girl.'

He held up his hand as I began to speak.

'Wait a minute. I haven't finished yet. I went around and talked to some of the other fellows.' He began pawing over the papers on his desk until he found a slip of paper. 'Miss Gellert has similar policies with the same coverage with nine other insurance companies, and that gives her a total coverage of one million dollars for a premium of one hundred and fifty dollars a year. Now, how do you like it?'

II

The desk clock ticked loudly in the silence that followed. I stubbed out my cigarette, lit another and pushed the pack over to Maddux.

'A million!' I said, and whistled softly. 'That's money, but it doesn't prove the deal's crooked.'

'It's crooked all right,' Maddux said grimly. 'It's more than that: it's a blue print for murder!'

I gaped at him.

'Now, wait a minute . . .'

'That's what it is,' Maddux said, thumping the desk. 'I haven't been wrong about this kind of thing; not once in twenty years. I smell murder!'

'You mean – Denny?'

'Could be. I don't now. All I know is this set-up reeks of murder. Let's take a look at Denny. He's a small-time theatrical agent, probably broke. He thinks of some cute idea of killing this girl: a murder with a new twist. He sets his stage,

First, he sells her on the idea of being an owner of a million-dollar policy. He points out the publicity value of such a policy. Then he sells the idea to us and nine other companies. He waits a few months, then he kills her and collects. How do you like it now?'

'Sounds fine, but for one little thing. Tell me how he's going to murder her and make a claim on us. Tell me that.'

Maddux shrugged.

'Whoever's behind this set-up has thought up a tricky idea we're not going to think of in five minutes. I'm not worrying about that. I want to get this policy cancelled before they spring something on us. And that's where you come in. I want to know all about Susan Gellert and this fella, Denny. I want to know what makes them tick. If you can't find out anything wrong about them, and if we can't break this contract, then we'll have to sit tight and wait until something happens to the girl.' He thumped his fist on the desk, his face turning red. 'And when it does happen – as I'm damned sure it will happen – then we'll really go to work!'

'Hadn't we better have a word with the other companies?' I said. 'If something did happen to her and one or two settled the claim we wouldn't stand a chance if the estate sued for our end.'

'I'm taking care of that,' Maddux said. 'I've called a meeting for tomorrow morning, and I'll try to persuade them to let us do the investigating. We don't want ten investigators scratching over the ground.'

'I'm not entirely convinced this is premeditated fraud,' I said. 'If this girl came to us for a million-dollar accident policy to be used for publicity purposes even the old man would have turned her down. Maybe her idea of publicity is to have a million-dollar policy, and she's been smart enough to go to ten companies and get what she wants.'

Maddux showed his teeth in a grin that made him look like a wolf.

'And that's the reason why I'm in this office and you're work-

14

ing for me,' he said. 'I have years of experience behind me. I've developed an instinct that can smell trouble when it is a mile away.' He rattled the policy at me. 'I'm telling you this, Harmas, this damned scrap of paper is a blue print for murder!'

'Okay, so what do we do?'

'Apart from the enumerated causes of death,' Maddux went on, ignoring my interruption, 'which would arouse the suspicion of anyone who had any experience at all, there's this little item at the foot of the page. Take a look at it.'

He threw the policy over to me. Below the rather childish signature Susan Gellert had scrawled on the policy there was a smudge of ink and a well-defined thumb-print.

'Find out from Goodyear,' Maddux said, 'if that's her print. Find out why it's on the policy. It looks to me the print has been placed there for a reason, and that reason could be to make certain we don't try to avoid payment on a question of identity. I tell you, Harmas, the more I look at this policy the smarter and smoother it becomes, and that thumb-print damns it!'

I had a sudden idea.

'Did you say the policy excludes death by electricity?'

He picked up the policy again.

'That's right. The wording is: death caused by faulty electrical wiring or any faulty electrical apparatus. It's the same thing.'

'Oh, no, it isn't! There's nothing faulty about the wiring or the mechanics of the electric chair!'

Maddux stiffened, his scowl became ferocious.

'What are you talking about?'

'Suppose this girl has committed murder, and she knows sooner or later, she'll be found out? Wouldn't she feel a lot safer to know ten powerful insurance companies were behind her when she comes to trial?'

'Why should she? What are you getting at?'

'If we knew we'd lose a hundred thousand bucks if this girl went to the chair wouldn't we organize her defence, pay for the best lawyers, hire the best counsel, do everything in our power to get the verdict whittled down to a second-degree rap or even an acquittal?'

Maddux looked startled.

'We might.'

'You mean we would! And so would the other nine companies. Every one of us would be working like niggers to keep her from going to the chair. Take a look at that wording. It says faulty wiring. Why not electrocution?'

Maddux scratched the side of his jaw.

'It's an idea, but I don't like it a lot. Go and look at the girl. Dig around. Make inquiries. Remember, this may be a very clever fraud, and you won't crack it if you don't figure all the angles. And another thing: try to find out who will benefit if the girl dies. Find out if she's made a will. You can bet whoever gets the money is behind this. Find that out and we're half-way home.'

'Where do I find her?'

'She's given an address in Los Angeles.' He consulted the policy. '2567, 4th Street.'

'Is Goodyear in town?'

'How should I know where he is? In some bar, I guess. Now get out of here and let me work, and keep this under your hat. I don't want the old man to know I'm investigating this policy. If I can prove fraud I want to be the one to go in there and beat him over the head with it!'

As I made for the door, he stopped me.

'Why don't you take your wife along with you? She's nobody's fool, and I'd back her judgment against yours any day. Take her along. She'll enjoy the trip.'

'I dare say,' I said, pouncing on the opening, 'but I can't afford to take her. What do you imagine I'm made of – bullion?'

Maddux pulled at his nose.

'Well, you can have up to thirty bucks a week expense-money for her,' he said generously. 'Put it down as entertaining.'

'Thirty bucks?' I said, and laughed. 'Why, that wouldn't keep her in food. Since she stopped working for you, she's developed a hearty appetite. Make it a hundred a week, and I will take her.'

'Thirty dollars!' Maddux barked. 'Not a dime more! Now, get out!'

III

It wasn't until seven o'clock that evening that I finally tracked Alan Goodyear down, and, oddly enough, I tracked him down in a bar.

Alan was a good-looking young husky; tall, leggy, with the energy of a buzz-saw. His genial personality got him into homes where most other agents had to stand on the doorstep. He was about six years younger than I was, and was already earning three times as much money. He had only been in the insurance racket for three years, and in that time he had acquired the reputation of being the smartest and most successful salesman of them all. The year before he had carried off the coveted Williams trophy, the award given by the President of the Insurance Guild to the most successful salesman of the year, and I had heard rumours he was likely to snag it again this year.

He waved to me as I crossed the bar and headed his way.

'Hello, Steve,' he said, pushing a chair towards me. 'What are you doing here? Where's Helen?' He signalled to a waiter to bring me a beer.

'I've been hunting for you in all the low taverns,' I said, sitting down. 'Helen's at home, wondering where I've got to; at least, I hope she is.'

The waiter came up and put a pint of beer at my elbow. Alan paid. 'Cheerho,' I said, took a long drink, sighed and put the can down. 'I wanted that. About this Gellert girl, Alan.'

He looked surprised.

'What about her? You're not interested in her, are you?'

'Very much so, and so is Maddux.'

'Why? The policy was okayed three months ago. She's paid three premiums. It's pasted down now. You can't unstick it. What's the trouble?'

'I have orders from Maddux to unstick it fast.'

Alan got red in the face. He disliked Maddux as much as Maddux disliked him.

'You can't!' he said heatedly. 'The old man himself okayed that policy, and I won't have Maddux sticking his nose into it!'

'Take it easy. Wait until I tell you what's happened.'

I told him what Maddux had found out at the convention.

'That gives her a coverage of a million dollars, Alan. You can't blame Maddux for wanting to check up when a sum that big is involved.'

'Check up on what?' he demanded. 'What's wrong with it? Now look here, Steve, you haven't met Miss Gellert or Denny. I have.' He leaned forward earnestly. 'Do you think I'd have taken that policy unless I was convinced they were on the level? Ever since I've been in this racket I haven't had one dud sale, and I don't intend to have one. I'm after that trophy again, and if this policy turned sour I wouldn't get it. Those two are on the level; make no mistake about it!'

'Maybe they are, but there's no harm in making the usual routine check.'

'Oh, make a check if you want to,' he said angrily. 'I don't care. But I know what's at the back of this. Has that fat punk Maddux asked himself how much I'm getting out of the deal? Well, let him figure it out, and then perhaps he won't be so damned sure all I think about is making commission. There's nothing in the deal for me. It's been so much waste of time, but I wanted to help those two. They're a couple of decent people, and they need help, and that's the way the old man saw it, too.'

'Imagine me telling Maddux that.'

'To hell with Maddux! These two need publicity. They're at the bottom of the ladder, and they're struggling to get somewhere. They haven't much money. They travel around the small towns, playing in dreary little halls, having to keep on the move and having to sleep in a different bed every week. Competition in their game is cut-throat. Imagine what it would mean to them if they could get some sort of notice in the papers: get themselves talked about. That's why they hit on this insurance idea. All right, I admit I didn't know they were getting coverage elsewhere, but what of it? Why shouldn't she go to other companies? Can you imagine we'd give her a million-dollar coverage?'

'Yeah, that's what I told Maddux. He says the set-up is a blue print for murder.'

'Murder?' Alan gaped at me. 'The man's crazy! He should be retired. It's fantastic. Well, all right, go and talk to these two. I don't care. See them for yourself, and I'm willing to bet you'll agree with me there's absolutely nothing phoney about them.'

'I'm sure you're right,' I said soothingly. 'Anyway, it gives me an opportunity to go to Hollywood. Where do I find her? Is that her permanent address on the policy?'

Alan looked malicious.

'No, it isn't. It's Denny's office address. They're on tour right now. They go from town to town. I haven't the vaguest idea where they are right now. You have a nice little chase in front of you.'

'That suits me,' I said, finishing my beer. 'I'm due for a vacation. By the way, Alan, that clause about faulty electrical wiring. Was it your suggestion or theirs?'

'It was Denny's suggestion, I believe,' Alan said, looking puzzled. 'What's wrong with it?'

'It just struck me the wording was a little odd. Why not death by electrocution?'

'I can't see it matters,' he said impatiently. 'If you're going to be killed accidentally by electricity the apparatus or wiring has to be faulty. If it isn't, and you still insist on dying, then it's suicide. We're covered both ways, so what's biting you?'

'Forget it,' I said. 'Just an idea that floated into my mind. One more thing, Alan. Why the thumb-print on the policy?'

He sat back and looked at me, exasperated.

'You know, you're getting as bad as Maddux. The print got on the policy by accident. The pen leaked and she smeared her thumb in the blot accidentally. What does it matter, anyway?'

But the print bothered me. It didn't look as if it had got on to the policy by accident. It was too well defined for that.

'You're sure it was an accident? She didn't deliberately put her print on the policy?'

'For Pete's sake!' Alan exploded, and I could see he was fast losing his temper. 'What are you driving at now? Of course it was an accident. I saw the whole thing. And even if it wasn't what the hell does it matter?'

'Maybe you're right,' I said. 'Don't get so heated. I have an investigation on my hands, and you're the only one who can help me.'

'I'm sorry, Steve, but it's enough to make anyone get sore. The way Maddux goes on, you'd think he didn't want me to sell policies.'

I lit a cigarette, asked abruptly, 'Did Miss Gellert say who would get the money if anything happened to her?'

He deliberately fastened the straps of his brief-case and reached for his hat.

'There's no question of a claim,' he said with restrained quietness, 'and therefore no question of a beneficiary. If you will take the trouble to study the policy you will see that fast enough. This is a publicity stunt, and nothing more than that.' He got up. 'Well, I must be running along. I have my packing to do.'

I walked with him to the sidewalk where we had parked our cars.

'So long, Alan. Take it easy. It'll come out all right.'

'It had better come out all right,' he said. 'If Maddux makes trouble I'm going straight to the old man. I'm fed to the teeth with Maddux. If I have much more of him I'm going to quit. There are plenty of other people who want me to work for them. So long, Steve.'

He got into his car, revved the engine and drove off with an angry clashing of gears.

IV

Maddux was quite right when he said he would back Helen's judgment against mine. She had been his personal secretary for five years, and had acquired one of the keenest eyes in the business for a phoney claim. She was a very smart cookie, and the way she could calculate a premium without the help of tables made my head swim.

I still haven't worked out why she married me, but I know why I married her: she could cook like an angel, run a home economically, talk insurance when I wanted to talk insurance, tell me how to handle Maddux when he needed handling, and that was quite often, look like a movie star, make her own clothes, and keep me out of debt, something I had never been able to do myself.

We owned a four-room apartment, twenty minutes' car drive from the office, and, because we were a little short of money, we dispensed with help: Helen ran the place herself. What we saved on the help was spent in hard liquor and an occasional movie.

I arrived home over an hour late for dinner, but I had a good excuse and a good story to tell, so my conscience was as clear as it ever will be.

Helen is a little fussy about me being late for meals; about the only thing she is fussy about: that, and my habit of scattering cigarette ash on the carpet in spite of the ring of ashtrays she builds around me.

I opened the front door, stepped into the tiny hall and took a long, deep sniff for the first savoury smell of cooking.

No appetizing smell greeted my inquiring nostrils. The shock was a severe one. It looked as if the table offering was going to be something cold, and the Harmas stomach isn't partial to cold snacks.

I walked into the sitting-room.

21

'Is that you, darling?' Helen sang out from the bedroom.

'No, it is not,' I shouted back. 'It's a bunch of Croatian refugees who haven't had a square meal in months and who expect to be fed on a lavish scale.'

She appeared in the doorway. I looked at her because she's always worth looking at. She is just over medium height, square shouldered and dark. Her hair is parted in the centre and falls clear of her shoulders, her skin is smooth ivory, her mouth large and not over-red, and her eyes are as blue as forget-me-nots. Apart from looking like an intelligent movie star – if there is such an animal – she has a figure that is a nicely proportioned blend of Betty Grable, taking charge of the ground floor, and Jane Russell, influencing the upper region.

'You're late,' she said, advancing on me. 'I thought you were eating out. Are you hungry?'

'Hungry? That is an understatement. I am starving, and the reason why I am late is because I have been working like five Negroes in a cotton field.'

'Yes, darling, I can smell it on your breath. I'll get you something at once. I'm afraid it will have to be a scratch meal. I've been very busy, and dinner went right out of my mind.'

As such a thing had never happened before in our three years of married life I felt justified in looking hurt.

'Let's go into the kitchen, and while you get something substantial in the shortest possible time, you can tell me why you have been too busy to think about my stomach,' I said, taking her firmly by the arm. 'You realize, of course, this gives me grounds for a divorce?'

'I'm sorry, darling,' she said, patting my hand, 'but I can't always be thinking of your stomach. I have been packing for you.'

'Packing? How did you know I was going away?'

'I have my spies,' she said, breaking six eggs, one after the other, into the frying-pan with a dexterity that always leaves me gaping. 'There's not much I miss.'

'Did Patty Shaw call you up?'

'Well, she did phone.'

'I thought so. I suppose Patty told you I was going to Holly-wood? Might be my big chance. Some movie director might spot me. How would you like me to be Clark Gable the second?'

'I think it would be very nice, darling.'

I paused in my hunt for the can-opener and looked sus-piciously at her.

'But think of all the women who'll lie at my feet.'

'So long as they lie at your feet I wouldn't mind.'

'Maybe some of them might do more than that, of course. It's a risk most movie stars have to take.' I broke off to swear at the can-opener. 'Why we can't afford a decent can-opener beats me. This thing's absolutely useless.'

'Patty said you'd be away for about a week. I packed your evening clothes. You might feel like a night-club in your leisure moments,' she said, taking the can from me and opening it expertly.

I beamed at her.

'Now, that's what I call being a really thoughtful wife. Yes, a night club or two might be an idea. I wonder if Hedy Lamarr ever goes to a night club.'

'I expect she does, darling.'

I suddenly felt a little guilty.

'Do you think you'll be lonely?' I asked. 'I tell you what I'll do. I'll hire a dog to keep you company. No use wasting money buying one as you'll have me back in a week. There's a guy down the street who'll let me have his airedale for a buck a day. You'd like that, wouldn't you?'

'I don't think we could take an airedale to Hollywood,' Helen said, considering the point. 'Hotels – if they're high class – don't favour dogs.'

'We? Where do you get this "we" stuff from? Who said you were going?'

'Your boss for one, and me for another. That makes two of us, so you're in the minority, darling.'

'Now, wait a minute,' I said feverishly, 'we haven't the dough. You know that. We have bills to pay. We owe fifteen more payments on the car. There's that television set you insisted on buying we haven't paid for yet. We can't do it. Mind you, I'd love to have you with me, but let's be sensible about this.'

'I know it will be difficult since I am such a hearty eater,' Helen said dreamily, 'but perhaps you can cut down your eating and we'll economize that way.'

'Did that serpent Patty Shaw tell you that?' I said. 'You don't believe a word she says, do you? Why, everyone in the office knows what a liar she is. Only the other day . . .'

'Dinner is served, Mr Harmas,' Helen said coldly, and carried the dish into the dining-room.

It wasn't until I had got back my strength by eating most of the eggs and half the ham that I returned to the attack.

'I know Maddux is anxious for you to go with me,' I said, pushing back my chair and reaching for a cigarette, 'but as he is only offering thirty bucks for your services, and that is below Union rates, we must be reasonable about this. If I had any spare dough . . .'

'You don't have to worry,' Helen said, smiling. 'I am going with you, and it won't cost you a dime. I have got myself a job.'

'You mean you're going to earn some money?'

'Yes, dear. Fortunately, I still have a little influence in the insurance business, and, in spite of being married to you, my reputation is still untarnished. After Patty had told me what was cooking, I called Tim Andrews and asked him if he would like me to represent him in this investigation. He was delighted with the idea, and is paying me a retaining fee of a hundred dollars and I can run to an expense account.'

I gaped at her.

'Why, that's princely! Does Andrews think the Gellert policy is phoney, too?'

'He didn't at first, but I talked him into it,' Helen said shamelessly.

'A hundred bucks! Why, we can pay off some of our bills now. But, wait a minute. I know Andrews. He's a wolf who doesn't even bother to put on sheep's clothing. He doesn't expect you to do a bubble dance on his desk as well as work for him, does he?'

'Would you object?' Helen asked, raising her eyebrows.

I considered the point.

'Well, for a hundred bucks one should be prepared to make sacrifices. It would depend on how big the bubble was, and what my cut is to be.'

She came around to stand behind me and put her arms around my neck.

'Sure you don't mind me coming, Steve?'

'I can stand it if you can.'

'I'll let you off the leash if you want to run wild.'

'I'm pretty satisfied running wild in my own backyard,' I said, pulling her down on my knee. 'Allow me to give you a practical demonstration, Mrs. Harmas.'

CHAPTER TWO

I

WE got into Los Angeles around three o'clock in the afternoon, and while Helen took our luggage to the Culver Hotel, where I had booked a double room, I reported to Tim Fanshaw, head of our branch office.

Fanshaw was a big, fat, blue-chinned bird who seemed to think the Gellert policy was about the funniest thing he'd ever run into. I didn't blame him. The dog wasn't barking up his tree.

'Maddux phoned about an hour ago,' he said, after we had gone over the details of the policy together. 'He's had that thumb-print checked, but it's clean. I gather he was hoping the girl had a record.'

'I didn't think she had,' I said. 'She wouldn't have got her print on the policy if it was recorded. I still don't believe that print was an accident. It's all very well for you to sit down and grin, but you haven't to hold the baby, if there is a baby to hold.'

Fanshaw continued to grin.

'I'm not taking this seriously,' he said. 'The trouble with Maddux is he's too suspicious to live. Why doesn't he show a little faith in Goodyear? Now, that fella's a damned fine salesman. It's a swell break for me he's been transferred to this office. I don't know if you've heard, but he's landed a terrific sale with Joyce Sherman. It's about the most complete policy I've ever seen, and it covers her from every angle. The premium he's got off her is hair-raising. And he landed the sale because he took the trouble to come down here and remind her in person to renew her fire and theft policy. Most of the bums who work for me would have telephoned her or sent her a written reminder, but Goodyear went in person. He deserves to be trusted instead of being kicked around.'

'I know. He's the best in the game, but it's no use expecting Maddux to trust anyone. Anyway, I'm not grumbling myself. This is going to be a soft job, and it's got me out of the office and out of Maddux's clutches.'

Fanshaw beamed.

'If you want to kick the can around in your spare time, just let me know. I've a book full of telephone numbers of warm, willing wantons who'd be glad to show you a good time.'

'Thanks for the offer, but I've brought my wife with me,' I said, getting to my feet. 'She's warm and willing enough for me. I guess I've got time to call on Denny's office. May as well make a start. I want to impress my wife with the way I work.'

'If you two have nothing better to do, come round to the Athletic Club tonight. I'll buy you a drink.'

I said I'd see how things worked out, shook hands with him and went down to the street.

As I drove up Long Beach Boulevard I thought it mightn't be a bad idea to try for a transfer to Fanshaw's office myself. He seemed a pretty good guy, and it would be nice to get away from Maddux, but I knew I was kidding myself. Maddux wouldn't part with me, and the old man himself wouldn't let me go either.

I was sweating gently by the time I had walked back.

The building that housed Denny's office was sandwiched between a drug-store and a Chinese restaurant. The entrance was equipped with double swing-doors and some brasswork that hadn't been cleaned this year nor last year from the look of it. I pushed open the doors and walked into a dim, hot atmosphere that offered a variety of smells from stale garbage to unwashed bodies.

A sign-board by the stairs informed me that Denny's office

was on the sixth floor. It was a modest little notice, written in uneven capitals on a piece of paper and stuck over the name of a previous tenant. It read:

BRAD DENNY
AGENT   RM. 10. FLR. 6

Not the kind of sign that would attract the custom of stars like Joyce Sherman, but then, it took all kinds of agents to fill a hall.

Denny shared the sixth floor with the Fire Exit and the Gentlemen's retiring room. His office door faced the Fire Exit.

It wasn't much of a door. Maybe it had been painted when it had been put up, but it certainly hadn't been touched since then. A visiting card was gummed to the door, bearing the same modest legend as the sign downstairs.

I rapped on the panel without much hope, and after a long pause in a silence you could lean against, I turned the handle. The door remained shut, and I concluded without a great deal of mental effort that it was locked.

I stood back, fumbled for a cigarette and stared at the door. It was fitted with a Yale lock, and I didn't think it would give me a lot of trouble to open, but I decided now wasn't the time.

I made a long, lonely journey down the stairs.

I paused in the lobby and looked around. A door by the elevator seemed to be what I was looking for. I went over to it and knocked. Nothing happened.

I knocked again, then turned the handle and pushed. The door opened and the smell of stale beer and ripe drains jostled past me and joined the other smells in the lobby.

Ahead of me was a passage that led to stone steps. I walked to the head of the steps and peered over the iron banister rail. Below me was a big concrete-floored room full of pails, brooms, empty kegs, boxes, wooden crates and the smell of mice and greasy, long-forgotten meals.

Seated on one of the crates was an elderly man in shirt-sleeves, tin spectacles, a bowler hat and worn trousers. He was reading a racing sheet, and humming to himself as if he hadn't a care in the world. In his left hand he held a can of beer, and, as I watched him, he dragged his eyes from the racing sheet and took a pull from the can.

I waited until he had finished, then walked down the steps.

He looked up sharply, adjusted his spectacles, put the can down and blinked. He seemed harmless enough, but to be on the safe side I started a wide, friendly smile long before I reached him.

'Hello,' I said, coming to rest at his side. 'I was looking for the house-manager. Is that you?'

The heavy, bloodshot eyes blinked again.

'Eh?'

'The janitor,' I said patiently. 'The guy who runs this joint. Is that you?'

He didn't seem at all certain, but after thinking it over he said he guessed he was.

I was feeling pretty hot and sticky by now. The atmosphere in the room was thick enough to slice up with a carving knife. I reached out and drew an upturned keg towards me, blew off the dust and sat down.

'I could use a can of beer if you'd sell me one,' I said.

'Ain't got one to spare,' he said promptly.

I dug out my pack of Camels, took out two and offered him one. He snapped it up faster than a lizard snaps up a fly. After we had lit up and had breathed in each other's faces for a time, he took the initiative and said, 'You looking for me?'

'That's right,' I said, and took out my wallet. I selected a business card and poked it at him. He took it, peered at it, brooded over it and poked it back at me.

'I don't want any,' he said. 'I don't believe in insurance.'

I wondered how Alan Goodyear would have handled him. He'd probably have finished up by selling him the whole works. I was glad selling insurance wasn't my job.

'I'm looking for Brad Denny,' I explained. Because I've trained myself to watch people whenever I speak to them I spotted a slight tensing in his thin, stooped frame. No more than that, but it told me I'd surprised and possibly startled him.

'Sixth floor,' he said. 'Room 10.'

'I know. I've been up. He's out.'

'Nothing I can do about that then,' he said, and rustled his racing sheet. In his sloppy, weak way he was attempting to give me the brush-off.

'Know when he'll be back?'

'Guess not.'

'Know where he is?'

'Nope.'

'I want to get into touch with him. It's important.'

He actually took a peep at his paper, although he hadn't the nerve to make a job of it.

'Nothing to do with me, mister.'

'It could be,' I said, and took out two dollar bills.

He jumped up so fast I thought he had driven a nail into himself. He went over to a hidden hoard and came back with a can of beer which he thrust into my hand. I gave him the two bucks.

'Let's start again,' I said, as I levered off the cap. 'Where's Denny?'

'It ain't my business to talk about key-holders,' he said, 'but I don't mind obliging . . .'

'Okay, skip it,' I said. 'Let's take that part as read.' I took a pull at the can. The beer tasted as flat as a bishop's tea-party. 'When did you last see him?'

'Last month. He came in to pay his rent.'

'Know where he is now?'

He tried to look regretful.

'I guess not. He gets around a lot. He was telling me when I saw him he'd been all over – Stockton, Oakland, Jackson: places like that.'

'You've no idea how I can get into touch with him?'

'No. I was telling the other fella . . .' He stopped, squinted at me, shifted uneasily and sucked his teeth.

30

'What other fella?'

'It ain't my business to talk . . .'

I stood up.

'Okay, give me back my money and I'll blow,' I said. I wasn't going to let an old ruin like him shake me down. 'Come on, grandpa, hand it over and make it snappy.'

His dirty fingers clutched on to the bills with the ferocity of a bear-trap.

'A couple of days ago some fella was asking for Mr. Denny,' he said hurriedly. 'He was in yesterday, and again this morning. He's awful anxious to talk to him.'

'Did he give his name?'

'No, and I didn't ask him. He was a tough egg; a real bad man. I didn't like being down here alone with him.'

I became slightly interested.

'Maybe he was an actor, keeping in character. Denny deals in actors, doesn't he?'

The janitor shook his head.

'This guy wasn't an actor,' he said seriously. 'He scared me. There was something about his eyes that sent chills up and down my spine.'

I wasn't particularly interested about the way his spine reacted, but I didn't say so.

'He was here this morning?'

'That's right. He didn't see me, but I was watching him. He sneaked up the stairs when he thought no one was around. There's not much I miss in this building.'

'What was he doing up there if Denny's away?'

The weak, elderly face turned blank.

'How should I know? You don't think I should have asked him, do you? He's dangerous. I know. He's bad.'

'What's he look like?' I took another pull at the beer.

'Look like?' the janitor said, frowning. 'I've told you, haven't I? What more do you want?'

'How was he dressed? Was he tall, short, fat or thin? Was he clean-shaven or did he wear a beard?'

The janitor brooded.

'I'm not good at describing people,' he said at last. That didn't surprise me. From the look of him there would be very few things he would be good at. 'I guess he was around your build, dark, with eyebrows that joined up over the bridge of his nose. It gave him a frowning look. As far as I can remember he had on a light-blue and white check coat, light-brown trousers and a brown slouch hat.'

To me he sounded like an actor, and a bit of a ham at that.

'Well, never mind him,' I said, lighting another cigarette. 'It's Denny I'm interested in. Know where he keeps his baggage? Doesn't he have some place where he dumps his personal stuff when he's on tour?'

'If he has I don't know it.'

'How about his mail?'

'It waits here for him: he doesn't get much.'

I seemed to be getting nowhere fast.

'Miss Gellert ever come here?' I asked, without much hope.

'Who's she?'

'Some girl he goes around with.'

'I don't know nothing about girls.'

That didn't surprise me.

'Hasn't he any friends who call on him? Someone you know?'

'I mind my own business. I ain't interested in the keyholders.'

I wondered what he *was* interested in.

'This guy seems hard to find,' I said, getting to my feet. 'Well, thanks for your help.'

'You paid me for it.'

'So I did. If I go on giving money away for nothing I'll be glad of a couple of bucks myself. I guess I'll be getting along.'

He pointed to the can of beer at my side.

'You haven't finished that yet.'

'But it's damn near finished me,' I said, and steered myself towards the exit.

32

The clerk at the Culver Hotel, a polished, sleek-looking bird, pushing sixty, told me Helen was in the cocktail bar. Obviously she didn't intend to waste any time padding out her expense sheet. I hurried across the lobby to give her some help.

There was no sign of her in the glittering bar, and I concluded she was patronizing the retiring room. I picked a quiet table in a corner where we could talk when she reappeared and sat down.

There were about a dozen mixed couples in the room: all of them trying to kid anyone interested that they were in the movie business. My entrance caused quite a flutter. A couple of elderly men hopefully showed me their sagging profiles. A young red-head in a green off-the-shoulder evening-gown that fitted her like a second skin showed me her leg as she hunted for a run in her stocking that wasn't there. A blonde paraded her talent by smiling with empty sweetness up at the ceiling. I was startled for a moment, then remembered, in Hollywood, any stranger is a casting director until he's found out.

Even the barman began to juggle bottles, and he was still tossing them around as he asked me what I'd have. His flashing smile was as bright as a neon sign.

'Some Scotch,' I said, loud enough for anyone in the room to hear. 'A handful will do to get on with. Take its clothes off. I'll have it in the nude.'

'Yes, sir; certainly, sir.' The barman was pointing like a gun-dog now. 'Working in pictures, sir?'

Everyone else in the bar began to point like gun-dogs. If Helen had been with me I might have bluffed it out, but without her moral support I lost my nerve.

'Who wants to work in pictures, for Pete's sake?' I said.

The interest I had created went away like a fist when you open your fingers. The girl who was showing me her leg hid it from sight with one quick sneering movement. My moment had passed.

The barman came around the bar and put a tall glass half full of whisky and crushed ice before me. He took my money as if it had been seeped in plague germs.

I was very, very glad to see Helen drifting towards me, looking lovely in a severely cut, olive-green frock and a white bandeau around her dark hair. She sat down beside me.

'Are you ahead of me or will this be your first?' I asked suspiciously.

'I'm one up,' she said brightly. 'I'll now have a dry martini.' She patted my hand. 'I'm so glad I've come. I love the hotel. The room's marvellous, too, and I've been mistaken for a movie star twice already.'

I signalled to the barman.

'That's nothing. I've been taken for a casting director, and let me tell you a casting director is the most important man in Hollywood.'

The barman came over and lifted indifferent eyebrows. I ordered a large dry martini.

While he was fixing it without any show of enthusiasm, Helen said, 'You haven't been hobnobbing with Fanshaw all this time surely?'

'I don't know about surely,' I retorted. 'I could have spent a riotous evening with him. He tells me he has a list of telephone numbers as long as his arm, and he's willing to share them with me.'

'And you said . . .?' Helen regarded her nose in her purse mirror, seemed satisfied with it and put the mirror away.

'Well, of course I was tempted,' I said airily, 'but second thoughts convinced me a bird in hand's worth two in the phone book. I'm not all that enterprising.'

The barman set the martini down on the table, collected the swag and returned to the bar.

'I thought I'd look Denny's office over,' I went on. 'You will learn, as we work cheek by jowl, that your husband doesn't let grass grow under his feet. It would appear our friend Denny is going to be hard to find. The janitor could supply no clues, and as it's essential to find Mr. Denny as soon as possible I propose

34

having a good dinner and then returning to his office in the hope I can find from a personal survey of his private papers a clue to his whereabouts. Do you think that is a good idea?'

'Do you mean you are going to break in?' Helen asked, her eyes widening.

'I suppose you would call it breaking in. The door didn't look very substantial.'

'I'll come with you.'

'Certainly not,' I said firmly. 'This isn't a job for a girl. You will stay here, and I'll give you a round-by-round commentary when and if I return.'

'I'm coming,' she said with equal firmness. 'In fact, it might be better if you stayed here and I did the job on my own. A girl can handle this kind of thing much more easily than a man, and with a lot less fuss.'

'Now look,' I said, 'this is a job for a trained investigator, and not for an amateur. You won't be able to walk in. It means breaking in, picking locks; tricky stuff like that. I'd like to see your sex open a locked door.'

'Then you'd better come along and watch me,' she said.

III

We left the Culver Hotel just after eleven o'clock. Between eight o'clock and that time we had had a few more drinks and an excellent dinner, and while we ate we discussed the Gellert policy. I was interested to hear Helen's views now she had had time to think about the set-up, but she wasn't to be drawn.

'I know it looks suspicious,' she said, 'but that doesn't necessarily mean it is. The policy could have been taken out as a publicity stunt. That's believable. Alan is a good salesman, and he has everything to lose by making a dud sale. If he is satisfied, and it'd take a lot to fool him, then it looks as if these two are on the level. When I talked to Tim Andrews he told me he was satisfied the policy was all right. He spoke very highly of Alan. He told me he was prepared to accept the policy on its face value simply because Alan handled it in the first place. I think he's right. Of course, Maddux doesn't like Alan. Maddux picks holes in any policy, but, at the same time, we mustn't forget he has a wonderful nose for smelling out trouble. He hasn't been wrong yet, and it is possible Alan has been fooled.'

'I know,' I said, 'but what worries me is if this is fraud, how is the girl going to be murdered? So far, I have only one angle.' I went on to tell her about the faulty electrical wiring clause, and how it could exclude a state execution.

Helen didn't think much of the idea.

'But how often is a woman executed? If this is fraud, surely whoever is behind it is going to make sure he or she will collect the money?'

'My idea is she has already committed a murder,' I explained, 'and she's taken out these policies to ensure she gets the best possible defence if she's caught. I agree the chances of her going to the chair are remote, but so long as there's a doubt, we and the other companies would organize a defence for her to protect ourselves against a possible claim.'

But Helen wasn't sold on this idea. She thought it was too fancy.

'If this is fraud,' she said seriously, 'then it's for the money. I'm sure of that. I have an idea that this set-up is like a smart conjurer who is setting his stage for a clever illusion. While he attracts your attention with his right hand he does his trick with his left. I may be wrong, and it's a waste of time to speculate until we have met these two, but remember what I've said. If it is fraud we'll have to be very careful the card they are now showing us isn't going to be substituted later on for one they have up their sleeve.'

'Are you being clairvoyant?' I asked. 'Or is this the much-renowned instinct at work?'

She laughed.

'I don't know, darling. I'm just speaking my thoughts out loud. I may be entirely wrong.'

We left it at that.

After dinner we went up to change. I collected a jemmy and

a .38 police special from my suitcase, while Helen slipped on a pair of slacks and a dark windbreaker. She tucked her hair up under a close-fitting beret.

We took the elevator down to the underground garage. The attendant sprang to his feet when he saw Helen and beamed on her.

'Okay, miss, I'll get her for you,' he said eagerly, and went off at a run.

'If I had come down here alone, he wouldn't have moved,' I said. 'Have you been working on him?'

'I've been polite to him; nothing more,' Helen said coolly.

'I'd like to have seen you,' I said, as the attendant drove the vintage Buick down the corridor of cars. 'He's even cleaned it.'

'I filled her up, lady,' the attendant said, jumping out and starting to polish the windshield, 'and she's had a wash.' His eyes ran over Helen's figure that was something to look at in that rig-out. 'Did you notice the tappet? Well, I fixed it.'

She thanked him with a bright smile while I pushed a buck into his hand which he took without taking his eyes off her.

As I drove up the ramp, I said, 'I nearly punched that punk in the nose. Did you see the way he was looking at you?'

'There are times, Mr. Harmas, when you look at me in exactly the same way,' she returned, 'and I don't remember having punched you in the nose.'

'Never mind. We are now approaching 4th Street. There's a parking lot on Boyle Avenue. We'd better leave the car there in case some cop gets curious. And don't forget, honey, if anything goes wrong, run. Don't let's have any misunderstanding about this. I'll take care of the trouble: that's what I get paid for. You use your pretty legs.'

'And what kind of trouble do you anticipate?'

'I have no idea, but it's well to have a plan of action ready in case. If the cops turn up or something happens, skip out fast. Go back to the hotel and wait for me.'

'And suppose you don't come back?'

'Then you phone up Fanshaw and get him to bail me out.'

We didn't say any more until we had parked the car, then, as we retraced our steps to 4th Street, Helen said, 'You'll be careful, won't you Steve? I'd hate to have to start hunting for another husband.'

'If you get yourself another husband I'll come back and haunt him. Let's take a look at the back of the building. There may be a window left open. Here's an alley that should take us to the janitor's entrance.'

Having made certain there was no one in the street to watch us, we ducked down a dark, evil-smelling alley. We were half-way down when out of the darkness I heard a scurry of footsteps. We both came to an abrupt standstill while we peered ahead.

Without warning a woman came quickly out of the semi-darkness, brushed past me and went on towards the end of the alley and to the street. It was too dark to see what she was like except to see she wore a scarf over her head and a long dark coat.

Appearing so suddenly, almost like a ghost, she had startled me. She had also startled Helen, who was clutching my arm.

'Where the devil did she spring from?' I said, and started back down the alley. I had only taken a couple of strides when I heard a car start up. I quickened my pace and reached the end of the alley in time to see a vast dreadnought of a car, without lights, shooting away from the opposite kerb.

Helen joined me and we stood looking after the car.

'What was all that in aid of?' I said. 'No lights, and going like a bat out of hell.'

'Did you smell her perfume?' Helen asked. 'Joy – the costliest perfume in the world.'

'Let's have a look at this alley,' I said, and we retraced our steps.

Twenty yards brought us to a blank wall. The alley only led to the janitor's entrance.

'Looks as if she must have come out of here,' I said, pausing before a door on which was printed in white paint:

'Unless an essential piece of elastic broke and she ducked down here to fix it,' Helen said.

'Wouldn't she have fixed it in the car?' I said, and took out my torch to flash on the door. 'Why, it's open.' I pushed the door and it swung inwards. 'You know, I think she's been here.'

'Maybe she owns an office here,' Helen said, lowering her voice. 'Do we go in?'

'Yeah.' I stepped into the lobby. 'Close the door behind you.'

Helen did so, then, bending, she slid a small wooden wedge under it.

'That'll hold it if a policeman tries it,' she said. 'I learned that one out of a book.'

'Very smart,' I said. 'Now keep quiet and close to me. We'll walk up. I don't trust the elevator.'

We went up the stone stairs, silently; she two steps behind me. Every now and then I flashed on the torch, but most of the time we climbed in darkness.

Helen jerked at my coat as we reached the fourth floor. I paused.

'What is it?' I asked, my head close to hers.

'I thought I heard something,' she whispered. 'I have a feeling someone's in the building.

'For Pete's sake, this isn't the time to exercise your instincts now. You're making me nervous.'

We stood side by side, listening, but there was no sound to be heard.

'Forget it,' I said. 'You're just jumpy. Come on, let's get up to the top floor.'

We went on, and by the time we had reached the sixth floor we were both breathing heavily.

'Now if you'll just give me a light,' I said, 'I'll show you how

I open a locked door. It's something people a lot poorer than you have paid good money to watch.'

'You can have the light,' she returned, a temor in her voice, 'but it doesn't seem necessary, does it?'

For the door stood half open.

We looked at it, and I admit the hair on the back of my neck bristled.

'Who's been in there?' I whispered. 'It was locked this afternoon.'

'What makes you think he isn't in there still?' she said, stepping behind me.

I slid my hand inside my coat and yanked out my gun.

'Let's have a look,' I said, thrusting the door open with my foot, and swung the beam of the torch around the small, dusty room. It contained a desk, two chairs, a strip of threadbare carpet and a filing cabinet. No one was lurking in there.

'That's odd,' I said, and walked into the room. 'I wonder if Denny came back this afternoon.'

Helen closed the door, crossed to the window and pulled down the blind, then turned on the electric light.

'I don't think it was Denny,' she said. 'It was that woman we ran into. Can't you smell the perfume in here?'

I sniffed, but I couldn't smell anything. I knew my nose was nothing like so sharp as Helen's for smells.

'You sure?' I don't notice anything.'

'I'm positive, Steve.'

I looked around the office. Nothing seemed disturbed.

'A woman who uses that sort of perfume wouldn't be one of Denny's clients,' Helen went on. 'That stuff costs money.'

'Then who was she? What was she doing here?'

I walked over to the dusty desk and pulled open a drawer. It was full of junk: paper-clips, bits of scrap paper, dirty pipe-cleaners, some empty tobacco tins, but nothing to interest me. I went through the other drawers. One of them contained a soiled shirt; another a towel, razor, shaving soap and a mirror.

'Just a small-time agent with very few assets,' I said, taking out a cigarette and sticking it on my lower lip.

Helen had opened the filing cabinet and was going through some letters. After a while she closed the drawer, shaking her head.

'Nothing here to tell us where he is now,' she said.

'Try the bottom drawer,' I suggested.

She pulled out the lower file. Tied up with red tape was a neat bundle of insurance policies.

'The cause of the trouble,' I said. 'Let's have a look at them.'

We spread the ten policies out on the desk and bent over them.

A few minutes' scrutiny told me they were an exact copy of the policy Goodyear had negotiated.

'The most sensible thing they could do,' I said. 'If they were going to accept her as a risk, they couldn't improve on our wording. I wonder if any company turned her down.' I turned one of the policies over to look at her signature. 'Hey! Look at this. A smear of ink and a thumb-print!'

'They've all got it,' Helen said, rapidly examining the other policies.

We looked at each other.

'Alan swore that print was an accident. This proves it wasn't. I think we have something, although I don't know what it is.'

Helen frowned down at the policies.

'Perhaps the first print was accidental,' she said. 'She might have liked the idea of having her print on the policies, and put it on the rest of them.'

'Is that what your instinct tells you?'

She shook her head.

'No. We'll have to find out from the other agents if they are also under the impression the prints got on their policies by accident,' she said, folding up the policies. 'I think as you do, Steve. There's something very slick about these prints.'

I returned the policies to the drawer.

'There's nothing else to see. Let's get out of here. At least we haven't wasted time, but we still haven't a lead where to find them.'

We left the door as we had found it and walked out on to the landing. We stood for a moment listening to the distant hum of traffic. Then we started down the stairs. We moved silently and fast.

On the third-floor landing Helen stopped and caught hold of my arm.

'Wait!' she whispered urgently. 'Listen!'

I snapped out the light, and we stood side by side in the darkness. Then I heard what she had heard: a soft, scraping noise coming from somewhere downstairs; a sound like a sack being dragged very slowly over a stone floor.

Helen clutched my hand.

'What is it?' she breathed.

I stepped to the banister rail and peered into the dark well, down to the ground floor. Nothing but darkness, a black empty pit, met my eyes. The scraping noise went on.

'Someone's down there,' I whispered. 'Sounds as if he's moving something.'

We waited, leaning over the rail, our ears strained.

More scraping noises drifted up out of the darkness, then a sudden clash of metal against metal nearly made us jump out of our skins.

'The elevator,' I said. 'Someone's coming up.'

I pulled Helen away from the banister rail.

'Who can it be?' she asked, and I could feel her trembling against me.

'Take it easy. Let's get out of sight.'

As we stepped back we heard the elevator coming up slowly and creakily. I tried one of the office doors, but it was locked.

'The stairs,' Helen whispered. 'We can go down as he's coming up.'

I took her hand and we groped our way to the head of the stairs. As we fumbled with our feet for the first step, another sound froze us rigid: a horrible, gasping groan that drifted up the elevator shaft and seemed to fill the whole building.

'Someone's hurt,' Helen said. 'I'm scared, Steve.'

I held her to me while we listened. The elevator came up

42

slowly. It was close to our landing now. I caught a glimpse of it outlined against the landing window, drifting upwards towards us, moving slower and slower, until it came to rest within a couple of yards of us.

A little flurry of sound came from it: a sound that made Helen catch her breath: a gasping sigh and a sliding, flopping noise.

I jerked out my gun, pushed Helen behind me and turned on my torch. The light fell on the grill of the elevator. Helen gave a faint scream. Blood ran over the elevator's step and dripped down into the well.

I took a step forward, the light shaking in my hand and peered into the elevator.

The janitor lolled up against the wall of the cage. His tin spectacles hung from one ear. There was blood on his face and his eyes were sightless. As I began to move forward, his limp body suddenly shifted, and he rolled away from the wall and slumped in a heap against the grill.

Somewhere in the distance, cutting sharply through the silence of the night, came the high-pitched wail of a police siren.

CHAPTER THREE

I

'WHO is it?' Helen asked, a little quaver in her voice. She moved forward and stood by my side.

'The janitor,' I said, listening to the sound of the approaching siren. 'Here, hold the light.'

I pushed the torch into her hand, took out my handkerchief, and, covering my hand with it, I opened the grill. I bent over the still body and turned it over. He had been stabbed in the hollow between his neck and shoulder. Although I lifted his eyelid I needn't have bothered. I knew he was dead.

The police siren became deafening, and I caught a glimpse of the red spotlight as it flashed across the transom of the front door.

'Upstairs!' Helen breathed, catching hold of my arm. 'We'll walk right into them if we use the alley. Quick!'

There came a hammering on the front door. I jerked away from the janitor's body, and together we darted up the stairs. A bell rang sharply from the janitor's room and more hammering came on the door.

We pelted up the stairs, making no sound.

'Top floor,' Helen gasped. 'There's a fire exit there.'

We reached the top floor as sounds below told us the police had entered the building. Helen was already drawing the bolts as I swung the torch on the fire-exit door.

'Know where it leads to?' she asked.

'We'll soon find out. Can't bolt it after us, and that'll tell them the way we went.'

She opened the door and peered out into the night sky, dimly lit by distant neon signs and the flood-lit roofs of the better movie houses and restaurants.

As I followed her on to the roof, a voice yelled from the ground floor, 'Anyone up there?'

I hastily shut the door. A quick look at the iron fire-escape showed me it led to the alley. I also spotted a patrolman standing in front of the building, watching the street.

Helen had gone to the back of the building, and now she waved to me. I joined her.

'There's a cop watching the front entrance,' I said. 'We can't use the escape.'

'We can get down here,' she said, pointing. 'It's a bit of a drop, but we can manage it.'

Some twenty feet below us was another flat roof. From the smell that came to us through the half-open skylight, I guessed it belonged to the Chinese restaurant I had noticed in the afternoon.

'We'll break a leg,' I said doubtfully.

'Not if we fall right,' she returned, and, before I could stop her, she sat on the edge of the roof, grabbed hold of the guttering and lowered herself into space. Then she let go and dropped a jiu-jitsu fall, landing on heels, arms and shoulders in quick succession. A moment later, she was on her feet.

'There's nothing to it,' she called up in a whisper. 'Come on, darling.'

I swore softly as I lowered myself over the edge of the roof. I was a lot heavier than she, and I visualized at least a broken ankle. I let myself go, trying to imitate her fall. I landed with a jar that shook the breath out of me. For a moment I sat, stunned, then, as she pulled at my arm, I got slowly to my feet.

'That's no way to fall,' she said. 'Did you hurt yourself?'

'I've probably fractured my spine and both legs,' I said with feeling, 'but don't let that worry you.'

Obviously it didn't, for she wasn't even listening. She was bending over the skylight, and, as I joined her, she got it open.

'Let's pretend we're hungry,' she said, smiling. 'At least, it smells good.' She swung her legs through the open skylight and dropped out of sight.

This was getting a little out of hand, I thought. She was showing a shade too much initiative, but I followed her down. We found ourselves in a long, dark passage, at the bottom of which was the head of a flight of stairs. We peered over the banister rail. Two flights below we could see waiters moving about, carrying trays.

'We can't go down there,' I said. 'They'd know we came this way.'

'They wouldn't think of it,' she returned briskly. 'They're too busy to spot us. Come on, darling, it's the only way.'

She went down the stairs to the next landing. I followed her.

'I'm going in there to powder my nose and get rid of my beret,' she said, pointing to a door marked *Ladies*. 'You go on down and get a table.'

She had gone before I could argue with her. I leaned over the banister rail for some moments, then when the landing below was deserted I whipped down the stairs, darted to the next flight, went down ten stairs, turned quickly and began to saunter up them as a tall chink in an ill-fitting tuxedo appeared from behind a bead curtain that led to the upper restaurant.

'Good evening, sir,' he said, with a little bow. 'Did you reserve a table?'

'I didn't,' I said. 'Should I have done?'

'It's quite all right,' he said, bowing. 'There are plenty of tables tonight.' He looked me over. 'Is there something wrong next door? I thought I heard a siren.'

I took out my pack of Camels, selected one and lit it before saying, as casually as I could, 'A couple of cops playing at robbers. I don't know what the excitement's about. Maybe someone shut the cat in.'

Helen appeared, her hands in her pockets, a bored expression on her face. She had removed her beret, and her dark, silky hair made an attractive frame for her face.

'Two, sir?' the chink asked, looking admiringly at Helen.

'That's right. We left our six children and the dog outside.'

He blinked, looked again at Helen, and then led the way into the restaurant.

'Must you talk rubbish?' she whispered fiercely as we followed him.

'Nothing like the domestic touch to lull suspicion,' I whispered back, grinning.

The restaurant was large and gaudy. Across one of the walls was a hideous red and yellow dragon, breathing fire and brimstone out of its open mouth. A number of people were still eating in spite of the late hour, and they glanced up as we came in. The men, without exception, eyed Helen with ferocious interest. I noticed regretfully that none of the women paid any attention to me. They were too busy trying to get their escorts' eyes off Helen.

We sat down at a corner table and made an effort to show interest in the yard-long menu the chink flourished before us. Finally, in depression, we ordered a savoury and highballs. The chink went away, his back stiff with outraged indignation.

It took a few minutes for the people at the other tables to lose interest in us, and when we felt it was safe to talk I said in an undertone, 'I don't know if it was smart to run like that. This could put us right in the middle of a jam.'

Helen shook her head.

'We had to get out. We'd have been in a worse jam if we'd stayed. After all, we did break in, and if we had told them why and the press got hold of it, we would tip our hand.'

'Someone must have told the cops for them to turn up like that. Think we were seen going in?'

Helen made a little grimace.

'It's possible. We'd better stay here a while. If they have a description . . .'

'Yeah.'

The chink came back and put plates before us. I asked him to bring me another highball in five minutes. I wanted a drink badly.

When he had gone, Helen said, 'You're sure he was dead?'

I nodded and took a long drink. It hit the spot all right.

'No doubt about it. The artery was cut. He must have bled to death.'

'How did he get into the elevator?'

'Probably crawled there and tried to pull himself up to a telephone,' I guessed. 'He hadn't one in his room.'

Helen cut into her savoury.

'I wish I didn't have to eat this,' she said. 'Do you think his death has anything to do with Denny?'

But I was scarcely listening, for my whole attention was riveted on a man who had appeared from around the corner where other tables were hidden from our sight. He was tall and built like a prize-fighter. His beetling brows met across the bridge of his thick nose. His heavy, sullen face was sun-tanned and set in a cold, blank, poker-faced expression. He wore a blue and white check leisure coat and fawn trousers, and he carried a light-brown slouch hat in his hand.

I knew at once who he was. The janitor's description fitted him like a glove. This was the man who had been so anxious to meet Brad Denny.

II

The sound of sirens, wailing up the street, came blasting through the open windows of the restaurant. Some of the diners jumped up and went over to the windows to see what the commotion was about.

'Don't look now,' I said rapidly to Helen, 'but our pal in the check coat is with us. He's on his way out. I'm going after him. You stay here. We'll meet at the hotel. Okay?'

She opened her bag, took out the car key and slid it to me.

'You may need the car. I'll take a taxi.'

Once again I gave her full marks for quick thinking.

The man in the check coat was moving to the exit. I pushed

back my chair and got up, walking over to the cash desk. The chink looked at me impassively.

'I want to see what the shindig is outside,' I said, and tossed a five-dollar bill on the desk. 'Give the lady the change.'

'Yes, sir.'

I pushed aside the bead curtain and stepped out on to the landing. The man I was following had paused just inside the door leading to the street. I watched him from over the banisters, and then, when he moved out of the doorway and walked away from the building the police were investigating, I ran down the stairs three at a time and reached the street in time to see him rapidly disappearing into the darkness.

I looked quickly at the ambulance and the three prowl cars outside the building. There was a crowd of people standing in a half-circle outside the entrance. Two cops were struggling to keep them back, and they were far too busy to bother about me.

I set off after the man who had just left the restaurant. He was moving fast, and was heading towards the car-park where I had left the Buick.

He strode along, his hands in his pockets, his hat on the back of his head, and he didn't once look around. While I legged it along in his rear I wondered what he was doing in the restaurant. Had he broken into Denny's office? Had he killed the janitor? He might have spotted us and had slipped into the restaurant to phone the police so we would run into trouble. I was only guessing, but I liked the idea. But who was the woman who had come running out of the alley? Was she hooked up in some way with the killing?

The tall, broad-shouldered figure ahead of me paused at the entrance to the parking lot to look back over his shoulder. I had just time to flatten myself against the wall. I was pretty certain he hadn't spotted me. He walked through the big gateway and disappeared. I broke into a fast, silent run, and reached the parking lot in a dozen strides.

The man in the check coat had vanished, but I knew he was in there. The fence was too high to climb easily, and I reckoned I'd have heard him if he had made the attempt.

I decided he was either groping around for his car or else was aware I had been following him and was waiting to see what my next move would be.

Knowing he had very probably just committed a murder and another wouldn't make a lot of difference to him, I didn't feel any too easy. I slid my gun out of its holster and dropped it into my pocket, shifting off the safety-catch as I did so.

For some minutes I stood in the darkness, sure he couldn't see me, and trying in vain to see him. As the minutes ticked by I became more and more convinced he knew I was following him and was baiting a trap for me to walk into. I began to move along the fence, keeping in the shadows, and straining my eyes for a glimpse of him.

I could just make out six cars in a row in the middle of the lot, and I watched them for a few moments for any sign of movement, but saw nothing. I kept on, and whenever I came to within seeing distance of a car I stopped to watch it.

I had been at this game for about five minutes, and I was sweating freely, when suddenly the headlights of a car swept the entrance to the parking lot and lit it up like a Christmas tree. I flung myself flat, looking quickly to right and left. There was no sign of the man in the check coat.

The car pulled up and the lights went out. A girl and a man got out and hurriedly walked towards the exit.

I heard the girl say excitedly, 'Imagine a murder on 4th Street! Do you think we'll be able to see the body?'

'We'll have a damn good try,' the man said, and, taking her arm, he started to run.

I watched them disappear, and then I straightened up. Somehow the man in the check coat had fooled me. He must have climbed the fence without my hearing him. My immediate reaction to this was to wonder what Helen would say. I didn't relish telling her I had let this guy slip through my fingers. I wanted her to keep her illusions that I was a pretty smart investigator.

Cursing myself, I turned towards the exit and began to walk rapidly along the row of six cars parked in the centre of the lot.

As I reached the third car I heard a soft whistle that seemed to come from behind me. I stopped as if I had run into a brick wall. Turning, I peered into the darkness, holding my breath so I could hear better, suddenly aware that I was right out in the open, a beautiful target for a sharp-eyed gunman.

I was about to drop on my hands and knees when I heard a faint rustle behind me. My hand flew to my pocket for my gun as I spun around.

The broad-shouldered, shadowy shape was right on top of me. A fist thumped my chest, sending me off balance. I clawed the gun out of my pocket as another fist whistled out of the darkness and smashed against my jaw.

I went out in a sky full of stars and bright lights.

III

Helen was pacing up and down in our bedroom when I walked in. She took one look at my bruised face and dusty clothes and rushed to me, her eyes wide with alarm.

'Oh, Steve! What happened? Are you hurt?'

I gave her a twisted grin. It was the best I could manage at the moment, as I was feeling very sorry for myself.

'It's okay,' I said, sinking on to the bed. 'Did you think to pack that bottle of Scotch I've been hoarding? I could do with a snort.'

She flew to the suitcase, unearthed the bottle, ran into the bathroom and came out with the glass full of the precious stuff.

'Can you manage, darling?'

'I'd have to be dead and buried not to manage a glass of Scotch,' I said. 'Relax, sweetheart. I'm okay.' I drank some of the Scotch, set down the glass and rubbed the lump on my jaw. I was lucky not to have lost some teeth. 'Right at this moment,' I went on bitterly, 'you're looking at Public Sucker No. One. Take a good look.'

'All of which adds up to the fact you lost him?' Helen said, sitting on the bed by my side. 'Even the best detectives don't always get their man.'

'I didn't lose him,' I said. 'I wish I had. I let him find me. I followed him into the car-park. It was as black as a hat in there, and he vanished. I hunted around, but couldn't see him. Then a car drove in and lit up the place; still no sign of him. All the time, of course, he was crouching behind a car, well out of sight, hoping I'd think just what I did think: that he had gone. As I was leaving the place, chastened and down-hearted, he stepped out from nowhere and slugged me.' I wobbled my jaw to and fro. It felt very loose. 'He has a punch like a sledge-hammer and he's as fast as greased lightning. It took me a good half-hour to come round, and another ten minutes to get the thing I have humorously called a brain up to now working. He had gone through my pockets, scattered my belongings to the four winds, and decamped.'

'What was in the wallet, Steve?'

'That's it. I always did say you were the brains of the family. You've put your finger on the wound. The whole works was in the wallet: my business cards to tell him who I am; Fanshaw's address to tell him I'm here on business; my licence to tell him I'm an investigator and – and this will kill you – the list of the causes of death against which the Gellert girl can't claim. The whole works! If he is one of Denny's stooges, I've blown the lid right off the set-up.'

'Well, it can't be helped,' Helen said, and kissed me. 'It's just one of those things. Anyone could have walked into a trap like that. You mustn't blame yourself.'

'That's very nice of you to put it like that, but if Maddux hears about it he'll pop an artery. Well, I'm going to turn in. I've had quite enough of the Gellert case for one day.'

As I began to strip off my clothes, Helen said, 'When you left me I went down and joined the crowd. I did a little gaping myself and got friendly with one of the policemen. He told me an attempt had been made to open the safe in a diamond broker's office on the third floor. The policeman said the burglar was an amateur. Apart from scratching the safe, he didn't get anywhere. The police think Mason, the janitor, heard him, went up to investigate and got knifed.'

I paused as I was getting out of my trousers.

'Sounds a pretty desperate amateur. That yarn doesn't make sense to me. Anything said about Denny?'

She shook her head.

'No, the police are convinced the killer's object was to get at the diamonds in this broker's office.'

I continued to undress.

'If that is so, and I doubt it, the janitor's murder has nothing to do with Denny. Of course we don't know for certain the gent in the check coat was in the building or that he did kill Mason. The fact he has been hanging around for three days looking for Denny and is on the spot tonight points to him being the killer, but we have no proof. Then there's the lady of the Joy perfume. Where does she come in?'

While I was talking Helen had slipped out of her things and into a nightie. The speed she could undress at always left me gaping. I followed her into the bathroom.

'Come to think of it, the gent in the check coat may have nothing to do with our case at all. He might have used Denny's name from the sign-board as an excuse to look over the broker's office.'

Helen nodded vigorously as she cleaned her teeth.

I went back into the bedroom and got into my pyjamas.

When Helen came out of the bathroom, I said, 'We've got to find this Gellert girl. Our best bet would be to call on the smaller theatrical agents. They may know where she is. We'll draw up a list of the agencies and see what we can find out about her. Any better suggestions?'

'Yes,' Helen said, jumping into bed. 'Quit acting like a detective and let's get some sleep. Do you realize it's after two o'clock?'

'I'll have you know, Mrs. Harmas,' I said, drawing myself up, 'a detective can't afford to sleep. He must be at it every hour of the day and night.'

'I thought we agreed you were Public Sucker No. One, and not a good detective.' Helen said, pulling the bedclothes up to her shoulder. 'Get off your high horse, and come to bed.'

The next morning, a little after nine-thirty, and after breakfast served in bed, we got hold of the classified telephone book and made a list of the various theatrical agencies in town. Their name was legion, and by the time we were through we had a list as long as my arm.

'You'll have grandchildren by the time we've worked through this lot,' I said in disgust. 'Jeepers! How do these punks ever earn any money with so much competition?'

'We may be lucky and hit on someone first shot who knows them,' Helen said hopefully. 'Tear the list in half. I'll do one half and you do the other.'

'That's very sporting of you,' I said. 'You're not compelled to do this, understand. Walking the sidewalks, asking idiotic questions and pounding up and down stairs is what I get paid for. You've been hired for your brains.'

'Oh, I shall use them,' Helen said. 'Give me the list, and let's make a start. Shall we meet here for lunch at one o'clock?'

'We'll do that. Concentrate on the one-man agencies. The big stuff won't know this girl. Take care of yourself.'

Armed with my list, I started off on the job. It wasn't the kind of work I liked, but it was something that was always cropping up, and I knew from experience that it paid off dividends if you kept at it and had enough patience. Trying to trace a missing person, as any cop will tell you, is ninety per cent leg work, five per cent inspiration and five per cent luck.

After a couple of hours slogging up and down stairs and in and out of offices I came to the conclusion I was getting all the leg work and absolutely no luck. By now I had visited ten agencies, only to be met with a blank, disinterested, 'Never heard of her', when I asked about Susan Gellert, and neither had they heard of Brad Denny, and what was more they didn't seem to want to either.

It was a hot day, and by half-past eleven I was feeling like an old man who has spent an hour too long in the steam-room of a

Turkish bath. I took time out to rest my feet and have a coffee at a drug-store. I was working a street that contained twenty-two theatrical agents; all of them on the top floor of various buildings that hadn't got around yet to installing an elevator. I decided it might be worth while to consult the elderly attendant who served me with coffee.

'I'm trying to trace a show girl,' I said, mopping my face and neck. 'Name of Gellert: Susan Gellert. Ever heard of her?'

'Susan Gellert?' he repeated, then shook his head. 'Can't say I have. Corrine Gellert, but not Susan. Maybe they're sisters. I heard somewhere Corrine Gellert had a sister.'

'Who's Corrine Gellert?' I asked, not too hopefully, although the name wasn't one you heard every day.

The guy grinned, showing three teeth and a lot of gum.

'She was some baby in her day. Used to come in here every so often. A real wild one if ever there was a wild one.'

'In what way – wild?'

'Didn't give a damn for anyone or anything. She used to do a strip act at the Keyhole Club on 10th about six or seven years ago. Got drunk one night and walked right out of the club and down the street as bare as the back of my hand. Luckily for her, the cop she ran into knew her, and got her off the street quick. A real tough baby, believe you me.'

'Know where she is now?'

'No idea. I haven't seen her for getting on three years. I heard she got married. I know she quit show business or maybe show business quit her.'

'Ever run into a guy named Brad Denny? He's an agent I believe.'

'I guess not. But why not go over to Mossy Phillips's joint across the street. I guess he's photographed everyone in show business at one time or the other. Not the big stars, of course, but all the smaller ones. They all go to Mossy. He may be able to help you.'

That sounded like a good idea. I paid for my coffee, thanked him and went out into the blazing sun again.

Across the way was a small, single-fronted photographic

studio with a lot of glossy prints in the window. The facia carried a sign in a faded gilt lettering that read:

M. PHILLIPS.   PORTRAITS.   EST. 1897

I pushed open the door and entered the tiny shop consisting of a counter that divided what floor space there was in half, and four large boards on which were pinned photos of show girls, hoofers, peelers, muscle-dancers and comics. A bell pinged sharply as the door opened, but it was some time before any one appeared.

I was browsing over the photos, wondering how many of these people were alive today: most of them looked as if they had patronized Mr. Phillips about the time he got himself established, when I heard a gentle cough behind me.

I turned.

A tall, sad-faced, white-haired negro stood behind the counter looking at me with hopeful inquiry. He was pushing seventy-five in a gentle way, and his frock-coat, string tie and spotless dicky were relics of the past.

'Good morning,' he said, resting two bony hands on the counter. 'Can I help you?'

'I'm hoping you can,' I said, and tentatively tried my wide, friendly smile on him. He reacted to it the way a friendly dog reacts when you snap your fingers at it. His teeth were a lot whiter and bigger than mine. 'I'm looking for a little information,' I went on and laid my card on the counter in front of him.

He studied the card and then nodded his head.

'Oh, yes, Mr. Harmas. I know your company well. My son insures with you. He speaks very highly of your people.'

'That's fine,' I said, and shook hands with him. 'I'm trying to trace a show girl. It's to do with a policy.'

'Would you care to come into the studio? You can make yourself comfortable and we're not likely to be disturbed.'

He lifted the counter flap, and I followed him into a comfortably furnished room, one end of which was obviously the studio. A big, old-fashioned camera, covered with a velvet cloth, stood on a tripod, facing a large strip of grey canvas on which were painted some very phoney-looking clouds.

We sat down opposite each other in tub-chairs which are comfortable enough if you don't mind sitting bolt upright.'

'You mustn't pay any attention to this place,' Phillips said apologetically. 'I know it looks very old fashioned, but show people like it this way. They're very conservative and superstitious, and it wouldn't do for me to change anything or try to change anything or try to bring things up-to-date.'

I wasn't kidded for a moment. I said I knew how show people were.

'Who was the girl you're interested in, Mr. Harmas?' The sad eyes told me he knew I wasn't kidded.

'Her name's Susan Gellert, and her agent's Brad Denny. I don't know anything else about her.'

'Susan Gellert?' Phillips wrinkled his forehead. 'Why, yes. Corrine Gellert's sister. Is that the one you mean?'

'I've no idea. I don't know if she had a sister or not.'

'It must be. Corrine was the clever one. She had a lot of talent. Susan was a pretty little thing, but I'm afraid she hadn't much up here,' and he tapped his bony forehead. 'They were twins, and, apart from their colouring, you couldn't possibly tell them apart.'

'Twins?' I sat forward.

'Yes. Really remarkable how alike they were. Susan is blonde and Corrine dark. They once did an act together. Susan wore a dark wig. She mystified the audience.' He got up. 'I have a photo of them somewhere. Perhaps you would like to see it?'

I said I would. I was trying to make up my mind if I had discovered anything important.

The old Negro spent some time fiddling with a mass of prints he had taken from a file. His eyesight wasn't as good as it should have been, and he had practically to rub his nose on each print before he could identify it. I was fit to climb up a wall with impatience before he suddenly gave a pleased little grunt and came over with a glossy twelve by eight in his hand.

'Here it is,' he said, handing it to me. 'You will see the kind of act it was. It wasn't very successful. I believe Susan hadn't the talent to compete with her sister.'

The photograph showed a girl admiring herself in a gigantic mirror. It wasn't until I had studied the print carefully that I realized the girl was standing before an empty frame and there was no mirror. The reflection was, in fact, her twin sister, holding the same pose. It certainly looked effective, and the girls were identical: good-looking kids, good figures and neat legs. They were dressed in the usual pie-dish frilled skirt and spangled bodices you see in hundreds of Honky-tonk shows.

'I have a photo of Susan without the dark wig,' Phillips went on. 'I'll see if I can put my hand on it.'

While he was hunting for the photograph I asked him if he knew where I could find Susan.

'I'm afraid I don't,' he returned. 'I haven't seen her for a long time. Corrine got married about three years ago, and she's left show business. I heard she went to Buenos Aires. I don't know what Susan is doing now. I can't imagine she would be very successful without her sister who was, as I think I told you, the talented one of the family.'

'Ever heard of Brad Denny?'

'Why, yes. Mr. Denny had been in here once or twice.'

'Did he have his photograph taken?'

'He's one of the newcomers, and I think he considers my methods are a little old fashioned. He came only to buy some prints.'

'What kind of fella is he?'

'A very pleasant young man,' Phillips told me, his nose still in the photographs. 'He's quite a clever dancer.'

'I thought he was Susan's agent.'

'He may be. I don't know. When I met him, about six months ago, he did a song and dance act. He's only been a few years in the profession. I doubt if he is more than twenty-three or four.'

'Would you trust him, Mr. Phillips?'

The old Negro straightened and blinked at me.

'Trust him? I don't think I understand.'

'Would you say he's honest?'

'As far as one can trust anyone these days,' he returned gravely, 'I would trust Mr. Denny. I have had no personal dealings with him, but I would say he was an honest young man. He has a very agreeable personality, and I liked him.'

I nodded. He was merely confirming what Alan Goodyear had said.

'How about these Gellert girls? What sort of reputation have they got?'

Phillips began to look a little uncomfortable.

'Well, I don't think I care to express an opinion. They may have changed a lot now they are older. They were a little wild, but then, so many show people are. I haven't seen them for some time now. I would prefer not to say more than that.'

I had an idea he was holding back quite a lot, but I could see by his expression I wouldn't get it out of him, so I let it ride.

Eventually he found the photograph. I studied it with interest. Susan was a pretty girl with laughing eyes that could be reckless when she happened to be in the mood. It certainly wasn't a bad or vicious face, and I had a distinct feeling I had seen her somewhere before, although I couldn't place where.

'Could I buy this off you: and the other one?' I asked. Seeing his hesitation, I took out a five-dollar bill and laid it on the table. 'My company's anxious to have these prints, Mr. Phillips, if you can spare them.'

'Certainly, but that's far too much for them. A dollar is ample.'

'That's okay. Thanks for the information. You can't give me any idea how I can get into touch with either Susan Gellert or Denny?'

'You might ask at the Vaudeville Club. It's on Firestone Boulevard. They may be members, and the club keeps forwarding addresses.'

'I'll try it. Thanks.' I shook hands with him, accepted an envelope for the prints, and hurried back to my car.

The time was now five minutes to one, and I decided to call on the Vaudeville Club after lunch. I was hot and tired, and I thirsted for a drink. I drove to the hotel as fast as the mid-morning traffic would allow.

I found Helen sitting in the lounge, reading a newspaper. She looked so cool and fresh that I stood over her, staring suspiciously.

'There you are, darling,' she said, looking up and smiling. 'How hot you look. Have you had a hard morning?'

'I have,' I said. 'I've been walking my feet to the bone. You don't look as if you've even started work yet.'

'I thought it was a little too hot for walking, so I didn't go out.'

I sat down beside her, and clawed at my damp collar that was threatening to strangle me.

'You mean you've been sitting on your fanny all the morning?' I said gaping at her. 'You've been resting while your poor husband has been slogging up and down thousands of stairs? You have the crust to sit there and tell me that? Didn't you promise you'd work on that list I gave you?'

'I know I did, darling,' she said, patting my hand. 'But after you had gone I decided to use my brains instead of my feet. You did say I was hired to use my brains, didn't you?'

I wiped my face with my sodden handerkerchief.

'Go on – tell me. You know where they are?'

'Certainly I do. They are playing at the Palace Theatre, Willington.'

'Are you sure?' I snarled. 'You wouldn't be making this up?'

'I'm quite sure.'

'Then how did you find out?'

'I looked in *Variety*. I remembered artists usually advertise in the Personal column where they are next appearing. It was in there. I did try to get into touch with you, but you seemed to have covered an awful lot of ground.'

I walked towards the bar, speechless.

CHAPTER FOUR

I

WHILE I had been walking my legs off all the morning, Helen hadn't been as idle as she had made out. As soon as she had found out where Susan Gellert and Denny were playing, she had consulted the hall porter about the best way to Willington, bought a map of the district, packed our luggage, settled the hotel bill, phoned the only hotel in Willington and booked a room for the night.

Willington, it seemed, was a hick town about a hundred and twenty miles from Los Angeles, and Helen reckoned we could get there in time to catch the evening performance at the Palace Theatre if we left the hotel immediately after lunch.

I was too busy eating and drinking to tell her what I had discovered, but as soon as we were in the Buick and heading up Figueroa Street I gave her a detailed description of my meeting with Mossy Philips.

'Twin sisters!' she exclaimed, when I had concluded my recital. 'Now my imagination is going to run riot! This could be the key to the fraud, Steve. I'm not saying it is, but it could be an impersonation.'

'For crying out loud!' I said. 'Don't make this more complicated than it is. We haven't even seen Susan yet, and Corrine is in South America.'

'We don't know that for certain, but it would be fun, wouldn't it, if we could go out there? I've always wanted to see South America. I hear the men are wonderful.'

'Will you watch where you're driving and let your husband

get a little sleep?' I said. 'You've sat around all the morning, but I haven't; besides, I think I've eaten too much.'

'Very well, darling, you go ahead and get some sleep,' she said sympathetically. 'An idea's just occurred to me. If it is any good I'll wake you up and tell you about it.'

'Save it until we get to Willington,' I said, and closed my eyes.

We reached Willington just after seven in the evening. It wasn't much of a town, but a shade better than I had expected. We found the only hotel on a side street off the main street.

After a wash and a quick snack, we set off for the theatre which the reception clerk told us was a hundred yards or so along the main street.

'Imagine living in a dump like this,' I said, as we walked along the dusty sidewalk. 'How would you like it?'

'Not for me,' Helen said, shaking her head. 'What are your plans, Steve? Are you going to be an investigator when you go backstage or a bewitched fan?'

'An investigator. Having heard about the other policies I am a little anxious about Miss Gellert's safety. That's the angle. I shall point out the dangers of being insured for a million; remind her of the temptation some other party may have to get rid of her. It'll be interesting to see her reaction. If I give her a straight warning we are aware of the possibilities of the set-up, she may lose her nerve if she is planning something and not go through with it. I also want to find out who will come into the money if anything does happen to her.'

'Do you want me to come or shall I be in the way?'

I grinned.

'You're never in the way, sweetheart. You come.'

The Palace Theatre seemed determined to give value for money. Besides Hopalong Cassidy, there was a singer who set my teeth on edge, a comic that made Helen blush, and now the lights went down for Brad Denny, described in the programme as 'The Boy with the Happy Feet.'

To judge from the whispered conversations going on around

us, the audience had come to see Susan. I noticed the men outnumbered the women by about six to one. There was a buzz of impatience when Denny's name flashed up on the lighted sign.

'I wish she'd come on,' I muttered to Helen. 'This sweat-box is killing me.'

Her reply was drowned by the five-piece band blaring into life. The lights flashed up on the stage and a young fellow in a tuxedo came on in a tap routine.

We both watched him with interest.

He was a good-looking youngster: a typical college boy; fair, broad-shouldered, with a flashing smile and alert, bright eyes. Although he was no Astaire, he managed to put over his dance with enough vigour to earn a good hand from the sweating audience. But his encore was received with less enthusiasm. The audience had come to see Susan, and were getting restless.

'Nothing the matter with him from his looks,' I said, as Denny came to the footlights to make his final bow.

'I think he's a pet,' Helen returned.

As the last of the applause petered out, Denny raised his hands.

'And now, ladies and gentlemen,' he said, 'it is my great pleasure to present to you that brilliant, courageous and beautiful young dancer who twice nightly risks her life to give you the most sensational dance of the century! Ladies and gentlemen: Susan Gellert in the Kiss of Death!'

He stepped back as the drummer crashed two ear-splitting cymbal beats, followed by a roll on the drums. As the audience began to stamp and clap the lights went down slowly until the stage was in darkness.

Sitting in the hot, stifling atmosphere, I sensed a sudden electric tension spreading through the ghastly little theatre: the kind of tension you get at a first night of a Broadway play. I noticed also the complete stillness of the audience, and the quiet that had fallen.

63

Then the lights flashed up. In the middle of the stage stood a blonde girl in a G-string and a snake: that's the best description I can give of her complete nudity.

The snake was a six-foot cobra. She had it draped around her neck and over her shoulders. One hand held it behind its hissing neck while the other held its tail.

For fully twenty seconds she stood there while the drums rolled and the audience yelled and clapped. She had a beautiful little figure. Watching her, as she stood motionless, the snake's scaly length twined around her body, had me and all the other men suddenly sitting on the edges of our seats.

'If I'd any idea you'd be so carried away,' Helen said a little tartly, 'I'd have brought a pair of field-glasses for you.'

'I would have brought them myself if I'd known she was going to be this good,' I returned, 'and keep quiet, please; my line is busy.'

Susan began to move around the stage: a mistake. The moment she began to move I realized she had about as much talent for dancing as I had, and that's not saying much. She lacked rhythm; she was awkward; she was amateurish. But not a man's eyes shifted away from her. If she hadn't any talent, at least she had a body a sculptor would rave about. As the music broke into a lilting waltz, she moved quicker, swaying from side to side, still holding the snake's head at arm's length. Then suddenly, she released its tail, and the brute lashed the air angrily, before coiling around her arm, squeezing into her flesh and bringing an involuntary gasp of horror from some of the women.

On went the naked, beautiful figure, round and round, spinning and weaving, and it wasn't until she had slowed down that I saw the snake's neck, just behind its vicious-looking head, had dilated, forming a hood, a sure sign it would strike if given the chance.

I told myself the snake was harmless, that the poison sac had been removed, but, even with that assurance, I was gaping and clutching on to the arms of my seat as she came to a standstill once more at the footlights while the scaly, hideous body of the snake twined and untwined itself around her arms and neck.

The drums began to roll as she slowly went down on her knees, and then with a smooth, unhurried movement she uncoiled the snake from her and set it on the floor in front of her. She swayed away from it as with a quick movement it coiled itself into a tight circle, its hooded head rearing up, its forked tongue darting at her.

For a long moment she knelt motionless, facing the snake. Then, very slowly, she began to lean towards it.

'Sweet grief!' I muttered, unable to control myself. 'If that brute spits at her . . .'

'Quiet!' Helen snapped, and from the tone of her voice I knew she wasn't entirely unmoved herself.

Somewhere in the darkness a woman stifled a scream. A man jumped up, but was immediately jerked back into his seat by those behind him.

The girl continued to lean forward, not more than a foot separating her from the hissing, vicious head. The drum suddenly stopped rolling, and in a silence you could cut into slices, she suddenly froze into a rigid stillness.

The snake, too, was motionless. Helen put her hand on my arm and dug her fingers into my flesh. There was now the kind of atmosphere you find in a bull-ring at the moment of the kill. This was no longer a corny dance with a corny snake. Suddenly, it was as if Death had walked into the stifling little theatre and had taken a seat at your side. People around me were gasping. One or two of them were moaning as if they were having a fit.

The girl moved again; inch by inch she brought her face closer to the snake. Its forked tongue darted in and out: inches separated them now. Then, as she moved even closer, the forked tongue flickered over her lips. It was the most gruesome thing I've ever had to watch. That was obviously the climax of the dance, for there was a clash of cymbals and the lights went out.

For a long moment nothing happened. I flopped back into my seat, feeling as if I had run up ten flights of stairs. The only sound that could be heard was the heavy, gasping breathing coming from all over the theatre. Then someone began to clap; a man whistled; another yelled. It was the signal for a release of sound that shook the building.

Up went the lights, and Susan stood bowing and smiling. The cobra had disappeared, and she was now wearing an emerald-green cloak that covered her down to her heels.

She stood bowing and blowing kisses for fully five minutes while the audience, now on their feet, yelled, whistled and clapped. Then the curtain fell, and the house lights went up. Even then most of the men continued to yell and whistle.

'Let's get out of here,' Helen said. 'Ugh! I hated that. There was something depraved about it.'

I realized I was sweating and my heart was banging against my side. Helen was right, of course. There had been something depraved about the dance. In some mysterious way it reeked of death and sex.

We were glad to get into the cool night air, and we lit cigarettes, standing against the wall to let the crowd move off along the sidewalk.

All of them were talking excitedly, their eyes gleaming. Some of the men had a hungry, animal look that made me wonder uneasily how I was looking myself.

'Sure she hasn't a hope of putting an act like that on in New York,' Helen said.

'I doubt it. The police wouldn't stand for it. But I do think the audience were to blame. It was they who created that atmosphere. Let's go and talk to her. Do you think the snake was harmless?'

'Of course it was. You don't think anyone in their right minds would fool around with a cobra unless it was harmless, do you?'

'I'm glad we're covered against snake-bites,' I said. 'It would be easy to substitute another snake. Come on, let's take a look at her.'

There was a small crowd of men around the stage door. A cop kept them off the sidewalk. Most of them were elderly, obviously from out-lying farms on a night out.

I showed the cop my card.

'I want a word with Miss Gellert.'

He looked at me, then at Helen and decided we were at least respectable.

'Report to the manager's office,' he said, and opened the door. We ducked under his arm and walked down a dimly lit passage to the office.

The manager and the elderly doorman were standing just inside the office, talking. They looked up as I entered.

'I'm looking for Miss Gellert,' I said.

The manager shook his head.

'I don't think she's seeing anyone. Got a card?'

I gave him one and he glanced at it, then handed it to the doorman.

'Slip down to Miss Gellert's room, Joe, and find out if she'll see this gentleman.'

The doorman went off. There was no slipping about it. You could almost hear his bones creak.

'Some show you've put on,' I said, offering the manager a cigarette. He was a big, flabby bird with a bald head and purplish patches under his eyes.

'You liked it? Well, that's something. Some cranks have been writing me abusive letters. A couple of them have been to the sheriff's office, but they didn't get any change out of him. Of course, the majority have been knocked sideways, but they don't bother to come round and tell me.' He lit the cigarette and eyed Helen with interest. 'We've never done better business in the history of this house. Did you like the act, too, miss?'

'I'm afraid I didn't. Female nudes don't interest me,' Helen said. 'But I liked Denny.'

'Yeah, he's not bad,' the manager said indifferently. 'He's a lucky guy to have hitched himself to Miss Gellert. That girl's going to go far.'

'Unless she lands herself in jail,' Helen said tartly.

The manager looked uneasily at her.

'Did you think it was a little raw?'

Seeing Helen was about to make an acid remark, I broke in hastily, 'I wouldn't care to get my face as close to that snake as she does. Of course, it makes a difference when it has had its poison drawn, but, even at that, I wouldn't like it.'

The flabby white face looked shocked.

'What makes you think it isn't poisonous? Did you miss the publicity outside the house? We're offering a hundred bucks to anyone who can prove the snake isn't poisonous. Anyone can examine it at any time.'

'Has anyone?' Helen asked.

'Sure. Some farmer who reckoned he was a snake expert took a look at it through the glass top of its box. He wouldn't handle it. The snake spat at him, and it was poison on the glass all right. I guess that's why people get so worked up. They're waiting to see her bitten, and I don't know why the hell she hasn't been bitten.' He mopped his face with a soiled handkerchief. 'Yeah; it's some act.'

The doorman returned.

'She'll see you,' he said, jerking his thumb down the passage. 'First door on the right at the far end.'

'Thanks,' I said, and slipped him a buck.

We nodded to the manager and went out into the passage.

'Maybe she keeps two snakes,' I said under my breath. 'One harmless and the other for show.'

Helen didn't say anything. She walked ahead of me, her back stiff.

We arrived at the first door on the right at the end of the passage and I knocked.

'Come in,' a girl's voice called out.

Helen pushed open the door, and we looked into a small untidy room that was typical of the usual hick dressing-rooms you can find in any part of the country. There were two chairs, a dressing-table, a curtain-covered recess that served as a closet, a strip of carpet and a toilet basin with running water.

Susan Gellert sat at the dressing-table, rubbing her hair vigorously with a towel. From its appearance it was obvious she had just washed it, and I couldn't help giving Helen a prod in the back. There was no question this girl was wearing a wig, and Helen's idea that the girl was Corrine impersonating her sister was exploded right away. By the way Helen stiffened I knew she had realized the significance of the vigorous towel-rubbing as I had.

Susan was wearing a blue sweater and a pair of black flannel slacks. She was smoking, and, although she had on no make-up, she looked fresh and very young.

'Come on in,' she said, smiling. 'This is a surprise.' She looked at Helen. 'Are you his wife?'

'Yes,' Helen said, 'but at the moment I am representing General Liability.'

Susan's blue eyes opened wide.

'Oh!' She looked quickly at my card. 'And you're from National Fidelity? Oh, dear! Is there anything wrong? But do sit down. I'm afraid there isn't much room.' She pushed the only other chair towards Helen and waved me to a big cabin trunk standing against the wall. 'You must excuse me. I didn't expect visitors. I must look a sight.' Then, before I could re-assure her, she raised her voice and shouted, 'Hey, Brad! Come in here.'

We heard a door open somewhere along the passage, and a moment later Denny came in. He was still in the tuxedo, which looked pretty shabby at close quarters. He seemed surprised when he saw us, and glanced quickly at Susan.

'This is Brad Denny,' Susan said, and smiled at him. 'He's my agent and partner. This is Mr. and Mrs. Harmas. Mr. Harmas is from the National Fidelity, and Mrs. Harmas is from General Liability.'

For a moment Denny looked taken aback, then he grinned.

'Well, I'll be damned!' he said. 'I didn't know you insurance companies inter-married. That rather lets the cat out of the bag, doesn't it? I guess you know about the other policies?'

'Yeah,' I said. 'I know.'

I was watching these two closely, but there was no look of guilt or consternation on their faces. They weren't quite certain of themselves, and were obviously a little embarrassed, but at the same time, I could see by the way they smiled at each other, they both found the situation a bit of a joke.

'I don't know if we should have told you,' Denny said, leaning up against the wall. 'We didn't want to scare you. No one asked us if we had insured with any other company, so we kept quiet about it.'

'With the kind of policy you hold,' I said, 'it's not strictly necessary to have told us about the other companies. I understand Miss Gellert is now insured for a million dollars?'

'Yes!' Susan's face lit up. 'Isn't it marvellous? It's going to knock the press sideways when we spring it on them. What did you think of the act? Didn't I slay them tonight? It's like that every night, isn't it, Brad?'

'Sure is,' Denny said, looking at her with pride. 'I've been telling her, Mr. Harmas, she's got to be patient. We must have this act absolutely right before we spring it on New York. She wants to start now, but I think we should go for another month around these hick joints. You see, Bellarius isn't absolutely reliable, and we don't want anything to go wrong when we get into the big time.'

'Bellarius?' I said, staring at him.

Susan giggled.

'That's my snake. Isn't he wonderful. Don't you think I've trained him beautifully? But I guess Brad's right. Sometimes Bellarius gets moody and won't kiss me.'

I pushed my hat to the back of my head and blew out my cheeks.

'That doesn't seem to me anything to grieve about. They tell me he's poisonous. I've always heard a cobra's bite is fatal.'

'Well, it is, I guess,' Susan said mildly, 'but he wouldn't bite me.'

'That's very trusting of you,' I said. 'But why don't you make

70

sure and remove the poison sac? Wouldn't that be a sensible thing to do?'

'But it wouldn't be fair,' Susan said, shocked. 'Why, the people would feel cheated.'

'I know how you feel,' Denny said, as I turned to look at Helen. 'I felt that way myself when I first saw her act. It took me weeks to get used to it. In the first two months I worked with her I guess I lost a stone, but now I'm used to it. She's got that cobra just where she wants it. It'll do anything for her.'

'You haven't said how you liked the act,' Susan said, as she began to comb her hair. 'Did you get a bang out of it?'

'That's putting it mildly,' I said. 'It's dynamite. What makes you think you'll get away with it in New York?'

Both of them looked at me sharply.

'Why shouldn't we?' Denny demanded. 'Gee! Mr. Harmas, no management in his right mind would turn away a crowd as big as we can drag into his theatre. Of course, we'll get fixed up. This act is a natural.'

'Maybe the police will have the final say in it.'

'Oh, you mean . . . ' Susan stopped and looked embarrassed. 'Well, I reckon to wear clothes in New York. I know it's a bit raw now, but then, we're playing in the hicks, and that's the way they want it, but, in New York, it's going to be refined. Brad is going to get me fixed up in a night-club.'

'That's the idea,' Denny said. 'I know it's strong meat, but people want strong meat. That's why I think a night-club would be just the thing.'

'I wish you both luck,' I said. 'Now about this policy . . .'

'There's nothing wrong with it?' Susan asked anxiously. 'Mr. Goodyear said it'd be all right. Isn't he nice? I think he's real cute. The trouble he took . . .'

'There's nothing wrong with the policies,' I said, 'but my people thought it only fair to warn you of the dangers of being insured under this coverage for a million. Quite frankly, the set-up could be turned to an unscrupulous person's advantage.'

Both of them stared blankly at me.

71

'I don't know what you mean,' Susan said.

'Putting it bluntly,' I said, 'you are insured against accidental death for a million. If someone gets the idea to murder you, it'll be just too bad for you and for us.'

'Murder her?' Denny said. 'You can't say a thing like that!'

'A million dollars is a lot of money. It may not seem to you any of my business, but I'd be glad to know who would come into the insurance money if you died accidentally,' I said, ignoring Denny and speaking to Susan.

'Why, no one,' she said, looking uneasily at Denny. 'Mr. Goodyear explained that to us. Didn't he tell you?'

'Yeah, I know all that,' I said, 'but this policy isn't foolproof. It states if you die from any cause except those mentioned we are liable.'

'But it's impossible for you to be liable,' Denny broke in. 'That's why we're paying such a low premium. Mr. Goodyear said he had covered all recognized risks.'

Unless these two were superb actors, they appeared to believe what they were saying.

'That's just the point,' I said patiently. 'All recognized risks, but we can't be entirely sure there isn't a risk we haven't covered that some clever crook can turn to his advantage.'

'Oh, Brad!' Susan exclaimed, jumping up. 'He's scaring me.'

'Look, Mr. Harmas,' Denny said sharply, 'this is no way to act. We don't reckon to tell you how to run your business. We put ourselves in Mr. Goodyear's hands, and he assured us there was no possible way for us to make a claim. What do you want to frighten her for?'

I ran my fingers through my hair and looked helplessly at Helen, handing the ball to her.

'I think we're wasting time,' Helen said, her voice cold. 'Let's not argue about this, Miss Gellert. The fact is you're insured for a million dollars for all unrecognized risks. Let us assume the impossible happens; never mind how, but let us assume it does, and you are accidentally killed, and a claim is made against us. Who will get the money?'

'What's the use of talking about it?' Susan said. 'There won't be any money. There can't be, and you're frightening me.'

'Who will get the money?' Helen raised her voice.

'I don't know.'

'Have you made a will?'

'No.'

'Have you a mother or father?'

'No, I haven't.'

'Any relations?'

'I have a sister; nobody else.'

'Then your sister would get it?'

'I guess so, but I don't see the sense of this. There won't be any . . .'

'Is your sister in show business?' I asked, anxious to stop the conversation going around in circles.

'Yes, but she quit some years ago,' Susan said, and sat down again. She looked worried and kept glancing at Denny for support. 'We used to work together. She got married.'

'I'd be glad if you'd tell me where she is living,' I went on. 'You must blame yourself if I seem inquisitive. If you will insure yourself for a million dollars I guess you must expect to answer a few questions.'

'Oh, I don't mind, but I keep telling you '

'Yeah, I know. What's your sister's address?'

'You won't go and see her? She doesn't know about this idea of ours. I want it to come as a surprise.'

'I only want her address for our files.'

'She's Mrs. Corrine Conn, and she lives at Dead Lake, Springville, California.'

I jotted down the address without showing my surprise. I had been expecting an address in South America.

'That's fine,' I said, and glanced inquiringly at Helen, who shook her head. 'I guess that's about all. Now we know who benefits there's nothing more for us to bother you with. Thanks for giving us so much of your time.'

They both looked expectantly at me.

'But there is something wrong, isn't there?' Susan asked. 'You talked about murder. You frightened the life out of me.'

I grinned at her.

'I don't believe that,' I said. 'Seriously, when a young woman in your circumstances insures her life in such a secretive manner for a million dollars at a fantastically low premium, the Claim department is inclined to raise its eyebrows. This investigation is largely your own fault. If you had told us you had other coverage I wouldn't be here. But now I have had your explanation and I know you haven't been persuaded against your will to take out this policy, I am satisfied. That's all there is to it.'

'You mean: it'll be all right?' Susan asked. 'It's important to us. I'm sure we're going to have a lot of publicity through the insurance, and that's what we need more than anything.'

'Why did you put your thumb-print on those policies, and make out it was done accidentally?' Helen asked abruptly.

'Well what do you know?' Denny said. 'You certainly are suspicious. Is that another thing that's worrying you?'

'Why did you make out it was an accident?' Helen repeated, without paying any attention to Denny.

'Why, it was an accident,' Susan said, round-eyed. 'I dropped a blot on Mr. Goodyear's policy and smudged it with my thumb. He seemed quite pleased about it, so I thought it was a good idea to put my print on the other policies.'

'Why a good idea?' Helen persisted.

'Mr. Goodyear said there could be no doubt then about my signature.'

'If you are so sure no claim can be made on any of the policies why should it matter if there is a doubt about your signature?' Helen rapped out.

While she was speaking I watched Susan intently: only bewilderment showed on her face.

'I'm only telling you what he said. I guess I'm not used to signing important papers. Brad does all that for me. So when Mr. Goodyear said it was a good idea to have my thumb-print I

74

thought the other companies would be pleased, too. Shouldn't I have done it?'

Helen looked exasperated.

'Oh, sure,' she said. 'Maybe it is a good thing.'

Susan looked at her, her eyes worried.

'Well, I'm very sorry if I've given you any trouble. I just thought it was kind of cute at the time.'

'Oh, it's cute all right,' Helen said, and made for the door.

Susan looked appealingly at me.

'Is that all, Mr. Harmas? I should be changing. It's getting late.'

I decided to try a shot in the dark.

'Just one little thing before we go. Do you happen to know a tall, powerfully built man who wears a blue and white check coat? He has heavy eyebrows that meet across the bridge of his nose.'

Both looked blankly at me.

'Why, no,' Susan said. 'I don't know anyone like that. Who is he?'

'He's been looking for you,' I said to Denny. 'I hear he's been hanging around your office for several days.'

Denny shook his head.

'Maybe some actor looking for a job. I don't recognize his description. I'm only just starting up as an agent, and I don't know half the people who call on me.'

'Okay. We won't keep you any longer.' I opened the door and Helen walked past me into the passage. 'It's been nice to have met you. Good luck to the act.'

Silently we walked down the passage to the street.

'Well, that's that,' I said, after we had pushed through the crowd of men who were still waiting hopefully outside the stage door. 'I guess that blows your impersonation theory sky-high. That certainly wasn't a wig she was wearing. I don't know how you feel about it, but I'm sold. They're a nice couple, just as Alan said. I've always had a feeling this was a screwball suspicion right out of Maddux's maggoty brain. If I'd been in Alan's place I'd have sold them that policy myself.'

75

'Know what I think?' Helen said. 'I think those two could be too good to be true.'

'That's just like a woman. You have a cock-eyed theory, and you don't want to admit it is full of holes.'

'While she was sexing you,' Helen said coldly, 'I swiped her mirror. It had a couple of beautiful thumb-prints on it. Want to check it against the policy's print?'

'I certainly do. That was very smart of you, pet. I didn't think of getting her print.'

It didn't take us long to reach the hotel, and we went immediately to our room. I unlocked my brief-case and took out a photostat of the policy. Helen produced the small purse mirror she had taken off Susan's dressing-table. There were several good prints on it, and it was easy enough to spot the thumb-print.

'Can I borrow a little of your face powder?' I asked, and when she had given me her compact I blew some of the powder over the surface of the mirror. 'This one's a beaut. Absolutely made to order. Now, let's see if there's any outstanding characteristic. Look, there's a ridge forking upright to the left, and a sharply defined whorl right in the centre.' I took the policy to the light and examined the smudge print under Susan's signature. 'It's the same print all right. Here's the forked ridge and the whorl. Well, now are you satisfied?'

'Not entirely, Steve. I think we should have a look at Corrine Conn before we report back to Maddux.'

'Springville's about a couple of hundred miles from here. Why waste any more time?'

'But we can't give Maddux an honest report unless we've seen Corrine, Steve. I admit neither Susan nor Denny appears suspicious, but I still have a feeling there's a trick in this somewhere. I think they are on the level, but you're forgetting the man in the check coat, and that woman. You're forgetting the janitor had been murdered and his murder could easily be connected with these two. I want to satisfy myself about Corrine, and I want to take a look at her husband. Don't forget, if anything does happen to Susan, and Corrine comes into the money, her husband will share it with her. He might be at the back of this fraud – if it is a fraud.'

I shrugged.

'Okay. May as well make a job of it while we're at it. I'll call Fanshaw right away and tell him where we're going.'

CHAPTER FIVE

I

WE arrived at Springville at six-forty in the evening, after a drive through some of the finest country in the world. Springville lies about twenty miles east of Grapevine Grade, and is three thousand five hundred feet above sea level.

'As I swung the Buick over to the big, sprawling wooden building bearing the sign, *Springville Hotel*, Helen checked her watch. 'I guess it's not bad considering we lost the way at least half a dozen times.'

'And allow me to point out,' I said getting out of the car, 'that wasn't my fault. If I had been the map reader we might have got here hours ago.'

'You may remember,' Helen said, 'it was you who insisted on turning left outside Oakland and nearly drove us into a swamp. I may have given you a few wrong directions, but at least we still have the car with us.'

An elderly man in a brown check shirt, riding breeches and knee-boots came down the steps of the hotel. He was almost as broad as he was tall. A fringe of white hair circled a bald head that was deeply tanned by the sun.

'Welcome to Springville,' he said, his keen blue eyes looking Helen over appreciatively. 'I'm Pete Eagan, owner of this hotel. I hope you've decided to stay with me.'

'If you can put us up for the night, we'll be glad to stay,' I said. 'This is my wife. I'm Steve Harmas. We're up here on business.'

'Well, come on in,' he said, shaking hands. 'I bet you're

hungry. The mountain air gives even me an appetite.'

After we had signed the register, Eagan said, 'Supper'll be ready in about twenty minutes. How about a drink?'

'Just what I was going to suggest,' I said. 'We've been driving all day, and I've a thirst that'd slay a camel.'

He took us along a passage to a well-equipped bar.

'We're quiet just now,' he said, as he mixed highballs. 'Between seasons. We've only a couple of guys on a shooting trip and another guy on business. If you'd come last month or next month you'd have found the place full.'

We sat on stools at the bar.

'Do you know where we can contact the Conns?' I asked, after we had admired the bar-room, talked about this and that, and had another drink. 'They live up here, don't they?'

He nodded.

'That's right. They have a place up at Dead Lake: the loneliest spot in the country, I guess. You have quite a trip in front of you if you intend to call on them. If you can spare the time it'd be easier to wait here three days. Conn comes down here on the first of the month to collect mail and buy groceries.'

I shook my head.

'We can't wait that long. We have to be in Los Angeles tomorrow night. How do we get there?'

'You continue past the hotel for another five miles,' Eagan explained, 'until you come to a sign-post. Take the turning to the left and continue on for another three miles. You'll come to a fork in the road. Take the right fork. The road's only just wide enough to take a car. You'll see a contraption Conn's rigged up just before you enter the road. It's a rope and bell affair. Don't forget to ring the bell. It warns traffic you're coming. Not that there's any traffic to warn, but if Conn happens to be using the road, and you meet him coming down, one of you'll have to reverse a couple of miles, and it won't be Conn.' He grinned, shook his head, went on, 'There's another way to take the lake, but it's about twenty-five miles longer. Conn's place is on an island. You can't miss it once you get to the top of the road.

There's usually a boat moored to the jetty. You can row yourself across, but if the boat isn't there, you'll find a hand-bell. Ring that and Conn will come over. It's quite a place to get to, but I reckon it's one of the prettiest spots on earth.'

'What's Conn's business?' Helen asked casually.

'Well, I don't know,' Eagan said. 'He's running a mink farm on the island, but, from what I've heard, he can't make anything out of it. He's lost a lot of stock recently. He and his wife lead a pretty hard life, I'd imagine.'

'Mrs. Conn was in show business before she married, wasn't she?' I said, reaching for my highball. 'I wonder she wants to bury herself miles from nowhere after being on the stage.'

'Yeah, I've wondered about that, too. A nice-looking girl at that, but she seems happy enough. Mind you, I wouldn't care much to be shut away with Jack Conn month after month. He's a pretty tough customer, and his temper's fierce.'

'What was he before he came to the island?'

Eagan shook his head.

'I don't know. No one knows anything about him. He scarcely ever opens his mouth when he comes in here, and he's not the kind of guy you question. He arrived at Dead Lake about six months ago, and started the farm. I didn't even know he was on the island until a month after when he came in here for whisky. About six weeks later, Mrs. Conn arrived. She's a fine girl. We get on well together, but I don't make much of her husband. A little too ready with his fists to please me.'

'How does Mrs. Conn get on with him?' Helen asked.

Eagan shrugged.

'I don't know. I've never seen them together. They take it in turns to come down here.'

'I ran into her sister, Susan Gellert, the other day,' I said. 'We saw her act at Willington. Does she ever come up here?'

'She's been once,' Eagan said, 'about a month after Mrs. Conn arrived. Like as two peas, aren't they? Never seen anything like it. She came in here with Conn. He'd come down to meet her. I thought at first Mrs. Conn had bleached her hair. She's a nice girl, too. She's a dancer, I understand.'

'Got an act with a snake,' I said. 'Stood me right on my ear. A cobra. The things she did with it made my blood run cold.'

'Conn keeps snakes up on the farm. There's nothing that guy can't do with a snake. I've seen him tackle a diamond back with his bare hands. He's as quick as lightning and catches them alive.'

'What does he do with them?' Helen asked.

'Sells them to the canning factory at Fort Ford. Rattlesnake meat is a delicacy to some folk, although I don't fancy it myself. He goes out every day and thinks nothing of bagging a dozen rattlesnakes. He seems to know just where to look for them.'

I decided I wasn't going to like Jack Conn.

'Well, if you'll excuse me,' Eagan said, glancing at the clock over the bar, 'I guess I'd better see how supper's coming along. I've a good cook, but he's bone lazy unless I stand over him and make him work. How about a rare steak? They look good if you fancy them.'

We said steaks sounded fine.

'Can I fix you another snort before I go?'

'Thanks. How about you, Helen?'

She shook her head.

'Not for me.'

After he had made another highball, he went away and we were left on our own. We carried our drinks to the big bay-window that overlooked the fir forest, and in the distance, the snow-capped Dead Lake summit.

'Well, how are your suspicions now?' I asked, as we settled into basket chairs. 'We've still nothing much to go on.'

'We haven't seen the Conns yet,' Helen said. 'He doesn't sound as if he's going to be my favourite man.'

'They certainly live in an inaccessible spot. No one's going to take them by surprise. I wonder if that means anything?'

Helen was looking past me. Her face had suddenly become tense. I looked up.

The bar-room door had opened, and the man in the blue and white check coat came in. He glanced around the room, looked at us without any sign of recognition, and went over to the bar.

We sat like a couple of waxworks, watching him. He rapped on the counter impatiently, and, when Eagan appeared, he said in a hard, barking voice, 'Two packs of Luckies.'

Eagan gave him the cigarettes, took his money and offered him a drink.

'I guess not,' the man said.

'Supper will be ready in five minutes,' Eagan went on.

'Send it up to my room. I've got work to do,' the other said. He paused long enough to rip open a pack and take out a cigarette, then he turned and walked out of the bar as silently as he had come.

II

I slid out of my chair, crossed to the bar just as Eagan was returning to the kitchen.

'Mr. Eagan.'

He turned.

'Call me Pete. It's less formal. Another drink?'

'Not right now. I've seen that guy before. Know who he is?'

'Mr. Hoffman? Sure. He's been down here two or three times. He's in the movie business.'

'I guess I must have seen him in Hollywood. Is he here on vacation?'

'No,' Eagan said. 'Business. He tells me he's planning to make a film here, and is picking locations. He spends all his time driving around. Nice job, I reckon.'

'Must be,' I said. 'Has he been out to Conn's place?'

'Sure. He asked me how to find it first time he came here. Might be a break for Conn if Hoffman picks on his island for background stuff. These Hollywood people pay good money, and Conn could use it.'

'I could use some of it myself,' I said. 'How are those steaks getting along? I'm hungry enough to eat a horse.'

'Three minutes. If you care to go ahead into the restaurant, it'll be served almost by the time you get there. Through that door, and at the end of the passage.'

I beckoned to Helen, who joined me, and we walked down the passage to the restaurant.

'His name's Hoffman,' I said, 'and he's in the movie business: or so he says.'

'Think he's following us or just happens to be here?'

'I doubt if he's following us,' I said, as we sat down at a table near a blazing log-fire. It got cold at this altitude at nights, and a fire was welcome. 'He could hardly show himself if he knew we were here. Yet I can't believe it's a coincidence he is here.'

'Of course it isn't,' Helen said emphatically. 'Coming here ties him into this, and makes him suspect number one for the janitor's murder. He's either following us or is in touch with Conn. Do you think he's spying on Denny on Conn's instructions?'

'That's an idea. He could be Conn's man.'

A white-coated Negro appeared, pushing a trolley. He served the steaks with fresh salad, fried potatoes and young peas. When he left us, and we were eating, Helen said, 'He must have a car, Steve. How about looking it over, getting the licence number and checking on his registration tag?'

'I'll do it.'

After we had finished dinner I asked Eagan where I could garage the Buick.

'There are a number of lock-ups around the back,' he told me. 'Sam'll fix it for you if you give me the key.'

'That's okay. I'll do it. We thought we'd take a stroll before turning in.'

'You'll find it cold,' he warned us.

'We're tough,' I said, and, hooking my arm in Helen's, went down the steps to the Buick. We found ten lock-ups at the back of the hotel. Only one door was closed.

'I guess that's his,' I said, after we had put the Buick away. 'Let's have a look.'

She went to the entrance to the courtyard while I pushed open the garage door, went in, closed the door after me, and turned on the light.

A dusty, mud-splashed Plymouth faced me. It looked as if it had had plenty of hard wear and very little attention.

I wrote down the number of the licence plate, opened the driver's door and checked the registration tag. It read: BERNARD HOFFMAN, 55 WILTSHIRE ROAD, LOS ANGELES. I scribbled down the address, then opened the glove compartment. Inside were a pair of powerful field-glasses and a .38 police special. I picked up the gun, sniffed at it, broke it open and checked the barrel. The faint film of dust in the barrel told me it hadn't been fired for a long time. I put it back. Then I searched the car pockets, but found nothing of interest.

I joined Helen in under a couple of minutes. We strolled away from the hotel while I told her what I had found in the car.

'The field-glasses suggest he's spying on the Conns,' I said. 'I'm inclined to think he's working against the Conns and Denny. Think I should tackle him?'

Helen shook her head.

'It won't get us anywhere. If he's mixed up in the janitor's murder, he's not likely to tell us anything.'

'I wonder if he recognized me. He must have done, but he didn't give anything away. Maybe that's why he had dinner in his room. He intends to keep clear of us. I wish I knew what he is doing up here.'

'Let's go to bed,' Helen said, stifling a yawn. 'I'm dead beat after that drive, and I'm getting cold out here. Now we have his address we can get a check on him when we get back to Los Angeles. We'll call on the Conns first thing tomorrow morning, then with any luck we should be able to get home by the day after.'

'Okay, I could do with some sleep myself.'

We walked back to the hotel.

I watched her mount the stairs, then went along to the bar. I was surprised to see Hoffman sitting by himself in a corner by the fire. He was drinking whisky, and didn't look up when I came in.

Pete Eagan was polishing glasses behind the bar. He nodded to me.

'You haven't been long. Found it a little chilly out there, I bet.'

'Too chilly,' I said, rubbing my hands. 'I'll have a Scotch. Thanks for the steaks. They were certainly all you said they'd be.'

'That bum of a cook of mine can cook if he wants to,' Eagan said, as he poured the Scotch. 'Glad you liked them. Mrs. Harmas gone to bed?'

'Yeah. She's tired.' I looked across at Hoffman, aware he was now watching me. 'Good evening,' I said to him. 'Haven't we met before?'

He gave me a sour, blank stare.

'Maybe.'

'I want to talk to this guy,' I said under my breath to Pete. 'Excuse me.' I carried my drink across the room. 'Mind if I join you?'

He looked up; his coal-black eyes hard.

'Suit yourself.'

I pulled up a chair and sat down.

'That's quite a punch you pack,' I said, and touched the bruise on my jaw.

His eyes shifted.

'I can punch when I have to.'

'I hear you're in the movie business,' I went on. 'I'm in the insurance racket myself, but I guess you would know that.'

He didn't say anything.

'Did you finally catch up with Denny?' I asked, after a long pause.

'I'm not interested in Denny,' he returned curtly.

'Was it you who broke into his office? I was under the impression you had just left the building when we ran into you at the Chinese restaurant on 4th Street.'

85

For fully five seconds he sat staring at me, then he suddenly seemed to make up his mind, for he relaxed, and a sneering little grin lit up his hard face.

'Pretty smart, aren't you?' he said, keeping his voice down so Eagan couldn't hear him. 'Okay, maybe you and me could get together. How about coming up to my room where we can talk?'

'About what?'

'This and that.' He stood up. 'Coming?'

I nodded, finished my whisky and pushed myself out of my chair. He led the way out of the bar. I nodded good night to Pete as I followed him. Pete was watching with concentrated interest.

We went up the stairs, and Hoffman opened a door on the first-floor landing. He had a room smaller than ours, and it was a little chilly in there. He closed the door, jerked his head to the only armchair and sat on the edge of the bed.

'I'm sorry about that punch,' he said, looking up at me. He didn't look sorry. 'You kind of crowded me, and I'm a bad man to crowd.'

I helped myself to a cigarette, offered him the pack and lit up.

'Just where do you figure in all this?' I asked.

'I'm working on a job,' he said, and took out his wallet. He selected a dirty card and shoved it at me.

On it was printed:

BERNARD HOFFMAN
LICENSED INVESTIGATOR
55 WILTSHIRE ROAD
LOS ANGELES

'Strictly a one-man show,' he said, with his sneering little grin. 'Small beer beside your racket, but I turn a dollar now and then.'

'Let's look at your licence,' I said, surprised to find he was a private dick.

He showed it to me. It was in order and up-to-date. I handed it back to him.

'Who are you working for?'

'Mickey Mouse,' he said, and grinned. 'Never mind who I'm working for. Suppose you let me do the talking? I reckon you and me are working on the same set-up. Did your company issue one of those policies Denny keeps in his office?'

I nodded. So he had been in Denny's office.

'And you're not satisfied with the set-up?' he asked.

'Not entirely. We have nothing to go on, but we're looking things over. So far we haven't turned up anything. What are the policies to you?'

'I can't answer questions,' he said. 'I have to play this close to my chest. But if you can give me some information, anything I find out I'll pass on to you. How's that?'

I studied him. I didn't like him. There was something shifty about him. There are too many private dicks operating in Los Angeles who use the information they dig up to blackmail their clients. Hoffman struck me as one of that breed. I couldn't be sure, but I didn't like the sneering expression in his eyes or the hard tightness of his mouth.

'What do you want to know?'

'Is it right this Gellert twist has insured her life for a million bucks?'

I nodded.

'Who was the agent who sold her the policy?'

'What's that got to do with it?'

He shifted, looked down at his cigarette, then up at me.

'We won't get anywhere if you start asking questions. Who was the guy?'

'There were ten of them. She's taken out ten separate policies. I can't give you the names of them all.'

'Who do you represent?'

'National Fidelity.'

'And the girl you're with?'

'General Liability.'

87

'Well, who were the agents who handled the deal for your companies?'

'Alan Goodyear and Jack McFadden.'

He drew in a lungful of smoke, then blew the smoke in a thin stream to the ceiling.

'Who started it? Was it Goodyear?'

'Goodyear sold her the first policy if that's what you mean.'

He bit his thumb-nail while he thought.

'I've had a look at those policies,' he said, after a while. 'They're duplicates of each other. I guess when the girl landed your policy it was easy to land the others. That right?'

'More or less.'

'How come a girl like Susan Gellert is able to afford a million-dollar policy?'

'We quoted her special rates as the policy is for publicity purposes only. If she does run into an accident she can't claim.'

'I thought maybe it was something like that. I didn't get much time to study the policies. Those causes of death mentioned in them, they cut down the premium, is that it?'

I said it was.

'Didn't it strike you the set-up was phoney?'

'Do you think it is?'

He grinned knowingly.

'How should I know? You insurance people are pretty smart. You should know. Ever had a policy like it before?'

'No, but that doesn't mean much.'

'What makes you think the Conns are tied up to this?'

'Are they?'

He rubbed the side of his thick nose before saying, 'I guess they could be. That guy Conn needs watching. Have you seen him?'

'I'm going out there tomorrow.'

'Well, you watch him. I'm willing to bet a dime he has a record, but he's smart. I can't get a thing on him. I've been out three times now, watching him through glasses. I might just as well have stayed home.'

'How about Corrine?'

He shook his head.

'Nothing to her. It's Conn who's at the back of this.'

'At the back of what?'

Again he grinned knowingly at me.

'Maybe if you stick around long enough you'll find out. I've got instructions not to talk. What's the idea of the finger-print on the policies? Was it Goodyear's idea or hers?'

'Hers.'

He nodded.

'I thought as much. That Conn's nobody's fool.'

'It might save us a lot of time and trouble if you'd put your cards on the table,' I said. 'Who's your client?'

He shook his head.

'Can't be done. There's a pile of jack hanging to this, and I'm not putting a foot wrong. Well, thanks for the information. If I come across anything I think you can use I'll slip it to you.'

'That's pretty nice of you,' I said, without moving. 'Maybe I can slip you a little information right now. Remember Mason, the janitor at Denny's office block?'

He gave me a quick, hard look.

'What about him?'

'He was murdered the night before last.'

Hoffman's reaction was startling. He reared back as if I had socked him in the nose, and his face went the colour of tallow.

'Murdered?' His voice croaked.

'Yeah. He was knifed. Don't you read the papers?'

'What's it to me?' he said, clenching his fists. 'Why tell me?'

'You were in the building that night, and he heard you. He went up to see what was going on, and you stuck a knife into him.'

'That's a lie!' He leaned forward to glare at me. 'You were there, too. Suppose it was you who stuck a knife in him?' There was sweat on his face now and his eyes looked scared.

'I like you for the job,' I said. 'The cops would like you for it, too.'

His hand slid inside his coat. Then a gun jumped into sight. He covered me.

'Who was the woman with you?' I asked. 'Was she your rich client?'

He jerked open the door.

'Out!'

He didn't look as if he would need much persuasion to put a slug into me. I stepped past him into the corridor.

'You won't be able to keep her covered much longer,' I said. 'You're in a jam. Wake up! On your own you don't stand a chance. Throw in with me, give me the story, and get yourself some protection. The cops are pretty careful how they handle anyone backed by my company. Get wise to yourself. Come clean, and I'll do what I can for you.'

He stood glaring at me. I could see fear and greed battling in his eyes, but greed won as it usually does.

'Go to hell!' he snarled, and slammed the door in my face.

III

While I was dressing the next morning, I told Helen about my talk with Hoffman. She had been fast asleep when I had left Hoffman, and I hadn't the heart to wake her.

She sat up in bed, her eyes wide and alert, while I told her what Hoffman had said.

'I'm sure he didn't kill Mason,' I concluded, as I slipped on my jacket. 'If he didn't do it, then the odds are this mysterious woman did. The way I figure it is Hoffman was hired by this woman to case Denny's office. Then he and the woman broke in. While he was faking the attempted burglary on the third floor to cover up the real reason why they were there, the woman was examining the policies in Denny's office. Mason must have heard them. He probably ran into the woman as she was leaving, and she knifed him. That's why Hoffman looked so shaken when he heard the janitor was dead. I guess he realized this woman's dangerous. Maybe he was planning to put the bite on her. How do you like that for a theory?'

Helen looked admiringly at me.

'Shouldn't we try to make Hoffman talk?' she asked on her way to the bathroom.

'That's what I've been thinking. I should have got tough with him last night, but I'm never at my best when a guy waves a gun at me. I'll have another crack at him after breakfast.'

But it was during breakfast that Pete Eagan told us that Hoffman had gone.

'Must have cleared off during the night,' he said, as he served an enormous platter of grilled ham and eggs. 'I thought I heard a car start up. He went in such a hurry he forgot to settle his account.'

'What are you going to do? Tell the sheriff?' Helen asked.

Eagan shook his head.

'I guess not. Hoffman's been here before. I'll wait a while. Trade isn't all that good. It doesn't do to slick the sheriff on customers.' He went away, still looking worried.

'Now we've missed our chance,' Helen said, annoyed. 'We should have watched him.'

'Forget it,' I said. 'We know where to find him. He won't run far. I'll tackle him when we get back to Los Angeles.'

After breakfast we set off for Dead Lake, following Eagan's directions. We arrived at the first sign-post and turned left. It was a bad road, and we bumped and banged for three miles or so with thick forest land on either side of us. Eventually we came to the fork in the road Eagan had described. Facing us was a crude notice which read:

PRIVATE ROAD
SINGLE LINE TRAFFIC
RING BELL

'Are you going to ring it?' Helen asked.

'Not on your life. No point in warning them we're coming. We'll take a chance of running into anything.'

We drove on. The road was so narrow the bushes and shrubs growing on either side continually flicked against the sides of the car. After the best part of a mile, the road widened, and then after another couple of miles we saw ahead of us a glint of water.

'Looks as if we've arrived,' I said, slowing down. 'Let's take a look without showing ourselves.'

I parked the car out of sight under some trees and we walked to the head of the road. Before us stretched a vast expanse of water, glittering in the morning sunshine. The lake was a good two miles wide, and about a quarter of a mile from our side of the bank was a small island, hedged in by tall fir trees.

'What a lovely spot,' Helen exclaimed. 'Isn't it marvellous?'

'Certainly is, and as safe as a fort.'

We watched the island for maybe ten minutes, but we saw no sign of life. All we could see was a short jetty and a boat, equipped with an outboard motor.

'Well screened, too,' I said, lighting a cigarette. 'Let's see if there's a boat this side.'

There was a boat tied up to the jetty, but it had no outboard motor.

'You'll have to row,' Helen said maliciously. 'The exercise will work off that enormous breakfast you had.'

Gloomily I took off my coat and rolled up my sleeves.

I pushed the boat off, scrambled in and started the long row across the lake.

'It'd be nice nice if he had a rifle and started taking pot-shots at us, wouldn't it? We must make a tempting target,' I said, pausing to mop my face.

'It would be lovely,' Helen said tartly. 'Will you try not to ventilate your horrible mind? I'm enjoying this.'

'I'm glad someone is, because I'm not.'

It took me over half an hour to reach the island. Sweat was running off me as the nose of the boat bumped against the jetty. I sat, puffing and blowing, while Helen tied up.

'What really makes my day,' I said, as I climbed out of the

boat, 'is the thought of rowing back. The sun'll be three times as hot.'

'Think of the weight you will lose,' Helen said unsympathetically.

A path led up from the lake and into the thicket. A fifty-yard walk brought us to a clearing, and facing us was a small log cabin and some ramshackle out-buildings. On the wide verandah were lounging chairs and a log table. The place looked very rough and primitive.

'Well, thank goodness there's no fierce dogs,' Helen said, 'I was expecting dog trouble all the way over.'

'They don't need dogs. They keep rattlesnakes – remember?'

I was studying the cabin. The windows and front door stood open, and the sound of a radio playing swing came from one of the rooms.

'For a mink farm it's strangely empty of mink,' I said. 'Well, someone's at home. Let's call on them.'

As we mounted the three steps leading to the verandah, a girl appeared in the doorway. Pete and Mossy Phillips had prepared me for the extraordinary likeness, but, although this girl was almost the exact image of Susan, there were differences. She was fuller in the face, and her teeth projected slightly, giving her a pouting expression. Her silky hair was dark, and I fancied she was a little more solidly built than Susan, and she was very deeply tanned by the sun.

She wore a red halter and grubby white shorts. What I could see of her body – and it was as much as I or any other man had any right to see – was the colour of bronze.

She looked at Helen and then at me.

'Where did you two spring from?' she asked, smiling. 'Don't tell me you rowed over in this heat?'

'I did, ' I said, mopping my face, 'and it was certainly hot work. I hope you'll forgive us coming like this. We're staying at the Springville Hotel, and Pete Eagan was telling us about your mink. My wife had always wanted a mink coat. It's been her greatest ambition, so I thought I'd give her the chance of seeing some mink on the hoof in the hope she would stop pestering me to buy her a coat. Would it be too much to ask if she could see them?'

Corrine Conn moved out on to the verandah. Rather to my surprise, she seemed genuinely pleased to see us.

'Did you row all that way to see our mink?' she said. 'You poor people! The devils died ages ago.'

'They did? Eagan said . . .'

'Jack was so mad,' she said, laughing, 'he hasn't told anyone. It was entirely his fault they died. Do sit down. You must want a drink. Would you like some iced coffee?'

'That sounds wonderful,' Helen said, speaking for the first time. 'You're sure we're not giving you too much trouble?'

'I'll say not. If you lived here and never saw a soul from one month to the next you wouldn't talk about trouble. I won't be a moment.'

She swung around and disappeared inside the cabin.

'I give up, ' I said under my breath. 'Every move we make brings us up against a blank wall. What do you think of her?'

Helen lifted her shoulders in a shrug.

'She seems all right. She's pleased to see us, and that's a surprise.'

'Where's Conn? If he's pleased to see us then we are washed up.'

Corrine Conn came back, carrying a tray on which stood three tall glasses of iced coffee.

'Maybe we'd better introduce ourselves,' I said. 'This is my wife, Helen. I'm Steve Harmas. We're on vacation, and this is our first trip to Springville.'

'I'm Corrine Conn,' Corrine said. 'My husband's somewhere around. He's catching snakes. I think.'

'Snakes?' Helen said. 'Why, of course. I'm sure Susan Gellert is your sister. We saw her act in Willington last night. What a very odd coincidence.

I looked quickly at Corrine to see how she reacted, but her face only registered pleased surprise.

'You mean you actually saw Susie? It certainly is a coincidence. I used to be in show business myself before I married.' She sat down near me. 'I sometimes think I should have my head examined, leaving the stage for this. How did you like Susie's act?'

'A little meaty,' I said. 'That cobra gave me the shakes.'

Corrine laughed.

'Bellarius? He wouldn't hurt a fly. Jack fixed him before he let Susie have him, and the joke is she thinks he's dangerous.'

'Why, even the manager of the theatre thinks so,' I said. 'They had an expert to look at it.'

'I know. Jack fixed that, too. Susie takes herself far too seriously. She thinks she's cheating the public unless her snake is poisonous, so we thought we'd better do something and not tell her. Why, if Jack hadn't fixed Bellarius, the little numskull would be dead by now. Maybe I shouldn't have told you. It's a trade secret. If you ever run into her again, don't tell her for heaven's sake.'

'We won't tell her,' I said, laughing.

'How amazingly alike you two are,' Helen said, studying Corrine.

'Everyone remarks about it when they see us together,' Corrine said. 'We had a good act before I married. I'm trying to persuade Jack to give up this island and get back to civilization. Susie and I could team up again. It's time she gave up that corny snake. She'll never get anywhere with it. Poor kid, she imagines she's going to get to New York. Nothing I say discourages her.' She looked out beyond us across the clearing. 'Here's Jack now.'

We both turned quickly. A short, thick-set man was coming up the path. He wore a dirty white singlet and canvas trousers, tucked into high boots. Over his shoulder he carried a sack.

Although he couldn't have been more than thirty-three or four, he was going bald. His round, fleshy face was sunburned, and his small, deep-set eyes were as cold and as expressionless as pebbles.

He came up the steps and stood looking at us.

'Jack, this is Mr. and Mrs. Harmas. They came over to see our mink,' Corrine said. 'Pete Eagan told them to come.'

The cold little eyes were probing us.

'You're too late,' he said. His voice was unexpectedly soft. 'They're dead. You row across?'

'That's right,' I said. 'I thought of ringing the bell, but I didn't want to bother you.'

He nodded. His face was completely expressionless. It was impossible to guess what was going on in his mind, and yet there was something about the way he stood, and the way his head was thrust forward, that made him dangerous.

'Corrine will show you around,' he said, picking up the sack which he had dropped on the floor. 'I'm taking the motorboat over in about a quarter of an hour. You can come with me.'

He started to move towards the cabin door when Corrine said, 'But, Jack, they've scarcely arrived. I thought it'd be nice to invite them to lunch . . .'

He paused to look at her. Just for a moment the blank eyes came to life. They seemed to glow with a yellowish light.

'I'll take them over when I go,' he said, and went into the cabin.

There was an awkward pause, then Corrine laughed uneasily.

'You'll have to excuse Jack,' she said. 'He doesn't like visitors. I guess he's lived alone so long he's not used to behaving politely.'

'That's all right,' Helen said. 'The trip back by motorboat will suit Steve fine. He wasn't looking forward to rowing again in the hot sun.'

'Well, come and look at the island,' Corrine said. 'There's not much to see, but it might interest you.'

We followed her down the steps into the hot sunshine. As she had said, there wasn't much to see. The island was a lot smaller than I had imagined. There were about fifteen or sixteen wire cages at the back of the cabin, scarcely enough, I thought, to keep mink on a profitable scale. The cages were empty, and Corrine made a rueful remark about white elephants.

'Jack makes a good living catching snakes,' she said. 'I don't think he's going to bother with mink any more.'

We stood by the motor-boat until Conn joined us. He got into the boat without a word.

'Well, good-bye,' Corrine said. 'I'm sorry it's been so short. Look us up again when you're this way.'

While Helen was shaking hands with her, I took out my cigarette case, selected a cigarette and offered the case to Corrine.

'Oh, thanks,' she said, and made a move to pick a cigarette from the case.

Purposely, I let the case slip so she had to take it in her hands.

'Sorry,' I said. 'Can you manage?'

'It was my fault,' she said, smiling. She took a cigarette, closed the case and handed it to me.

Well, at least we hadn't wasted our time. I had her finger-prints now.

As I turned to get into the boat I heard a sound that made me stiffen and look over my shoulder. A faint but unmistakable scream that drifted to us from the direction of the cabin on the light wind that was blowing.

'What's that?' I said sharply.

I was aware that Conn, who was in the boat, had also stiffened, and was looking at me with a tight little smile on his lips. I looked quickly at Corrine. She was smiling.

'Did it startle you?' she said. 'It's my paroquet. I forgot to show it to you. It startles people at night. Sounds as if some-one's being murdered, doesn't it?'

'Yes,' I said, feeling a chill run up my spine for no reason at all. 'It certainly does.'

'Get in,' Conn said, a rasp in his soft voice.

He started the outboard motor with two savage pulls, and as soon as Helen and I got into the boat, he cast off.

Corrine stood on the water's edge and waved to us.

'Nice place you have here,' I said to Conn.

He didn't even look at me.

'A little lonely for your wife perhaps,' I went on, trying to draw him.

His reply was to open the throttle wide, so the noise of the engine made talking impossible.

The boat shot across the water, leaving a wide wash in our rear. It took less than ten minutes to reach the jetty, and during that time Conn stared straight ahead, ignoring us.

He cut the throttle a few yards from the shore and let the boat drift in.

'I'm going farther up the lake,' he said. 'You get out here.'

We got out.

'If you come here again,' he went on, looking up at us as we stood side by side on the shore, 'use the bells. That's what they're there for. We get a lot of poachers here, and I shoot first and apologize after.'

We watched him out of sight. He didn't once look back at us.

'Not what you could call an endearing type,' I said.

'A horror,' Helen said. 'He gave me the shivers.'

We walked back to the car.

'I got her finger-prints,' I said, as we got into the car. I took from my pocket the cigarette case. 'If you lend me your powder I'll check them right away.'

A minute's operation with the powder and a careful study of the prints Corrine had left on the shiny surface of the case convinced me she hadn't made the thumb-print on the policies.

'That lets her out,' I said, showing Helen the print. 'We're no further than we were when we first started this caper.' I lit a cigarette, and went on, 'Did that sound like the squawk of a paroquet to you?'

'I don't know.' She was looking worried. 'It gave me a shock. It could have been. It was funny she showed us the island, but didn't let us into the cabin.'

'Maybe. Some people aren't too proud to show the way they live. I'd feel happier if I'd seen that paroquet instead of just hearing it. For a moment I thought it was a woman scream-ing.'

I started the engine. As Helen got in beside me, I said, 'I wish I had got Conn's finger-prints. Hoffman's right. He looks as if he's been in jail. But I guess he was too smart to fall for that gag. I was surprised Corrine fell for it.'

'Unless she wanted us to have her prints,' Helen said thoughtfully, as I drove slowly down the narrow road. 'Come to think of it, Steven, we got to the island without any trouble, didn't we? If Conn doesn't welcome visitors why was that boat waiting so conveniently? As he has a motor-boat on his side, you'd have thought the last thing he would have done was to leave a boat this side of the lake.'

'Are you being complicated again? Why should they want us to have her prints?'

'Now we have them, where does it get us? Aren't we asking ourselves if we're not making a fuss about nothing? And isn't that just what they would want us to think if they are planning fraud?'

'Yes; there's something in that.'

'I still think this set-up could be like a conjurer's trick,' Helen went on. 'Nothing up my sleeve, a double shuffle, and out comes the missing ace. I have a feeling we are being shown only what they want us to see. I think it's time for us to get tricky ourselves, Steve, or we'll never crack this before the girl is murdered.'

I shot her a quick look.

'You think they plan to kill her?'

'That man gave me the shudders. He's capable of anything. I think she is in danger. Everyone has been too frank, too willing to admit there can't possibly be a claim against us, too wide-eyed and innocent and too pleased to see us for my liking. I keep thinking there's a million dollars going to someone who is smart enough to kill that girl in a way we haven't thought of. I keep thinking of Conn and those brutal eyes of his. He looks like a killer, Steve.'

'He's a tough bird all right,' I said doubtfully. 'But we have absolutely nothing to go on. I'm not saying you're not right . . .'

We were still arguing by the time we reached the hotel, and still getting nowhere.

'I guess we'll pack and go straight back to Los Angeles,' I said, getting out of the car. 'If I can't find Hoffman, the next move is to toss the set-up in Maddux's lap and see what he makes of it.'

'I'm going to stay here,' Helen said. 'Now, don't fuss, darling. I think one of us should stay and watch the island. I have a feeling something's going to happen there before very long that's important.'

'Now, look, Helen,' I said anxiously, 'I'm not leaving you here alone. That guy Conn's dangerous. Oh, no! I'm not having that. You go back to Los Angeles, and I'll stay here.'

'Please don't be absurd. I couldn't tackle Hoffman, and you know it. I'll be all right. He'll never see me. I'll keep this side of the lake and watch the island through glasses.'

Pete Eagan came running down the steps towards us.

'There's been a call for you from a Mr. Fanshaw,' he said to me. 'He wants you to call him right away. He says it's urgent.'

'Thanks,' I said. 'Now I wonder what's biting him,' I went on to Helen. 'I guess I'd better see what it's all about.'

It took me a few minutes to get Fanshaw's office.

'That you, Harmas?' he bawled, his voice excited. 'Come on back right away. Maddux says you're to drop the Gellert case and work with me.'

'What's up?' I asked. 'I was coming in, anyway.'

'Joyce Sherman, the movie actress, has been kidnapped, and Maddux wants you to represent us.'

'Why should we care if she's been kidnapped?' I asked blankly, then remembered he had told me Goodyear had sold her a complete coverage policy only recently. 'You mean we're liable?'

Fanshaw gave an exasperated howl.

'You bet we're liable. She's insured with us against kidnapping. If we don't find her quick we're down the drain for half a million. Come on back and get to work!'

CHAPTER SIX

I

JOYCE SHERMAN had had an extraordinarily meteoric rise to fame. Three years ago, so the story went, she had been a receptionist at a small but exclusive hotel in San Bernadino. Perry Rice, a talent scout working for Pacific Pictures, had been staying at the hotel and had spotted her. It had been a lucky break for Rice. He had been on the point of being fired for inefficiency; he owed money everywhere, and his prospects, before he met Joyce Sherman, were as black as the Siberian wind.

Inefficient or not, Rice had been smart enough to realize Joyce was star material, and he persuaded her to sign a contract, assigning the complete rights of her future career over to him with a large financial interest. Nor had he any difficulty in persuading Pacific Pictures to give her a screen test which she passed with flying colours. She was given the second woman's lead in a well-written thriller, and, with the help of a competent director, acted the leading woman off the screen with such devastating effect that Howard Lloyd, head of Pacific Pictures, immediately offered her a star contract to make a picture a year at $50,000 a picture.

On the morning of the offer, Perry Rice resigned his job as talent scout and called on Lloyd in his new capacity as Joyce Sherman's agent and manager: a revelation that caused Lloyd practically to foam at the mouth. A long and bitter financial battle waged behind closed doors. But by his foresight in getting Joyce under contract to himself, Rice held all the aces, and he finally came away with a contract that is still talked about in Hollywood with bated breath. Over-night, Joyce Sherman became one of the highest-paid stars in the business, and a week later, to make certain of his property, Rice married her.

Apart from being a brilliant and natural actress, Joyce also had the physical equipment for a star. Her flaming red hair (dyed) and her almond-shaped eyes (suspected of being faked) were attractive to men and women alike, and her shape was as feminine and sensational as it was seductive.

When I arrived at Fanshaw's office I was surprised to find Maddux there. Goodyear was also present, looking pale and depressed.

Maddux was roaring like an enraged bull, and, as I walked in, he broke off to yell, 'Where the hell have you been? I expected you here an hour ago!'

'Well, I'm here now,' I said, pulling out a chair and sitting down. 'I've been quick could you but know it. What's cooking?' I winked at Fanshaw and nodded to Goodyear.

'What's cooking?' Maddux said, thumping the desk. 'Nothing at all! We only sell a policy to this damned actress, guaranteeing the ransom if ever she happens to get kidnapped, and the bitch gets kidnapped three weeks later. That's all that's cooking!'

'You didn't complain when I brought the policy in,' Goodyear said wearily. 'How was I to know . . .?'

'You keep out of this,' Maddux bawled. 'You've done enough damage by selling her the policy.'

'Now, wait a minute,' Fanshaw chipped in heatedly. 'I'm damned if I'll stand for that. It's Alan's job to sell policies. If he didn't, we would throw him out. You've no right to talk to him like that, and you know it!'

Maddux opened and shut his mouth, glared at Fanshaw, then said, more mildly, 'Yeah, maybe that's right.' He looked over at Goodyear. 'Forget it. I guess I'm a little worked up. I apologize.'

'Oh, that's all right,' Goodyear said, but he didn't look happy.

'Suppose you give me some facts,' I said. 'When was she kidnapped?'

'Three nights ago,' Fanshaw said. 'They've only just discovered about the policy, and the kidnapping is being kept quiet for a moment at the Studios. She went out after dinner alone in her car without telling anyone where she was going. At two o'clock in the morning Rice became anxious or so he says. I can't imagine a slob like him having any feeling for anyone. Anyway, according to him, he phoned her various friends and the Studio, but no one had seen her. Then a report came in to police headquarters that a car had been found on Foothill Boulevard. It was Miss Sherman's car, and stuck on the windshield was an envelope addressed to Rice. He and the police went out there. The note stated Miss Sherman had been kidnapped and the ransom demand would be made today.'

'Has it been made yet?'

'No. The point is we're liable up to half a million, and there's no out for us unless Miss Sherman is found before we have to part with the money.'

Maddux made a furious, snorting noise, but no one paid any attention to him.

'Any clues?' I asked.

'Not a thing. The Feds have taken over in an unofficial capacity. Rice won't let them start anything. He says he wants his wife back alive, and nothing must be done until she's returned. I can understand how he feels. The note warned him to take no police action, threatening all kinds of unpleasant things to Miss Sherman if he does.'

Maddux, who had been trying to get a word in edgeways while Fanshaw was talking, now barked, 'I want you to get over to the Sherman house right away. You're representing us, and you're to work with the police. I've fixed it for you to have all the necessary facilities. If we're responsible for the ransom money, we'll damn well be responsible for running this show.'

'Okay,' I said. 'Just one thing: what makes you call Rice a slob?' I was speaking to Fanshaw now. 'Is he?'

'Maybe a slob is the wrong word. Louse might suit him better. He has a pretty murky record in Hollywood. He's never stayed with anyone longer than three months. His reputation for fooling around with young girls stinks. He's been involved in several scandals that he's managed to hush up somehow or other. At the moment he lives quite shamelessly on his wife's earnings, and because of the contract he talked her into signing, before they were married, she can't get rid of him.'

I turned to Goodyear.

'Did Rice have anything to do with the policy?'

Goodyear shook his head.

'Not a thing. In fact, Miss Sherman insisted that he wasn't to know about it. The policy was to receive no publicity. She didn't pull any punches. She said Rice was not to know.'

'Could he have found out?'

'I don't see how he could. The policy was signed at Miss Sherman's lawyer's office, and he kept charge of it. It was he who put in the claim as soon as he heard she had been kidnapped.'

'Who's her lawyer?'

'Leo Simon,' Goodyear said. 'Fanshaw will tell you he's okay.'

'Yeah; he's one of the best lawyers here. Rice had no idea of the policy,' Fanshaw said. 'But now he does know about it, he's pressing us.'

'Well, all right,' I said, pushing back my chair. 'I'll get over there.'

'Keep in touch with me,' Maddux said. 'I've got to get back to San Francisco. If anything breaks I'll come out again.'

'Want to hear about the Gellert case while you're here?'

'He looked at his watch.

'Not unless there's anything cooking. I've got a plane to catch. This is the job to work on now. We'll work on the Gellert case if and when there's a claim.'

'Suit yourself,' I said.

Goodyear and I left the office together. Outside, Goodyear said, 'Talk about a break! This would happen to me.'

'What are you worrying about?' I said. 'You're not blaming yourself, are you? Maddux was just shooting his mouth off. These things happen in our racket, and you know it.'

'I guess that's right,' he said despondently. 'But to have two of my sales investigated is pretty depressing. Did you find out anything when you went to see Miss Gellert?'

I shook my head.

'Nothing to work on. Did you know she had a twin sister?'

'No. What's a twin sister to do with it?'

'I wouldn't know. The sister's married to a guy named Jack Conn. He could be a crook.'

Goodyear snapped his fingers impatiently.

'Do I get the blame for that, too?'

I grinned at him.

'Don't bear down on it, Alan. Now I've seen Susan Gellert and Denny I would have taken the policy as you did. They're a nice couple.'

'I knew you'd think so.' His pale face lit up. 'Those two are genuine. I'd like to see them go places.'

'Did you see her act?'

'I wanted to, but I just missed it. Was it any good?'

'It's sensational for the public she's playing to now, but not for New York. She fools around in the nude with a snake.'

'I hear Helen is working with you.'

'That's right. We're trying to keep the money in the family. She got Andrews to give her a job. I left her at Springville where the Conns hang out. She's keeping an eye on them.'

'What's Conn got to do with it?' Alan asked blankly.

'I wish I knew. Helen thinks he has plenty to do with it. Woman's instinct or something. She thinks there's fraud around the corner.'

I had a sudden idea.

'Have you ever run into a guy who calls himself Bernard Hoffman?' I asked.

'I know of him,' Goodyear said. 'I haven't met him. Why?'

'He's working on the Gellert case. I ran across him, but he

wouldn't tell me who he's working for. What do you know about him?'

Goodyear looked startled.

'Only he's a private eye, and not a particularly honest one at that. Working on the Gellert case? Are you sure?'

'I know he's interested in the policies. He broke into Denny's office three nights ago and examined them.'

'Why?'

'Search me. He wouldn't say. When I have some spare time I intend putting pressure on him. Maybe I'll get him to talk.'

Goodyear looked at his wrist-watch.

'I've got to scram. I'm late for a date as it is. Let me know if you get anything out of Hoffman, won't you?'

I left him, disentangled my car from the car-park, and headed out to Beverly Glen Boulevard.

II

I drove up the long, winding drive that led to the Sherman residence. It was exactly the kind of house I had imagined it would be, with all the usual trimmings movie stars insist on having to prove their success and financial standing.

There were the usual flood-lit swimming-pool, the acres of carefully cultivated gardens, the wide verandahs, the lounging chairs, hammocks and gay umbrellas, and finally the big, sprawling house with its twenty or so bedrooms.

Police guarded the main entrance, but after they had checked my card they let me through. More police guarded the front door; bored men who looked a little bewildered to find themselves in such lavish surroundings.

I was shown into a main lounge by a white-faced butler where three men and a girl were talking in low tones before the open casement windows.

One of the men came over to me. He was tall and willowy, with a narrow, tanned face, a sharp chin, a pencil-line moustache and pale, insolent eyes. He had on a yellow-silk shirt, open at the neck, bottle-green whipcord trousers and brown, reverse calf shoes. On his thin, hairy wrist was a gold bracelet. He didn't have to tell me he was Perry Rice. I had seen photos of him from time to time with Joyce Sherman, and I decided I liked the look of him a lot less in the flesh than in newsprint.

'I'm Harmas, representing National Fidelity,' I said. 'Maddux of the Claim department sent me over.'

'You've taken your time,' Rice said, in a drawling voice. 'We had given you up as lost. Well, since you have arrived at last you'd better meet the others. Miss Myra Lantis, my wife's secretary.' He waved to the girl, who turned and looked at me without interest. She was small and dark, sufficiently swarthy to make me wonder if she hadn't some Mexican blood.

I said the usual things one says on such occasions. She didn't bother to reply.

'Mr. Howard Lloyd,' Rice went on, waving to the tall, white-haired man who came forward to shake hands.

I looked at him with interest. His name was as well known to me as Sam Goldwyn's, and, as head of Pacific Pictures, he rated as one of the richest men in the world. He looked pale and drawn, and his deep-set eyes searched my face with an intensity that was embarrassing.

'Glad to have you here, Mr. Harmas,' he said, in a deep, slow voice. 'Looks as if your people have been unlucky this time.'

'Yeah,' I said. 'But that's part of our racket.'

'And this is Micklin, of the Federal office,' Rice went on, nodding to a short, chunky man who jerked his chin at me and didn't offer to shake hands.

'Any news yet?' I asked him.

'No. We're expecting to get the ransom instructions any moment now. Until we get them, there's not much we can do.'

'As your company's responsible for finding the money,' Rice said, selecting a cigarette from a gold case, 'perhaps you can tell me how soon you can raise it?'

'It depends on how much it is,' I returned. 'Kidnappers want the pay-off in small bills, and they usually expect to wait.'

He lit the cigarette; his pale eyes wandered over me.

'I see. In the meantime, poor Joyce is in their hands. The sooner you make arrangements to have a large sum ready the better!'

'Have you any idea how much it is going to be?'

He glared at me.

'How should I?'

'Aren't we wasting time?' Lloyd broke in impatiently. 'We thought, Mr. Harmas, you had better deliver the ransom when the instructions are received.'

'You did? That's pretty thoughtful of you. So you've decided to pay?'

'Of course we're going to pay,' Rice said angrily. 'I want my wife back.'

I looked over at Micklin.

'How about you? Do you want the ransom paid?'

He shrugged.

'I'd rather try to find her before we part with the money, but, as I am here in an unofficial capacity, there's not much I can do about it.'

'We have been warned not to bring in the police,' Lloyd said. 'Mr. Macklin is here only as an observer. As soon as the money is paid and Miss Sherman is returned, then he takes over.'

I looked over at Micklin.

'Probably a little late,' I said. 'And what makes you think Miss Sherman is going to be returned?'

'I keep telling them that,' Micklin said. 'They won't listen.'

'Of course she'll be returned,' Rice said, stubbing out his cigarette and immediately lighting another. 'Why shouldn't she be? What use can she be to the kidnappers once they have the money?'

I looked at Micklin, but he shook his head slightly. There seemed no point in telling them that kidnappers feel safer if their victims are dead. If they hadn't arrived at that answer I agreed with Micklin they'd find out soon enough without us telling them.

'As we are responsible for the ransom,' I said, 'we're entitled to have a little information. Are you quite sure neither you nor Miss Lantis knew where Miss Sherman was going when she took the car out the night before last?'

'I have answered all the questions I intend answering,' Rice snapped, turning away. 'The police have tired me to death, and I'm damned if I'm going to let you tire me further.'

'We have no idea,' Lloyd said, 'but Joyce often goes off alone after working at the studios. Motoring at night seemed to soothe her nerves.'

'Did she take any luggage with her?' I asked.

Rice turned to stare at me.

'Are you insinuating that my wife was leaving me when she went away?'

'A half a million dollars is a nice slice of money. I want to satisfy myself she has been kidnapped.'

Both Rice and Myra Lantis stiffened. Lloyd made an impatient gesture. Micklin was the only one to remain impassive. Rice took a step forward and faced me, his pale eyes glittering.

'And what exactly do you mean by that?'

'I want to be certain she hasn't gone away and left the note to confuse you,' I said, staring right back at him. 'I want to be certain someone, knowing about the insurance coverage, hasn't murdered her and is using the kidnapping set-up to pick up an easy half-million. Miss Sherman isn't covered against murder; only kidnapping. I also want to be certain that you and she haven't put your heads together to make a little pocket-money. That's what I'm getting at.'

'Why, you . . . !'

Rice pulled himself together with an effort. The rage that jumped into his eyes went away as if he realized he was out on very dangerous ground.

'In other words you and your rotten company are going to get out of paying the ransom if you can,' he said, his voice unsteady.

'That's the general idea,' I said cheerfully. 'We never pay

unless we have to, and I'm not yet convinced we have to. I'd like to see Miss Sherman's room.'

'Just a moment,' Lloyd put in. 'I can set your mind at rest on one of the points you have raised. It is extremely unlikely that Joyce has run away. She's in the middle of making a picture, and she's far too much of an artist to give up the best rôle of her career. No, she hasn't run away. I'm quite sure of that.'

'You must be losing some money if the picture's held up,' I said.

'Thousands. More serious than you can imagine. We've already spent three-quarters of a million, and if she's not found, we'll lose the lot. She's got to be found!'

'I'd like to see Miss Sherman's room.'

Myra Lantis moved to the door. I followed her up the stairs and along a passage to a big, airy room done over in green lacquer, with brown drapes, lighted mirrors and a bed with a brown and green quilted head. A nice room for a movie star. I felt a little lost in it.

'Did she take any luggage with her?' I asked, as Myra clicked on the lights.

'No.'

She made a move to go, but I stepped in front of her.

'And you wouldn't know why she went out that night on her own?'

The dark, glittering eyes looked into mine. She moved a little closer.

'She drank like a fish,' she said softly. 'Half the time she didn't know what she was doing. She was drunk that night like all the other nights. Can't you see they're trying to cover it up? She used to take the car out and drive like a mad woman. All they think about is the picture. She should have been in a home.'

I stroked the back of my neck and looked down at her. She had quite a Bitter Rice frontage. I had an idea at the back of my mind I wouldn't get my face clawed if I kissed her.

'So that's what makes the skeleton rattle. How long has that been going on?'

'Months. This could be her last picture. Most of the time they've had to lead her about the set.'

'Then the kidnapping has come at a convenient time?'

She didn't say anything.

'Do you think she's been kidnapped?'

'Why not? She hadn't the brains to think up a note like that.'

'Unless appearances deceive me,' I said, 'I have an idea you don't like her very much.'

'I love her,' she said. 'Everyone loves her.'

'Including Rice?'

'He doesn't have to. She's under contract to him.'

'That would make a difference.'

She reached up and adjusted my tie. That brought her face close to mine. I moved it back six inches into comparative safety.

'I thought strong-minded detectives only existed in books,' she said, and, pushing past me, went quickly down the passage and down the stairs.

I lit a cigarette because I needed one and stood brooding for a moment or so. Then I closed the door and began to look the room over methodically, not knowing what I was looking for, but trying to pick up the atmosphere that had been in this room before Joyce Sherman had gone out on what I was pretty sure had been her last drive.

She had a lot of clothes: that was to be expected. I also unearthed a lot of bottles of brandy. They were hidden away behind dresses, in the shoe cupboard and under piles of silk underwear: the way a squirrel stores its nuts against a rainy day.

In one drawer I found a .22 revolver. It was loaded, but it hadn't been fired, anyway not for a long time. In the same drawer I also found three unopened bottles of Joy perfume, and this discovery made me pause. I unscrewed one of the caps and sniffed at the perfume. It conjured up a dark alley, a woman in a hurry and a big, swiftly moving car. That was absurd, of course. Half the movie actresses in Hollywood probably used

Joy. I replaced the cap and continued my search. Hidden away in a hat-box I found a nasty-looking dagger, shaped like an ice-pick, its point filed to needle sharpness. This discovery, together with the bottles of Joy perfume, made me quicken my search. I turned my attention to the desk that stood in the bay-window, overlooking the pleasure gardens. One of the drawers was full of papers: letters, old contracts, photographs and press-clippings. Under one pile of letters was a business card, a little grimy, its corners broken. I picked it up: Bernard Hoffman's card.

As I stood staring at it, a chill of excitement running up my spine, somewhere downstairs a telephone bell began to ring.

III

I was surprised to see the lights still burning in Fanshaw's office as I pushed open the door. The time was seven-forty-five. I hadn't expected him to work so late. But he wasn't working. He was reading a paper-back novel, his feet on his desk, a bottle of Scotch at his elbow and a tray full of cigarette butts within reach of his hand.

'There you are,' he said, swinging his feet to the floor. 'I thought I'd better stick around in case you wanted me in a hurry. Has the ransom demand come in yet?'

'Yeah, a little under an hour ago,' I said, pulled up a chair and sat down. 'If you can spare any of that Scotch I'd be glad to make a hole in it.'

He poured two drinks and pushed one of the glasses towards me.

'It scares me to ask. How much?'

'Maddux will probably have a stroke. They're not even trying to be subtle. It's my bet they know all about the cover-age. They're slugging us for the full amount – half a million.'

'Jeepers!' Fanshaw groaned. 'When?'

'Four days from today. The money's to be in five, ten and twenty-dollar bills. Nothing larger. I spoke to the guy myself,'

I said. 'He sounded very tough. Four nights from now he's calling again to give delivery instructions. He won't give us time to set a trap.'

'Well, at least we do see life, don't we?' Fanshaw said, yawning. 'Maybe Maddux won't pay.'

'He'll pay. Rice has phoned the newspapers. He's given them the insurance story. We'll have to pay.'

'Well, I guess I'd better break the news to him. It's going to be some job getting those bills together. Nothing higher than twenty?'

'That's right. This guy sounded as if he meant business.' I used some of my drink, went on, 'Did you know Miss Sherman was a drunk?'

'Bad?'

'From what I hear this movie she's working on could have been her last. Her secretary tells me they had to lead her around the set.'

Fanshaw stared thoughtfully at me.

'I've heard rumours, of course, but I didn't think it was as bad as that. How did you like Rice?'

'I love him. We got along fine together.'

'Any ideas?'

'The obvious one. A highly paid star drinks herself out of a job. Husband decides to cash in before it's too late. Arranges for her to be kidnapped and pockets the ransom.'

Fanshaw nodded.

'Yeah, could be. The one snag is he didn't know about the policy.'

'We haven't proved that. She might have told him. I like the idea.'

'So what do we do?'

'Nothing until we've paid the money. Then we've got to watch Rice. If he has the money it'll show if we wait long enough.'

'And Joyce Sherman?'

'It's my bet she won't come back.'

'My bet too. Well, I'd better call Maddux. I'll tell him what you think.'

'He'll love it. It's the kind of theory he'd dream up himself.' I stood up. 'I have a job to do before I turn in. If he wants me I'll be at the Culver Hotel in about an hour.'

'Okay. See you in the morning.'

I left him putting through a call to San Francisco, and went down the street. A passing taxi-driver leaned out of his cab and looked at me inquiringly. I waved to him.

'55 Wiltshire Road,' I told him and got into the cab.

Wiltshire Road lay at the back of South Boulevard, a dimly lit street of small bungalows. No. 55 was lonely and dark, with a small uncared-for garden and a rickety wooden gate.

I told the taxi-driver to wait, walked up the path and rapped on the knocker. I had to rap a second time before I heard movements, then the door opened and a woman peered at me.

'Who is it?'

'Mr. Hoffman in?'

'No.'

The front door began to close.

'You Mrs. Hoffman?'

'What's it to you who I am?'

'I have urgent business with Mr. Hoffman. Where can I find him?'

She hesitated, peering at me, then making up her mind, she stood aside.

'Oh, well, I guess you'd better come in.'

I followed her into a small untidy room full of shabby furniture and a lot of dust.

In the harsh light of the electric lamp I saw she was around thirty-five, dark, sluttish and sullen. She still had a cheap prettiness, and if she hadn't let herself go she could have been a looker. She wore an old grubby sweater that she had on inside out, and there was a big grease stain in the middle of her grey, wrinkled skirt.

'Are you Mrs. Hoffman?'

'Suppose I am?' she said curtly. 'Don't think it's anything I'm proud of. What do you want?'

I offered her a cigarette. She took it, accepted a light and sat down on the battered chesterfield.

'Say your piece and make it snappy,' she went on. 'I have to go out in a while.'

'You don't know where your husband it?'

'I've told you. What do you want him for?'

'A job. I ran into him at Springville. That was last night. I could put some money in his way if I could find him.'

She looked searchingly at me, interest suddenly jumping into her eyes.

'Are you the insurance fella?'

'That's right. Did he tell you about me?'

'Him?' She laughed scornfully. 'He doesn't tell me a thing. I heard him talking to someone on the phone. He said he had met you. You're Harmas, aren't you?'

I nodded and lowered myself gingerly into one of the armchairs. It held me, but only just.

'When was this?'

'Three nights ago.'

'Do you know who he was talking to?'

'I have an idea.'

'Who?'

She gave a crafty little smile.

'I don't talk about my husband's business. He wouldn't like it.'

'It happens to be my business too. Would a twenty-dollar bill be of any use?'

She licked her pale lips and shifted restlessly.

'It might.'

I took one from my wallet.

'Who was it?'

'That redhead he's been going around with.'

'Now look, this is important. Loosen up, will you? Don't make me drag it out of you. It rates forty: twenty now and twenty when you're through.' I slid the bill along the arm of the chesterfield. She picked it out of my fingers and tucked it down the front of her sweater.

'You're not to tell him I told you,' she said. 'I wouldn't tell you now only I'm pretty sure he's not coming back.'

'What makes you say that?'

'He packed his things. Someone threw a scare into him. He did a sneak when I was in the kitchen. No, he's not coming back, and damn good riddance.'

'This redhead. Who is she?'

'I don't know. She came here about a week ago. I let her in, but I couldn't see much of her face. She wore sunglasses and a big hat. I wouldn't know her again.'

'Has she been here since?'

She shook her head.

'But I know Bernie's seen her from time to time because of the money he's been getting. He meets her late at night.'

'Know why she hired him?'

Again she shook her head.

'You say he phoned her three nights ago?'

'That's right. I was in the kitchen. I heard him using the phone. I thought I'd see what he was up to. I listened outside the door. He was talking about a murder. I'm sure it was the redhead he was talking to.'

'Can you give me some idea of what he said?'

She thought for a moment.

'I don't remember exactly. I think he said something like this: "The guy was following me. His name's Harmas, and he's an insurance investigator. He knows I was in that building. He can't prove it, but he knows. He'll try and pin the killing on me. Well, I don't run that risk for nothing. I've got to see you. Yes, right now. Bring some money with you. See you in half an hour," and he hung up.'

'What happened then?'

'He went out. It was a quarter to twelve. He came back at half-past twelve, and went straight to his room. He imagined I was in bed. We have separate rooms now. About twenty minutes later he came down with his bags. I was watching him from the kitchen door. He put the bags in the car and drove away.'

'You said just now he was scared. Why did you say that?'

'Because he was. He was as white as a sheet and sweating and muttering to himself. I've never seen him look like that before. He was scared all right, and he's in some jam. I was glad to see him go. I don't want to get mixed up in anything.' She looked at the clock on the over-mantel. 'I'm seeing a movie tonight and I'll be late if I don't go now.'

'Just one more question. Was he working for anyone beside the redhead?'

'I don't know for sure. He did a few odd jobs. People were always calling him up.' She stood up. 'What's this killing he's talking about?'

'I don't know,' I lied. 'I should keep clear of it if I were you. You have no idea where he's gone?'

She shook her head.

'You said you met him at Springville last night,' she said. 'I didn't even know he was going there. Why didn't you talk to him last night?'

'I didn't get the chance.'

She looked suspiciously at me.

'Has he killed anyone?'

'No. I don't know what he was talking about.' I gave her the other twenty. 'Stick around for a few days. You may have to talk to the police.'

'Well, I guess I don't care,' she said, shrugging. 'They can't do anything to me.' She led the way to the front door and opened it.

'If your husband gets into touch with you, it's worth a hundred for me to know where he is, I said, moving past her and down the two steps leading to the path. 'You can reach me at the Culver Hotel.'

As I was speaking I looked to see if my taxi was still waiting. It was. On the other side of the road, in line with the open front door, was a big saloon car. It hadn't been there when I had arrived, and I looked curiously at it. It was parked in the shadows, and I couldn't see if anyone was in it. Then suddenly I saw something move through the driver's window: something that glittered in the faint light of the distant street lamp.

My taxi-driver gave a hoarse shout of warning. He was a lot closer to the car than I was, and must have recognized the thing that had moved.

'Look out!' I yelled, and threw myself backwards into the hedge that grew along the path.

The dark night was split open by a yellow flash. There came the choked bang of a shotgun and the air became full of whistling shot. Something that hurt bit into my left arm. I was only vaguely aware that the car was driving away. My eyes were on Mrs. Hoffman, who had taken the full blast of the gun. She had been thrown back into the hall. Her hands picked feebly at her shattered chest as her knees folded up under her. She spread out, face downwards on the shabby hall carpet. By the time I had struggled clear of the hedge and reached her, she was dead.

CHAPTER SEVEN

I

THE only light in the room came from the desk lamp that made a pool of light on the desk and carpet.

Police-Captain Ed. Hackett rolled a pencil across his blotter, then rolled it back again. In the shadows, away from the light, Micklin chewed a dead cigar and scowled up at the ceiling while Fanshaw kept rubbing his eyes with the palms of his hands, yawning. He had been in bed when I had used the police phone to get him down to headquarters. I sat by the desk and nursed an aching arm. I had had four bits of shot picked out of my left biceps, and I was feeling low.

'You have no idea who did the shooting?' Hackett asked abruptly without looking up.

'Not a clue. As the taxi-driver told you, he couldn't be sure if the killer was a man or woman and he was too scared to get the car's number. I was too scared even to think of trying.'

'Who was he after – you or Mrs. Hoffman?'

'I have an idea it was me.'

'Okay,' Hackett said, looking up sharply. 'Let's see if we can straighten this thing out. Let's start in at the beginning. Why did you go to Hoffman's house?'

'I found out he was working for Joyce Sherman. I hoped I could get him to loosen up and tell me what the job was.' I went on to describe how I had found Hoffman's card in Joyce's drawer, and what Mrs. Hoffman had told me. 'It's my bet Joyce was to meet Hoffman the night she disappeared.'

'Think he kidnapped her?' Fanshaw asked.

I shook my head.

'I'm beginning to think she hasn't been kidnapped. My guess is she and Hoffman cooked up the kidnapping between them to get the ransom money for themselves.'

'For the love of Pete,' Fanshaw exploded. 'How do you work that out?'

'From what Mrs. Hoffman told me. She heard Hoffman ask Joyce for money. He was set to blackmail Joyce. She and he were mixed up in the murder of a janitor of a business block on 4th Street.'

'You mean Joe Mason?' Hackett asked sharply. 'The guy who was knifed on Tuesday night?'

'Yeah. The night of the kidnapping. I happened to be in the district that night, and I saw a woman leave the alley leading to Mason's door. She was wearing a perfume called Joy. I ran into Hoffman in a Chinese restaurant next door. For some reason Joyce was interested in certain insurance policies held by a girl named Susan Gellert. Joyce hired Hoffman to find out where the policies were kept. When he had traced them to this girl's agent, Joyce went with him to the agent's office to examine them. Mason probably heard them break in. He was knifed while Hoffman was faking a robbery in another office to cover up the real motive of their search.'

'Are you telling me Hoffman killed Mason?' Hackett asked.

I shook my head.

'I'm pretty sure he didn't know Mason was dead until the police arrived.'

'Then who killed him?'

'Haven't you checked on that knife I gave you?'

Hackett hesitated, then reached for the telephone. He spoke into it, listened, said. 'Fine. Hang on to it, Jack,' and hung up. His grey eyes were hard as he looked at me. 'Where did you find that knife, Harmas?'

'It's the one that killed Mason, isn't it?'

'Looks like it. It fits the wound, and the blood we found on the handle checks with Mason's group.'

'I found it in Joyce's bedroom. It's my bet she killed him.'

The silence that followed was electric.

'Can you prove it?' Hackett asked softly.

'I guess not, but Hoffman can. Joyce's secretary told me Joyce is a drunk. When I searched her room I found plenty of evidence to support that. It's possible Mason surprised her, and she knifed him in a drunken panic.'

Hackett rubbed his blue chin. He didn't seem sold on the idea.

'We'll leave that for a moment. Who's this Gellert woman you're talking about?'

'That's a long story, but it hooks up somehow, although I don't know how.' I told him about the accident policies. I gave him all the facts, including our visit to Dead Lake, but I didn't tell him we had broken into Denny's office.

'But why should Joyce Sherman be interested in this woman?' Micklin asked. 'It doesn't make sense.'

'I wish I knew. If I found that out maybe I'd know why these extraordinary insurance policies were taken out.'

'We'll get after Hoffman,' Hackett said. 'That's the first move.'

'I still can't see why you should say Miss Sherman hasn't been kidnapped,' Fanshaw said.

'Look at it this way,' I said. 'Suppose Hoffman had decided to blackmail her for Mason's murder. Joyce realizes he could bleed her white. She agrees to meet him and give him whatever she's been able to raise, and then vanish. I don't know what her bank balance is, but judging by the set-up she keeps I doubt if she has a lot of spare cash. If she disappears she cuts herself off from the enormous income she's been used to. She must have a get-away stake. She remembers the insurance policy, covering her against kidnapping. A half a million is just the sum she needs. But she realizes she can't swing it alone. She decides to hook up with Hoffman. They meet and she tells him of her plan. He writes the ransom note. They leave her car on Foothill Boulevard, and go off in Hoffman's car. All they have to do now is to collect the ransom, divide the money and drop out of sight. How do you like that for an idea?'

'You're full of ideas,' Hackett said wearily. 'It's all guess-work. We haven't any proof. I'm not saying it didn't happen like that, but I'm not sold on it. I'm going after Hoffman. He's the key to all this.'

'I like the idea,' Fanshaw said. 'We'd better tell Maddux right away. I don't see why we need pay the ransom now. If Lloyd wants Miss Sherman back so badly, let him advance the money, and if the kidnapping turns out to be on the level we can refund it.'

'We've got to pay up,' I said. 'Rice has given the story to the Press. We can't afford to back out in the face of the publicity we're going to get. We'll have to pay the ransom unless we can prove she killed Mason, and we've only three days to do it in.'

'We have proved it, haven't we?' Fanshaw said. 'The per-fume, the card in her drawer, the knife in her hat-box. What more do you want?'

'Thousands of women use Joy,' I said, 'and the knife and card could have been planted in her room. That's not proof.'

Fanshaw appealed to Hackett.

'How soon can you find Hoffman?'

Hackett shrugged.

'Tomorrow, next month, next year. It depends on the breaks we get.'

'That's fine,' Fanshaw said bitterly. 'You realize if you don't find him within three days we stand to lose a half a million?'

'You don't have to tell me,' Hackett said, pushing back his chair. 'I'll get on the job right away.' He looked over at Mick-lin. 'In view of this new development maybe we should start looking for Miss Sherman.'

'Yeah,' Micklin said, 'and it had better be done quietly. If Rice thinks we suspect his wife of murder he'll sue the lot of us.'

'We'll leave you to get organized,' Fanshaw said. 'Come on, Steve, let's get some sleep.'

As we walked down the steps to the street I said, 'You'll have to go ahead and collect the ransom. Unless Hackett finds Miss Sherman and Hoffman we're sunk.'

'I'll talk to Maddux. And, Steve, watch your step. If they're gunning for you, they may try again.'

When I got back to my hotel I took the precaution of locking my bedroom door and putting my gun under my pillow.

II

As I had foreseen, all the morning newspapers carried the story of the ransom insurance, and what a splash they made of it! They had interviewed Maddux, and under pressure, he had been forced to admit that the company would pay the ransom if Joyce Sherman wasn't found before the ransom instructions were received.

There was nothing for me to do until the ransom instructions were received, and as my arm was now a little inflamed and stiff, I decided to take it easy until I was forced into action.

I called Pete Eagan for news of Helen. He told me she was up at the lake, and he had been up there with her from time to time, sharing her watch with her. From the way he spoke I gathered Helen had been doing her stuff, and he sounded as if he had been enjoying himself.

'She told me if you came through to say she's fine, and for you not to worry. She'll call you sometime tonight if you're around.'

When Helen did come on the line in the evening, I didn't tell her I had been shot. I knew if she thought there might be another attempt to fill me full of lead, she'd come back fast. As it was working out, it was a good thing she had decided to stay up at Dead Lake.

I told her Hoffman was missing, and how I had now definite evidence that Joyce Sherman had killed Mason. She was as startled as I had been.

'I can't understand it,' she said, her voice sounding far away on the crackling line. 'Why on earth should a famous movie star be interested in the insurance policies of an unknown stripper? What's the connection?'

'I can't figure it out myself. The whole set-up foxes me.'

And it did. The more I thought about it, the less sense I made of it.

Although I took it easy, the police department was going flat out to find Hoffman. But in spite of an intensive search, no trace of either Hoffman or Joyce Sherman was found. It became more and more obvious as the hours slipped by that we were going to be forced to pay out the ransom money.

If it hadn't been for the enormous publicity given to the insurance coverage by the Press, I am sure Maddux would have found some way of getting out of paying. He thought my theory that Joyce Sherman had murdered the janitor was the answer to her disappearance, and he was in a frenzy at being forced to honour the claim.

Fanshaw had collected the ransom which was now under armed guard. I had never seen such a pile of money. It had been packed in two big suitcases for easy handling.

On the afternoon of the third day – the day we expected to receive the ransom instructions – I, Maddux, Fanshaw and Micklin met at Fanshaw's office.

Micklin had nothing to report, and when Police Captain Hackett arrived, one look at his dark, scowling face told us he had nothing to report either.

'That guy must be somewhere!' Maddux raved, pacing up and down. 'A half a million down the drain because you're all a lot of damned incompetents!'

'He may be out of the country for all we know,' Hackett growled. 'If you have any ideas, trot them out instead of bawling at me.'

'I don't reckon to have to tell you your job!' Maddux snapped. 'I have my work cut out handling my own job with the kind of crazy policies my company accepts.'

'I'd better get over to the Sherman house,' I said, tired of listening to him. 'As soon as I get the instructions I'll phone you here. With any luck we may still be able to set some sort of trap.'

'Not a hope,' Hackett said. 'You'll be sent half over the country before you get the final delivery instructions. I know kidnappers. A trap's what they'll be expecting.'

'Why not let him have a short-wave radio car?' Micklin asked. 'He'll be able to keep in touch with us. We can have a fleet of cars within a mile of him, and yet be out of sight.'

'Now, that's a damned good idea,' Maddux said. 'The first bright idea I've heard. How about it, Hackett?'

'Sure,' Hackett said. 'I'll get that laid on right away. Not a word to anyone about this, Harmas. When Micklin brings the ransom over, he'll have one of our fastest and best equipped police cars for you. I'll have the radio mast dismantled. We don't want to give anything away.'

'Right,' I said. 'Well, if that's all, I'll get going.'

As I walked across the sidewalk to where I had left my car I ran into Alan Goodyear who was heading for Fanshaw's office.

'Hello there,' I said, stopping. 'Wish me luck. I'm on my way over to the Sherman place. We're expecting the ransom in-structions.'

'So they haven't found her?'

'No; nor Hoffman.'

'We're going to pay up then?' He looked pale and worried. 'I wish I'd never had the idea of selling her that policy.'

'Forget it. Take my tip and don't go in there unless you have to. Maddux is there, and he's doing his wild bull act as usual.'

Goodyear grimaced.

'Then I won't. I've had enough of him. What chances are there of tracing the money, Steve?'

'You mean once it's left my hands? Not a chance in the world. The notes are too small. Fanshaw didn't even have time to take the numbers.'

'Then if the kidnappers aren't caught we lose the lot?'

'I guess so, but that's the way it happens. At least we've had a lot of free publicity.'

'Can't the police set a trap for these devils? Surely something can be done?'

'They're giving me a radio car,' I said, 'only keep that under your hat. With any luck we may be able to corner them. I can keep in touch with the police who'll only be a mile or so behind me, but out of sight.'

Goodyear's face brightened.

'That's smart, but watch out, Steve. Sounds a little dangerous.'

'Well, I guess I have to earn my money somehow. I know what I wanted to ask you. When you talked to Miss Sherman, how did she strike you?'

'In what way?'

'I've heard she's a hopeless soak. Did she strike you that way?'

He shook his head.

'I didn't notice anything like that. She seemed very much all there when we talked business.'

'Did you meet her secretary: a dark girl with an hourglass figure and a Mexican outlook?'

'Why, yes. She took me to Miss Sherman.'

'So she would know Miss Sherman had taken out the policy?'

Goodyear again shook his head.

'She knew I was checking up on the theft and fire renewal. She didn't know anything about the new coverage.'

I blew out my cheeks.

'It's a hell of a life being an investigator. I come up against a blank wall ten times a day. Well, so long. I must get moving.'

'Good luck, Steve. I wish I were going with you. I feel this is my responsibility.'

'Forget it,' I said, slapped him on the back and got into the car.

It took me ten minutes or so to reach the Sherman residence. The time was six-fifteen. A couple of tough looking cops guarded the main entrance. They let me through when I had proved who I was.

Perry Rice, attired in white flannels and a sleeveless singlet, was pacing up and down on the terrace.

'Come on up,' he called, leaning over the balustrade. 'Have you any news?'

'Not a thing. Has the call come through yet?'

'No.' There was a feverish light in his eyes, and his fingers kept twitching at his sides. 'Have you got the money?'

'It's all ready. It's at our branch office at the moment. As soon as we hear from the kidnappers Micklin is bringing it over.'

'In small bills as they said?'

'Yeah.'

He took out his handkerchief and wiped his face.

'Good. I don't want anything to go wrong with this. I want my wife back.'

I made grunting noises and looked hopefully at a table loaded with drinks. He followed my gaze.

'Help yourself,' he said abruptly. 'You'll have to excuse me. I have a lot of things to do.'

He went away, along the terrace and disappeared through the casement windows.

I helped myself to a large whisky and soda and sat down. It was very quiet and hot on the terrace. The view of the garden would have held my attention if I hadn't had so much on my mind. I did wonder – if Joyce Sherman had killed Mason – how she must be feeling to give up all this luxury, and where she was hiding. I sat thinking for maybe half an hour, then realizing time was getting on, and I was feeling uncomfortably hot, I decided to see if I could find someone to talk to – Myra Lantis for preference, but anyone rather than wait out here on my own.

I walked along the terrace, peered through the casement windows into an empty room, went on to the end of the terrace.

Steps led down to the sunken rose garden, and I was hesitating whether to go down and examine the roses at close quarters for the sake of something to do when I heard voices.

A moment's listening told me the voices were coming from an open window near by. I drifted quietly towards it with the idea of seeking company.

Then a voice stopped me in mid-stride: Myra Lantis's voice.

'How can you talk like that?' she was saying. 'She may come back. You don't know for certain.'

I moved quickly and silently to the wall and edged closer to the window, keeping well out of sight.

'Now look,' Rice said, 'she won't come back. I can't tell you how I know, but I know. As soon as they've paid the ransom we can get out of here. You want to come away with me, don't you?'

'Yes, I want that more than anything else in the world, but I'm not moving from here until I'm certain she isn't coming back.'

'She isn't coming back I tell you!' Rice snapped, an angry rasp in his voice. 'Even if they haven't killed her by now, she couldn't stand being without liquor all this time. Look at the state she was in when she went out that night.'

'You shouldn't have let her go, Perry. I haven't any use for her, but it made me sick to see her driving away in that state. You should've stopped her!'

'To hell with her!' Rice said viciously. 'I'm glad she went. I wish she had killed herself that night instead of getting herself kidnapped.'

'Perry; I must know. Has she really been kidnapped?'

There was a sudden silence, then he said in a grating voice, 'What the hell do you mean?'

'Perry; Don't look at me like that.' Her voice sounded scared. 'Why are you sure she isn't coming back? And if we are going to Paris, where's the money coming from? Darling, please tell me the truth. I know there's no money here. I'm not a fool. I pay all the bills. She owes thousands, and so do you. How are you . . .?'

'Will you shut up?' Rice snarled. 'I'm fed up with this. If you don't want to throw in with me, say so, and I'll go alone.'

'Oh, Perry, please don't talk like that. You know I want to go with you. I love you. Please . . .'

'Then shut up and stop asking questions! Leave me alone. I've got things to do if we're leaving soon. Go and find something to do yourself.'

I moved quietly away from the window, and as soon as I was out of their hearing, I ran down the terrace to my seat, but before I could sit down the shrill sound of a telephone bell ringing shattered the tense, hot silence.

III

As I made for the open casement doors, Rice appeared. His face was white, and there was a wolfish, hard expression in his eyes that startled me.

'Could be the kidnappers,' he said. 'You'd better answer it. Hurry!'

He waved me into the room. I reached the telephone in three strides and lifted the receiver.

'The Sherman residence,' I said.

There was a long pause on the line, then a muffled voice said, 'Who's that speaking?'

'Harmas, National Fidelity,' I said, recognizing the voice I had heard before when the first instructions had come through.

'Got the money?'

'It's all ready.'

'In small bills?'

'Nothing over twenty.'

'Right. Now, listen. You know Elmo Springs?'

I said I did. Elmo Springs was a tiny town about a hundred miles north of Los Angeles, up in the mountains.

'You've three hours to get there so you've got to snap at it,' the voice went on. 'You'll get further instructions at the Blue Triangle filling station. And listen, if you try any monkey business it'll be just too bad for the Sherman twist.'

'Keep your shirt on,' I said. 'All we want is Miss Sherman back. You'll get your money, but what guarantee have we she'll be returned?'

'Think I want to keep her? The bitch is ruining me. The amount of liquor she's using would float a yacht.'

'Bring her to the phone. I want to talk to her.'

'She's not here, pally, and if she was, she'd be too tight to walk.'

'How do we get her back?'

'Pay over the dough and I'll tell you. Now get going. I want that money in three hours.'

There was a sharp click and the line went dead.

As I dialled Fanshaw's number I said to Rice, 'Elmo Springs in three hours. There'll be other instructions for me there.'

'What did he say about Joyce?' Rice asked in a strangled voice.

'As soon as he gets the money he'll tell us where to find her.'

Hackett answered my call. I told him where I was to go.

'Okay,' he said. 'I'll have the car sent right over. We'll have ten cars around Elmo Springs before you get there. Keep in touch, and good luck.'

I thanked him and hung up.

Rice came over to me.

'They're not setting a trap, are they?' he demanded.

I shook my head.

'It can't be done. Besides, we're as anxious as you to get your wife back.'

He stared fixedly at me, muttered something under his breath and went out.

I walked on to the terrace. After a ten-minute wait I saw a car coming rapidly up the drive. I ran down the steps to meet it.

Micklin and Maddux got out. On the back seat I could see the two suitcases containing the ransom.

'Okay,' Micklin said. 'Off you go. Keep in touch with us.

We'll be right behind you, but out of sight. With any luck we'll catch him.'

I got into the car.

'I'll call you at Elmo Springs . . .' I started to say when Rice suddenly appeared. Before Micklin could stop him he had wrenched open the car door and was glaring at the short-wave radio set.

'So that's what you're up to?' he snarled. 'God damn it! Didn't I tell you not to try anything smart? Get out of that car?'

'Stay where you are!' Maddux barked and shoved Rice back. 'I'm running this show. This is our money, and . . .'

'He's not to take that car!' Rice raved, struggling to get at me. 'If anything happens to Joyce . . .'

I started the engine, made a quick U-turn and drove fast down the drive, leaving Maddux and Micklin to cope with Rice.

It was close on seven o'clock when I left the Sherman residence. I ran into a certain amount of traffic in Los Angeles which slowed me up, but once clear of the town and on the highway, I made pretty good time. The long, twisting mountain road made fast driving difficult, but I kept a good average speed, and at the half-way mark, I had ten minutes in hand.

I pulled up on a deserted part of the road to familiarize myself with the radio set. After erecting the short, steel mast, I sent out the call sign. Almost immediately Hackett answered.

'I'm just outside La Canada,' I said into the mike. 'Just checking to see if I've the hang of this thing.'

'I'm receiving you okay,' Hackett's voice boomed. 'Keep going. We're about half a mile behind you.'

'I'll call you next at Elmo Springs.'

I switched out, took down the mast and continued on up the Angeles Crest Highway to Cajon. From there the road was easier, and I made good time, arriving at Elmo Springs five minutes ahead of schedule. At the far end of the main street I spotted a triangular sign in blue neon lights.

I drove into the short runway of the badly lit filling station. It was a lonely spot, with three pumps and a shack that served as an office.

A white-coated attendant came out.

'Fill her up,' I said and got out of the car to stretch my legs. 'My name's Harmas. I'm expecting a message some guy said he'd leave here. Anything come in?'

'Sure,' the attendant said. 'I got a letter for you. I'll get it.'

He went into the shack and returned immediately with an envelope addressed to me in block capitals. I took it from him and moved away from the car to the only lamp above the shack.

The message was brief:

Go on from here to Canyon Pass. Further instructions under a stone at foot of highway sign-post.

I tucked the note into my hip pocket and went back to the attendant who was screwing on the cap of the tank.

'What was this fellow like who gave you the note?' I asked.

'I didn't see him. I had a phone call about half an hour ago saying a note was being left here for you. I found the note ten minutes later and a couple of bucks on my desk. Sort of mysterious, ain't it?'

'Yeah. You're sure you didn't see him? You could make yourself ten dollars if you did.'

The attendant's face fell.

'Honest, mister, I didn't see him. Gee! Ten bucks!'

I gave him five bucks.

'Okay, and thanks. How do I get to Canyon Pass?'

He gave me the directions.

'How far is it do you reckon?'

'A good thirty miles. Once you get off the main road on to the mountain road, you can't miss it. There's only one road up there.'

I thanked him again and drove off. When I had gone a mile, I pulled up, got out of the car, set up the radio mast and put through a call to Hackett.

'I'm heading for Canyon Pass,' I said when I had got him. 'I've written instructions, but the attendant didn't see the guy who left the note. Know where Canyon Pass is?'

Hackett cursed softly.

'I know it. There's only one road up there and no cover. This fella's smart. We can't come after you, Harmas, without giving the game away. He'd spot us.'

'It'll be dark by the time I get up there. It's pretty dark now. Can't you make it without lights?'

'Not a chance. You wait until you see the road. It's bad enough with lights, but without them it's suicide.'

So what are you going to do?'

'Wait at the bottom. I'll send three cars around the mountain to block the other end of the road, but it's a hell of a way around and I don't reckon they'll get there in time.'

'So I'm on my own from now on; is that it?'

'Guess you are. All we can do is to block the road when he comes down. At least there's no other way for him to come.'

'That's fine as far as the ransom is concerned, but not particularly healthy for me. Suppose this guy takes it into his head to knock me off?'

'I warned you this could be a dangerous job,' Hackett said. 'If you don't want to go through with it, stay where you are until we reach you, and Micklin will take over.'

'I'm handling it,' I said. 'I'll call you when I get to Canyon Pass.'

'Right,' Hackett said. 'I'll get the cars off right away. Take it slow. I want a little time for my men to block the other road.'

I replaced the receiver and started the car. *Then something cold and hard screwed into the back of my neck.* The shock nearly killed me. I knew what it was – a gun! I sat frozen, my hands gripping the wheel, expecting to have my head blown off.

'Don't move and don't look around,' a muffled voice snarled in my ear, 'or I'll spread your goddamn brain in your lap.'

Okay, I was scared. I admit it. I was scared stiff. I recognized the muffled voice. I had the kidnapper right behind me!

He must have got into the back of the car when the attendant was filling the tank. That made the attendant his accomplice. It meant too that I wasn't going to get out of this jam alive to give the attendant away to the police.

'Get going!' the voice went on. 'Do what I tell you or it'll be the last wrong move you make.' The cold barrel of the gun screwed into my neck and sent chills up and down my spine.

I engaged gear and drove down the road. After a mile or so, the voice said, 'Turn left and keep going.'

Instead of heading for the Canyon Pass I was now driving away from it, and away from all possible help. Sweat trickled down my nose and fell on to my hands. I was glad Helen wasn't there to see me. There was nothing very dashing nor brave about me at the moment.

'So you figured you'd be smart, didn't you?' the voice said sneeringly. 'Well, we'll see who's the smarter. I know who I've got my money on.'

'I never bet with strangers,' I said, annoyed my voice sounded like the croak of a frog. 'Where are we going?'

'Drive – don't talk or I'll clip you!'

We drove along the back roads, turning left, then right, then left again. I hadn't the vaguest idea where I was now. I kept on driving for a good twenty minutes, then the voice said, 'Okay, this'll do. Stop here.'

We were on a narrow deserted road lined on one side with sage and brush and on the other, darkness and space. It was as lonely and as silent as a coffin. Far below I could see a few scattered lights of cars climbing the mountain road. A chill air fanned my face, and I wasn't sure whether it was the altitude or fear that made breathing difficult.

'What's happened to Joyce Sherman?' I asked as I stopped the car.

'What do you think? She died of home sickness. Now, shut up and do what I tell you. Call the cops and tell them you're at Canyon Pass. Make it sound good or I'll drill you.'

'Dead? You mean you've killed her?'

I got a bang on the head that made me see stars.

'Shut up!' the voice snarled. 'Call the cops!'

I got through to Hackett.

'I'm out at Canyon Pass,' I told him. Sweat was pouring off me. The gun was now screwed into my right ear, and I knew as soon as I had finished talking to Hackett I was going to be murdered.

'Tell him you're leaving the money as instructed by the sign-post,' the voice whispered.

'This is the pay-off, Hackett,' I said into the mike. My right hand moved slowly and cautiously to the door handle of the car. 'I'm to leave the money by the sign-post.'

'No one around?' Hackett asked.

'No.'

It was coming. In a moment Hackett would be off the air. We must be miles away from Canyon Pass by now. All this thug had to do was to knock me off and be free to take the money and blow.

'Well, okay,' Hackett said. 'Dump the money and come on back. When you see a red light, dip your head-lamps three times or you'll get shot. So long for now.'

I pushed down the door handle and felt the car door open. As the line went dead, I struck upwards, knocking the gun away, and threw myself out of the car. There was a flash and a roar of gunfire. I rolled frantically to the side of the road as the gun crashed again. A slug kicked up dirt into my face. I squirmed madly to the over-hang. I could see him now. He was out of the car: a squat, broad figure, running towards me. I hadn't time to pull my gun. He could see me, but he wasn't going to miss me a third time.

As he came up, the gun levelled, I gave a terrific heave and threw myself off the road into dark, empty space.

CHAPTER EIGHT

I

HACKETT tossed the cigarette butt into the trash basket and drew in a deep whistling breath through his nose.

'So you're sure the guy wasn't Hoffman?'

'No, it wasn't Hoffman,' I said and eased my aching legs.

The time was twenty minutes past two a.m. I was feeling as if I had been run over by a train. If it hadn't been for a carload of people driving down to Los Angeles who had heard my yells, I wouldn't be here now. The roll down the mountainside had been an experience that would haunt my dreams for many nights to come. 'Hoffman's tall and big. This guy was short and thick-set. Did you nab the filling-station attendant?'

'When we got there he wasn't any use to us. Your pal had shot him through the head.'

'Oh, hell! I was hoping we'd get him to talk. Well, it looks as if we've been out-smarted. How's Rice taking it?'

'He talks of going away,' Micklin said. 'He now seems certain his wife's dead.'

'He was certain of that before I ran into the kidnapper,' I said, and went on to tell them of the conversation I had overheard between Myra Lantis and Rice.

'Could tie him into it,' Hackett said thoughtfully.

'We have two theories to work on,' I said. 'One is that Joyce Sherman murdered Mason, was blackmailed by Hoffman, decided to duck out and staged a phoney kidnapping to get hold of the ransom for a get-away stake. The other is Rice, knowing Joyce was on the skids and wanting to get rid of her to marry this Lantis girl, engineered the kidnapping. Either of these ideas stand up. For all we know it could be a combination of both theories. If Rice is at the back of it, sooner or later the guy who tried to kill me is going to contact him. He has the ransom and Rice will want his share. Why not slick two of your best men on Rice and watch him night and day? Give him no chance of getting his hands on the ransom. He may lose his head and make a wrong move.'

'Yeah,' Hackett said, 'I'll fix it.'

'Well, I'm about all in. If there isn't anything more, I'll go to bed,' I said. 'I've had enough excitement for one night. What's the next move?'

'We have everything organized,' Micklin said grimly. 'We now go after the kidnapper and try to find Miss Sherman.'

I was glad to leave it to them. It was a job that called for a patient and systematic search. It wasn't a one-man show. Only the police could handle a job like that. I felt I could leave it to them with a clear conscience.

I took a taxi to the Culver Hotel. As I walked across the lounge I heard my name. Turning, I saw Alan Goodyear coming towards me.

'My God Steve! Are you hurt?' he asked anxiously, staring at my dusty and torn suit.

'I'm okay. Just in need of a lot of sleep. What are you doing here?'

'I kept thinking of you and wondering how you were getting on. I didn't like to bother Fanshaw so I've been sitting here, waiting for you to come back.'

'That's pretty nice of you, but you're letting this thing prey on your mind. Take it easy, can't you?'

'What happened?'

'The guy out-smarted me. I had instructions to go to Elmo Springs and pick up more instructions. The kidnapper got into the back of my car without my seeing him, and took charge of me with a gun. He skipped with the money and the car.'

'He didn't hurt you?'

I grinned ruefully.

'He had a damn good try, but I was lucky. I rolled off the mountain road. Don't ask me why I didn't break my neck. It was quite a warm moment while it lasted.'

Goodyear drew in a deep breath.

'Phew! Well, I'm glad it was no worse. I imagined all kinds of things happening to you. So he got away?'

'Yep. Before he started to play rough he told me Joyce Sherman's dead. The cops think it's on the level, but that won't stop them hunting for her.'

'You mean he murdered her?'

'I guess so.'

'Do the police think they'll find him?'

'You know what the police are. They have to be optimistic. It's my bet Rice is tied up in this. The police are putting a tail on him tonight and tapping his phone.'

'Rice?' Goodyear looked startled. 'What makes you think he has anything to do with it?'

'Something I overheard. He and the Lantis girl are planning to elope. Look, Alan, I'm about dead on my feet. Mind if I turn in?'

'Of course not. Sorry to have bothered you, but I was worried sick about you.'

While he was talking the night clerk came over.

'Oh, Mr. Harmas . . .'

'What is it?'

'A gentleman's been calling you for the past two hours. He says it's urgent.'

'Who was he?'

'He wouldn't leave his name.' The clerk looked outraged. 'He said you'd remember him because he once gave you a punch in the jaw.'

I forgot my tiredness.

'Hoffman!' I turned excitedly to Goodyear. 'That's Hoffman!' To the clerk I said, 'Did he leave a message?'

'He asked if you'd go to Black's Hotel immediately.'

'Where's that?'

The clerk looked down his aristocratic nose. Obviously he hadn't any use for Black's Hotel.

'It's on the waterfront, near Ocean Park. Not a particularly respectable place, Mr. Harmas.'

'Well, I guess that won't worry me,' I said. Turning to Goodyear I went on, 'I've got to talk to this guy. This could be a break.'

'It can't be as urgent as all that,' Goodyear said, following me across the lobby. 'Why not see him in the morning? It's getting on for three. You should get some rest.'

'You get some,' I said, grinning at him. 'This is import-ant.'

I broke away from him, ran down the steps and looked to right and left for a taxi. One came along as Goodyear joined me on the kerb.

'Like me to come with you?' he asked.

'I guess not. I can't imagine Hoffman talking before a witness. Don't worry about me. I'm fine. So long, Alan. I'll let you know how it works out.' I jerked open the cab door. 'Black's Hotel, near Ocean Park,' I told the driver and jumped in.

It took over twenty minutes to get down to the waterfront.

'Watch your step, bud,' the driver said as I paid him off. 'Ain't healthy around here at this hour. Want me to wait?'

'No, thanks. I'll watch out.'

I stood on the sidewalk until the red tail-light of the taxi had disappeared. It was quiet and deserted along the waterfront. Far out to sea the lights of the gambling ships gleamed against the black curtain of the sky. The smell of the ocean, the faint odours of fish, gasolene fumes and tar made me wrinkle my nose. The dark piers stretched out into a still, oily sea. A thin fog hung low, and drifted in patches, blotting out the lights of the gambling ships, making them appear and disappear at in-frequent intervals.

I turned to look at Black's Hotel. It was a tall, narrow build-ing with a flashing sign over the door. A light came through the glass panels of the entrance and spread out on to the greasy sidewalk.

I walked up four steps and pushed open the door, walked up six more steps to the reception lobby.

A small, skinny man sat behind the counter, a newspaper spread out before him, shell spectacles on the end of his nose. He watched me come all the way, his face as expressionless and as disinterested as a goat at milking time.

'You look lonely,' I said, draping myself over the counter. 'Or are your ancesters keeping you company?'

He pulled the newspaper towards him and his right hand disappeared under the paper. I knew he was dipping into a concealed drawer for a gun, and looking into his hard little eyes, I knew he wouldn't think twice about using it.

'What's that again?' he asked in a hoarse whisper, his eyes never leaving mine.

'Forget the artillery,' I said, careful not to move my hands. 'I was just trying to be sociable. I see it was a mistake. My name's Harmas. A friend of mine called me from here. He's expecting me.'

The clerk continued to stare at me. His hand remained out of sight.

'What's his name?'

'He's a little sensitive about that. I shouldn't imagine he's using it here. Does it matter?'

The clerk shifted his bridgework from right to left as he thought about it.

'Got a card?' he asked after an impressive pause.

'Sure, but don't shoot me as I get it out. My gun's in my hip pocket just in case you're interested.'

'Would you quit acting like you're in the movies?' he said taking his hand from under the newspaper. 'This is a tough neighbourhood, and you're making me nervous.'

'Entirely my own fault,' I said, relaxing. 'The approach was dead wrong.' I took out my wallet and gave him my card. He studied it, nodded his head and pushed it back again.

'Room three on the third floor. Knock four times or you might pick some lead out of your belly.'

'I must take a room here myself one of these days,' I said. 'It's time I gave up living soft.'

He pushed his glasses back up to the bridge of his nose and started in on the newspaper again. As far as he was concerned I wasn't there any more.

I walked up the stairs, moving quietly, avoiding the banister rail, which was coated with dust.

On the third floor I encountered a girl in a blue and yellow kimono, carrying a jug of water. Her feet were bare and dirty. Her hair fell to her shoulders, and made me itch to look at it.

She gave me a gaudy smile and let the kimono slide open so I could see how little she had on underneath it.

'Hello, handsome,' she said, pausing. 'Lost your way?'

'Just slumming,' I said, edging past her. 'Picking up local colour if you can call it colour.'

Her smile went away.

'Another punk full of fluff,' she said. 'In your hat, darling; in your nice new hat.'

She went on and I went on. Outside room three I paused to wipe the sweat off my face. I didn't like the place, and I liked the occupants a lot less. I rapped four times, slowly but not too loud. I had a horror of waking up anyone in the adjacent rooms. Nothing happened. I waited, listening, but heard nothing.

Across the way, from behind a door, came a steady snoring sound as harsh and as violent as an electric saw cutting into knotted wood.

I rapped again, a little more loudly, and looked furtively to right and left, expecting someone either to curse me or throw something at me.

The girl in the kimono came out of the bathroom without the jug. She walked towards me.

'Why don't you kick the so-and-so door down?' she asked as she passed. 'You'll make less noise.'

Only she didn't say so-and-so.

I watched her drift to the end of the passage, open the door and look back at me. She made a rude gesture before entering the room and closing the door. I scratched the back of my neck not because I was perplexed, but because my neck seemed to itch.

Then I very gently turned the door handle, but the door didn't move. Again I looked up and down the passage before bending to peer through the keyhole. The key was in position on the far side of the door, and there was a light burning in the room. That was all I could see. I drew in a deep breath and knocked again, loudly this time; so loudly that the gentleman with the buzz-saw snore stopped snoring. Still nothing happened.

I went down the passage to the stairs. I kept going until I reached the lobby. The clerk frowned at me and pushed his glasses to the end of his nose.

'Did he go out tonight?' I asked, arriving at the desk a little out of breath.

'Why should he? He was waiting for you,' the clerk said, pushing aside his newspaper.

'Well, he doesn't answer. There's a light on in the room and the door's locked on the inside. Feel like doing anything about it or shall I call the cops?'

The clerk jumped up as if someone had stabbed him with a bayonet.

'You don't have to do anything silly,' he said. 'I don't want the cops here. Maybe he's sleeping sound.'

'Not as sound as all that. Got a pass-key or do I have to shoot in the lock?'

'If you feel that strong about it I guess I'll come up,' he said. 'Think anything's wrong?'

'Let's go and see.'

I sent him on ahead of me, then trod on his heels so we went up the stairs fast. We were both breathing like men in need of an iron lung by the time we arrived on the third floor.

The girl in the kimono was making another trip to the bathroom.

143

'Hello, Curly,' she said to the night clerk. 'What's all the rumpus about?'

'Get under cover, you dirty little tramp, before I kick you hump-backed,' the clerk said without raising his voice.

I expected an explosion, but instead she gave him a nervous, ingratiating smile and went away fast, like someone who is expecting to be kicked hump-backed.

'What a sweet, fragrant bunch of people you have staying here,' I said as I hustled him to room three.

'Who asked your opinion? There's nothing wrong with them if you know how to handle them.'

He pounded on the door of room three, waited a moment, then stepped back and gave it a vicious kick with the flat of his foot. He seemed to be in a kicking mood.

'Suppose you open that door and quit acting like James Cagney,' I said.

He fiddled with the lock, and after a moment or so succeeded in pushing out the key that was in the lock. Then he thrust in his own key and turned it gently.

'Better stand aside. He might be nervous,' he said, getting to one side of the door himself. He turned the handle and pushed open the door. Nothing happened. No one started to shoot. We looked cautiously around the doorway into the lighted room.

Hoffman sat in a chair, his hands hanging limply, his head sunk forward on his chest. There was blood on his coat and on the floor.

'Why couldn't the bum have got himself knocked off anywhere but here?' the clerk said as he walked into the room.

I bent over Hoffman, lifted his head, then gently lowered it again. I touched his hand. It was still warm. He hadn't been dead very long.

'Jeepers!' the clerk went on, 'and this joint's as hot as a stove. Stick around until I clear some of the characters out. I've got to be clean before the cops arrive.'

He went out quickly and I heard him running along the passage.

I looked around the sordid little room. The window was open

and chilly sea air and fog drifted in. Crossing to the window I looked out on to a fire-escape. The killer must have arrived that way. It had been easy for him. I went back to Hoffman, opened his coat, pulled aside his shirt and looked at the wound just under his heart. He had been stabbed with something that could have been a butcher's knife. The blow had been dealt with considerable violence. The flesh around the wound was badly bruised. I looked around for the weapon, but couldn't see it. Then I went through his pockets, but found nothing of interest. There were two suitcases under the bed, and they contained nothing of interest either.

I felt suddenly tired and deflated. There'd be no sleep for me now. I would have to wait for Hackett to get here and spend the rest of the night watching him at work. I groaned softly and wished there was some liquor in the room.

I went down the passage. There was a lot of activity going on. Three powerfully built men, carrying suitcases, their clothes flung on over their pyjamas, pushed past me and went running down the stairs. On the second floor, two girls, also carrying suitcases, their overcoats scarcely concealing their nightdresses, jostled me to reach the stairs.

The night clerk was standing guard over the telephone when I joined him.

'Three minutes, bud,' he said gloomily. 'We've got to give some sort of service in this joint.'

The final fugitive was a fat man whose white, round face had a hunted expression as he made for the exit. He waved a fat, uneasy hand in the direction of the night clerk as he pushed open the door.

'That's the lot,' the clerk said, drawing in a deep breath. 'Shall I call them or will you?'

'I'll do it,' I said, and reached for the telephone.

II

A persistent knocking on my door brought me out of a heavy sleep. I peered blearily at the clock on the bedside table. It told me it was ten minutes past ten. The sunlight struggling to get past the drawn blinds of my hotel bedroom told me it wasn't ten minutes past ten at night.

Feeling like a wet rag, and probably looking like one, I struggled into my dressing-gown and staggered over to the door and unlocked it.

The bell-boy thrust a telegram into my hand and asked in a loud, shrill voice if there was any answer. He had all the heartless heartiness of a person who has been up and about for hours.

I told him if there was I'd call the desk, waved him away and closed the door. He walked off down the passage as if his shoes were diver's boots and with a whistle that went through my head.

I pawed the telegram open. It was from Helen.

Conns left island with luggage yesterday afternoon. Meet me airport noon.

The thought of seeing her again gave me enough strength to creep under a cold shower. Three cups of black coffee, sent up as I was dressing, freshened me a little, but I was still feeling woozy when I left my bedroom and went down to the reception lobby.

I hadn't got to bed until five-fifteen a.m.

Hoffman's death had depressed me. I was pretty sure he had been ready to talk. I had an idea he could have told me why Joyce Sherman had been interested in Susan Gellert's policies, and that information was the key to cracking the case. The police had found no clues. The killing had been neat and smooth. No one had seen the killer. He had come up the fire-escape, wiped Hoffman out and disappeared as invisibly as he had come.

I drove over to police headquarters and spent an hour with Hackett, getting nowhere. The most obvious suspect for Hoffman's murder was Rice. If Rice were at the back of the kidnapping, he would have had to stop Hoffman talking, but the two detectives who were watching Rice reported that he hadn't moved out of his house that night.

The search for Joyce Sherman and the kidnapper was still going on with no results, and Hackett was getting both worried and short-tempered.

'Take it easy,' I said after I had listened to him grouse for longer than necessary. 'Someone will make a slip before long. They've had it too much their own way up to now. We'll get a break.'

Hackett snorted. He didn't seem convinced.

I got down to the airport ten minutes to noon to be told Helen's plane was a little late, and I'd have twenty minutes to wait. As I was beginning to feel low again, I went into the buffet for a cup of coffee. I told the attendant to put a shot of whisky in it. He took one look at the circles under my eyes and reached for the bottle, clucking sympathetically.

A second cup was putting some stiffening into my spine when a voice at my elbow said, 'It's Mr. Harmas, isn't it?'

I looked up. A dark, smartly dressed young woman was standing at my side, smiling. For a moment I didn't recognize her, then I started to me feet.

'Why, Mrs. Conn! I didn't know you in your town clothes. How are you?'

She was the last person I expected to see, and I wondered if this meeting was accidental or intentional.

She gave me a bright smile as she slid up to a stool by my side.

'I'm fine. I bet you're surprised to see me. I wasn't sure if it was you. I hope you don't mind me butting in?'

'I'm glad to see you again. What brings you to Los Angeles?'

'I'm on my way to Buenos Aires.'

'You are? Is your husband with you?'

She made a little face, and shook her head.

'I've left him.'

'You have? Since when?'

'Last night.' She paused to order coffee, went on, 'I couldn't stand that island any longer. It's a funny thing you and your wife are largely responsible. You kind of unsettled me. Believe it or not you were the first visitors I'd seen in months. I got thinking, and decided if Jack wouldn't quit, I would. We talked it over, and I think he was glad to be rid of me.' She laughed. 'All he thinks about are his blessed snakes. It's not very complimentary to be put second to a snake, is it?'

I said I guessed she was right.

'Did you leave him on the island?'

'Oh, no. He came down here with me, but he couldn't wait to see me off. As a matter of fact he's taking Susan back with him. She wants a vacation, and he wants a cook, so she's staying with him for a couple of weeks.'

'If she puts on a dark wig, he'll think he's still got you.' I said, watching her closely.

Just for a split second her eyes shifted, then she laughed.

'That's an idea. Well, she's welcome. I got awful sick of Jack Conn and he got awful sick of me. I guess that island's too lonely for two people to live on. We kind of got on each other's nerves.'

'How is your sister?'

'Oh, she's fine. She's waiting to hear if Brad gets her fixed up in New York.'

'He's in New York now?'

Corrine nodded.

'I don't know if he'll be lucky or not. Anyway, he can but try.' She finished her coffee and accepted a cigarette I offered her. 'In a way I wish I hadn't to go to Buenos Aires,' she went on. 'I'd rather be with Susie, but my old boss cabled me the job was still open: I used to work for him before I married, so I thought I'd better take it.' She leaned forward as I flicked my lighter alight. 'Haven't you had something to do with the Sherman kidnapping?' she asked. 'I've seen your name mentioned in the papers.'

'That's right,' I said, suddenly on my guard. 'Some shindig.'

'It's terrible. Of course Susie's more interested than I am, but I was shocked when the news broke. Do you think she is dead?'

As calmly as I could I said, 'It's possible. Why should your sister be interested?'

'Why, at one time they were old friends.'

'They were? I had no idea.'

'This was before Joyce broke into the movies,' Corrine explained. 'About four years ago, they shared rooms together. Joyce was a hotel receptionist at the time and Susie was in an act with me. Joyce always said she'd beat Susie at her own game, and she did.'

'That was in San Bernadino, wasn't it?'

Again I thought her eyes shifted, but she nodded, and her smile was convincing enough.

'I guess it was. I don't remember exactly. Poor Joyce. So you think she's dead?'

'I think it's very probable. Did your sister keep in touch with her? Have they met lately?'

'Oh, no. When Joyce first broke into movies, Susie hoped she could get her in too, but it didn't work out. Joyce got high hat: you know how it is, and she sort of froze Susie out. They had a bit of a quarrel. Joyce froze all her old friends out. I guess being famous went to her head.'

'It happens to most of them,' I said, wondering just why she was telling me this. I didn't kid myself she was making conversation. She was telling me this for a reason.

'Did you leave your wife up at Springville, Mr. Harmas?' she asked casually. So casually I nearly fell for it, but I spotted the trap in time.

'My wife? Good Lord, no. What makes you ask?'

She was watching me narrowly, although the bright smile was still on her lips.

'I thought I saw her. There's been a girl wandering around on the mainland. I thought it looked like your wife. When I have nothing to do I fool around with a pair of field-glasses. I get a kick out of watching the birds. I thought it was Mrs. Harmas.'

'Oh, no,' I said firmly, and slid off my stool. 'She's been with me all the time. As a matter of fact she went to San Francisco for a couple of days, and I'm meeting her now. That's her plane just signalled. I must run. Send me a postcard when you get to Buenos Aires. One of these days I plan to visit it myself.'

As she shook hands, she said, 'If Susie ever gets to New York, you and your wife will try to see her, won't you? She will need all the support she can get.'

'Sure,' I said. 'So long and good luck.'

By the time I got on to the tarmac Helen's plane was taxi-ing in, and Helen was one of the first to come down the stairway.

We fell into each other's arms. After a completely unembarrassed and repressed greeting, regarded by the onlookers with a mixture of envy and amusement, I pushed her away and held her at arm's length to admire her.

'Honey, you look good enough to eat,' I said. 'Have you missed me?'

'I missed you all right,' she said, smiling up at me. 'But there's no need to tear me to pieces.' Rather breathlessly she straightened her cute little hat and firmly removed my hands. 'I would remind you I'm your property for many years to come, so don't try to telescope the years in this one, frantic greeting.'

'Wait until I get you back to the hotel,' I said, grabbing her suitcase. 'This is only a dress rehearsal for what's in store for you.'

'I've been expecting it,' she said and laughed. 'What's been happening, darling?'

'Plenty,' I said as we walked over to where I had parked the Buick. 'But don't let's talk business until we get back to the hotel. I have things to tell you: such as you look very lovely. I've been counting the hours since I left you, and I'm very proud to call you Mrs. Harmas.'

Back at the hotel I gave her tangible proof just how much I had missed her, and she seemed, convinced.

'Well, I guess that'll have to do to get on with,' I said, a little breathless myself. 'Now come and sit on my knee and tell me what's been happening to you.'

'I shall sit on a chair,' Helen said firmly. 'I know what will happen if I sit on your knee.'

'Maybe you're right. Okay, sit on a chair.' I flopped into one of the armchairs myself. 'Let's hear what's been happening up at Dead Lake.'

'Talk about patience going unrewarded,' Helen said, curling up in the armchair opposite. 'Pete and I shared watches, and we didn't let the island out of our sight all the time we were up there. We didn't see a thing of interest. Conn went off every morning, snake hunting. We caught an occasional glimpse of Corrine, and that's all. No one visited them as I had hoped. Yesterday afternoon they came down to the motor-boat with hand luggage, crossed over to where a hired car was waiting for them and drove off. I thought it might be a good idea to have a look at the cabin in their absence. I even got as far as the jetty, when I remembered the snakes, and I turned back.' She looked sharply at me. 'Don't you dare laugh! I know I was cowardly, but I couldn't bring myself to walk up that path, knowing a snake might appear.'

'I'm not laughing,' I said, and patted her hand. 'I wouldn't have gone up there myself.'

'I have discovered one thing,' Helen went on. 'Pete and I spent hours talking while we watched the island. I got him talking about the Conns in the hope he would remember something that might help. Well, he did, and this is important, Steve. He said when Susan came to Springville on her way up to Dead Lake, Conn and she went to Pete's place for a drink. Susan had a few drinks while Conn was outside fixing the car. There was some fellow in the bar who got talking about movie actresses to Susan. Pete was behind the bar, taking part in the conversation. This fellow said he thought Joyce Sherman was the finest actress in the world. Pete says Susan was a little tight, and became very abusive about Joyce Sherman. She said she was nothing better than a ham, and she had lived with her before she was on the movies, and she was a dirty little tramp.

The fellow argued with her, and Susan got into a rage. She said if it wasn't for a good director, Joyce Sherman wouldn't know how to walk across a room. Then Conn appeared and Susan suddenly dried up, and they went out together. Pete said he saw Conn talking to her outside, and she looked white and scared.'

I grinned at her. Now I knew why Corrine Conn had taken the trouble to tell me Susan had known Joyce Sherman in the past.

'I ran into Corrine Conn just before you touched down,' I said. 'She told me Susan lived with Joyce Sherman, and Joyce had frozen Susan out. She also asked if I had left you at Dead Lake. She claimed to have seen you.'

'I was very careful,' Helen said, looking annoyed.

'She was watching the mainland with a pair of field-glasses. That's probably how she spotted you. I think I have a job for you, darling. Would you mind going to San Bernadino on your own? I'd come with you, but I've got to stick around here in case something breaks on this damned kidnapping.'

'Of course I'll go,' Helen said. 'What do you want me to do?'

'All the time that girl was talking to me,' I said, 'I had an idea that meeting me was part of a calculated plan. It was too smooth; too much of a coincidence. The way she brought the conversation around to Susan and Joyce's relations was just a shade too slick. She guessed Pete had been talking, and was getting her story in first. I want you to go to San Bernadino and dig around. Find out which hotel Joyce was working at when Rice found her. Find someone who can tell you about her. I want to know as much about her background as you can dig up. There must be someone who'll remember her. See if you can trace Susan's movements there around four years ago. If you can find where those two girls lived and get talking to whoever owns the place you may get some pretty valuable information. Go to the smaller theatres, the agencies; dig back into the local paper files.'

'What exactly are you looking for, Steve?'

I lifted my shoulders.

'I don't know, but I want to be sure Joyce and Susan did share rooms together. On a set-up like this, if you dig carefully there's no knowing what you'll turn up.'

'I'll do it. I'll leave first thing tomorrow morning. Now I want to know all that's been happening to you. We have all the afternoon, so don't skip the details.'

'Make yourself comfortable,' I said, reaching for a cigarette. 'This is going to take a long time.' And I launched forth into the story of the paying of the ransom, how I had rolled over the mountain road, the murder of Mrs. Hoffman, the proof I had found connecting Joyce Sherman with the murder of Mason, and finally to the murder of Hoffman.

It took a long time, and the discussion we had after took even longer.

III

The following morning Helen left for San Bernadino. I was itching to go with her, but Fanshaw insisted I should remain in Los Angeles in case the police got a new lead on the kidnapping. There was nothing for me to do but to wait, and I found it an exasperatingly dull job.

Try as they might, the police couldn't get started on the kidnapping. Usually someone of the underworld has information and turns informer, but this time no one had for the obvious reason it wasn't an underworld job. Suspicion pointed to Perry Rice, but we couldn't find a thing to hang on him.

He made no attempt to contact the kidnapper. He was tailed day and night, and he didn't make one suspicious move. The only thing that gave us any encouragement was that he cancelled his proposed trip to Paris. This move pointed to the fact he hadn't been able to contact the other guy and get his share of the ransom. That was my guess, but we couldn't prove it.

Myra Lantis continued to live with him, to outward appearances as his secretary, but we knew better, although there was nothing we could do about that either.

Each morning I visited police headquarters, then went over to see Fanshaw. One day dragged past; another day dragged past. Helen telephoned me each night. So far she hadn't discovered anything sensational. She was still hunting for the hotel Joyce Sherman worked at when Rice discovered her. It was a slow job, and to her surprise as well as mine, no one seemed to know the famous movie star had once worked in San Bernadino as a receptionist.

Things happened on the third day. I had started the day as usual, getting up just after eight, having a leisurely breakfast, and then settling down in the half empty lounge to look over the papers.

I had been skipping through the headlines for about half an hour when a small item, tucked away at the foot of the page, caught my eye. I read the headline, my mind only half concentrating, passed on to some other paragraph, then stiffening to attention, read the headline again.

The second reading was like a punch in the face.

SNAKE DANCER'S TRAGIC END
BLEEDS TO DEATH ON LONELY ISLAND

Two seconds later I was rushing like a lunatic for my car.

CHAPTER NINE

I

THE atmosphere in Fanshaw's office was loaded with tension when I walked in. Maddux was sitting at Fanshaw's desk, and for a change he wasn't roaring, but there was a look in his eyes that brooded trouble for someone.

Fanshaw stood by the window, nervously flicking at a cigarette and scattering ash over the carpet. He looked relieved when he saw me.

'Seen this?' Maddux snapped, and tapped the newspaper on his desk.

'Yeah,' I said, hooking a chair towards me with my foot and sitting down. 'Doesn't tell us much, but it looks as if our policies are turning out to be a little expensive.'

'So you think they have a claim?'

'I don't know, but death by bleeding isn't one of the causes of death mentioned in the policies. Until I hear the details I'm trying to keep an open mind on the possibilities of a claim.'

'I have the details,' Maddux said. 'I got them from the Press Association just now. The girl died yesterday afternoon. Apparently she was staying on this island with Conn while waiting to go to New York. Conn says he crossed over to the mainland soon after ten o'clock in the morning. Susan told him she was going to clean up the cabin while he was away. She wanted to clean the windows and asked Conn for a step-ladder. He told her where to find it, but warned her it wasn't safe. One of its legs was on the blink, but as none of the windows was higher than seven feet, she said she wouldn't have far to fall. Conn told

155

her to please herself.' Maddux paused to bite off the end of a cigar. He lit it, waved away the smoke and went on, 'It wasn't until after lunch that she got around to the job of cleaning the windows. She was working on one of them when the leg of the ladder snapped and threw her forwards against the window. Instinctively she tried to save herself by putting her hands against the window-pane. The glass broke and inflicted deep gashes on both her wrists, severing the arteries.

'From a minor accident the incident developed into a highly dangerous one. Cutting arteries in both your wrists when you're alone is a nasty situation to deal with. Obviously there is a lot of bleeding, and Susan panicked badly. There's blood in every room in the cabin, showing she must have run about aimlessly, either looking for bandages or just in blind fear. Two blood-soaked towels were found. Some rag she had torn into bandages were on her wrists when she was found. They were not tied anything like tight enough to stop arterial bleeding, and that's not surprising. To tie a tight bandage on your own wrist when your hands are slippery with blood is practically impossible.'

'Pretty horrible,' I said.

Maddux shrugged his shoulders.

'The inquest's tomorrow. It's obvious what the verdict will be: death from misadventure. There's no evidence of foul play. At the time she was bleeding to death Conn was at the Springville Hotel, collecting his mail. He was seen by several witnesses. His wife was on her way to Buenos Aires. Denny was in New York, and Rice's movements are accounted for by the cops tailing him. They have all cast-iron alibis. Besides, on the evidence, there's nothing to make the sheriff think of foul play.'

'Except she happens to be insured for a million,' I pointed out.

'He doesn't know that,' Maddux said, puffing smoke to the ceiling. He brooded for a moment or two. 'This is a nice, tidy job, Harmas. I had an idea at the back of my mind they'd spring something like this on us. Well, they've done it. No jury is going to bring in a verdict of foul play on the evidence found on the island. To them it is a water-tight accident, but it wasn't.

It was murder. Make no mistake about that. From the moment Denny persuaded that ass Goodyear to draw up that goddam policy, the stage was set for murder. We have now to wait and see if they'll have the nerve to make a claim.'

'They'll do that all right,' I said. 'Why shouldn't they?'

'Come to think of it, bleeding to death is a very convenient form of murder. Convenient because it is silent; it takes a little time for the victim to die and gives the killer time to get clear, and it looks like an accident.'

'You haven't a shred of evidence that this is murder,' Fanshaw said, coming away from the window. 'If she was murdered, who did it? The only suspects we know of have cast-iron alibis. Who else is there?'

Maddux made an important gesture.

'That's nothing to do with me. I'm not a policeman. It's not my business to solve murders, but it is my business to smell out fraud, and this is fraud! Nobody takes out a million-dollar accident policy and then dies accidentally less than a month after the policy has been issued under these circumstances unless it is fraud. Oh, no, that cat won't jump. This is murder!'

'So what's the next move?' I asked.

'We do nothing. We sit tight. They've got to make the first move: not us.'

'They'll do that fast enough.'

'Let them. In the meantime we are going to ignore this paragraph.' He tapped the newspaper. 'None of us has seen it. We'll make it as hard as we can for them. We'll tell them the policies were for publicity purposes only, and that's why the premiums were so low. We'll remind them both the girl and Denny told you they didn't expect to make a claim, and we'll take down every word they say before witnesses. Then we'll tell them to sue if they dare, and we'll give the whole story to the jury and let them decide if it's fraud or not. We'll get Bergman to represent us, and if he can't handle them, no one can.' He leaned forward to glare at me. 'We've got to scare them into either not making a claim or if they make it, into withdrawing it.

We've got to hammer into them that if they fail to make the claim stick, they're going to be indicted not only for fraud, but for murder!'

'Do you want me to attend the inquest?' I asked.

'Inquest?' Maddux barked, jumping out of his chair. 'Don't you listen when I talk to you? I said we're going to ignore the whole thing. If we show up at the inquest we are telling the jury we are aware of our liability. We haven't seen this paragraph! We don't know the girl is dead! If you go to the inquest, and Conn spots you, we play right into his hands. When it comes into court, the jury will want to know why we showed up at the inquest if we didn't expect to settle the claim. We keep away. We do nothing. Understand – absolutely nothing!'

'By doing nothing,' I pointed out, 'we throw away some useful cards. I'd like to examine the cabin. I'd like to identify the body and check the finger-prints.'

'We do nothing,' Maddux repeated, growing red in the face. 'That's an order. I can't help it if we lose a trick or two. But if we show ourselves at the inquest or even ask for facilities we'll weaken our case when it comes into court. We've got to keep clear of it.'

I could see his point but I was very reluctant to yield to it.

'Let me remind you these two girls are as alike as two peas,' I said. 'Unless we identify the body we have no means of telling if there has been a switch. If Susan has cooked up this fraud, the body may be Corrine's.'

Maddux snorted.

'On your own say-so Corrine is on ship to Buenos Aires.'

'That's what she told me, but we don't know if she's on board. And another thing she could have been Susan wearing a dark wig, establishing herself an alibi. At least there's one thing I can do. I can find out if she's on board. It won't take long to check.'

Maddux shrugged.

'Check it if you like, but it's a waste of time. If Mrs. Conn told you she was sailing for Buenos Aires, you can bet your last dollar she has sailed. There's a million tied up in this swindle, and they're not going to slip up on an elementary point like that.'

'I guess you're right. All the same I'm going to check it. They must make a false move sometime. But don't you see how vitally important it is for me to identify the body?'

'I can't help that!' Maddux said, banging his fist on the desk. 'If we can prove in court we weren't asked to see the body, that we had no opportunity to identify it, we can raise doubt about identification. It may not get us far, but it'll cause delay, and even doubt, if Bergman handles it right.'

'I still think we should identify the body,' I said obstinately.

Maddux was about to explode when there came a knock on the door, and Miss Faversham, Fanshaw's secretary, looked in.

'Mr. Brad Denny is asking for Mr. Harmas,' she said.

Maddux smiled. He looked a cross between a wolf and a tiger.

'Here it comes,' he said, getting to his feet. 'He hasn't wasted any time, has he?' He turned to Fanshaw. 'You had better stay. I'm keeping out of this for the time being. You stay too, Miss Faversham, and take down every word that's said.' He looked over to me. 'Watch your step, Harmas. We admit nothing. Understand? Tell him to put the claim in writing. If he presses you, deny all liability and tell him it's up to him to sue if he wants payment. Okay?'

'Yes, I said.

We waited until he had left the office, then Fanshaw said, 'Show Mr. Denny in.'

II

Fanshaw waved me to his desk, and kept by the window.

'You do the talking,' he said under his breath. 'I'll chip in if necessary.'

The door opened and Denny came in. He looked pale and haggard. As he moved towards me, holding out his hand, Miss

Faversham went quietly to another desk and unobtrusively opened her notebook.

'Have you heard?' Denny asked as I shook hands with him.

'Nice to see you again,' I said, waving him to a chair. 'How did you make out in New York?'

'Never mind that,' he said curtly. 'Have you heard about Susan? She's dead!'

'Dead? What happened?'

Fanshaw moved quietly over to the desk and gathered up the newspaper we had both forgotten. He folded it and dropped it into the trash basket.

'It's horrible,' Denny said and sat down. I doubted if the grief and despair on his face could be an act. He certainly looked as if he had had a severe shock. 'The poor kid cut an artery. She was on that damned island. There was no one to help her. She – she bled to death.'

'Good God!' I said, sitting down. 'I can't say how sorry I am. When did it happen?'

'Yesterday. I only got back from New York just now and saw it in the paper. I telephoned Pete Eagan at the Springville Hotel and he gave me the details. Conn hasn't bothered to get into touch with me, and Corrine's on her way to Buenos Aires. I'm going up to Springville this afternoon.'

'Is there anything I can do?'

'No, there's nothing, thanks all the same. I came in to have a word with you about that insurance policy.'

Here it comes, I thought, and glanced over at Fanshaw. 'By the way, I'd like you to meet Tim Fanshaw. He's the branch manager here.'

Fanshaw came over and shook hands.

'What about the policy?' I asked when they had got through saying polite things to each other.

'Well, now Susie's dead, it's no further use to her, of course. I'm wondering about the premiums. Will I have to pay to the end of the year?'

For a moment I couldn't believe I had heard aright. From

the way Fanshaw had stiffened I knew he was as much surprised as I was.

Keeping my face expressionless, I said, 'Why, no. The premiums stop automatically at her death.'

Denny looked relieved.

'Well, that's a weight off my mind. I'm a little pushed for cash at the moment, and I was worrying I'd have to go on paying.'

We waited like a couple of dummies for him to start hinting about a claim, but he didn't. Instead, he said, 'You know, Mr. Harmas, I wish she had never thought up that insurance stunt. If it hadn't been for those policies she would have been alive today.'

That statement was so startling I gaped at him.

'What do you mean?'

'Why, if it hadn't been for the policies she wouldn't have quarrelled with me, and she wouldn't have gone to Dead Lake.'

'Did she quarrel with you?'

'Yes. You remember how keen she was to use those policies for publicity purposes?'

'Why, of course,' I said, sitting forward.

'The whole idea was to get some advance publicity so her name should be known to the New York managers. Well, when I was satisfied her act was as smooth as it'd ever be, I told her I was ready to give the story to the Press. To my surprise, she said she had been thinking it over and had decided her act was so good it wasn't necessary to cheapen herself with a stunt like that. Those were her very words! Can you imagine that? Cheapen herself! A million dollars insurance, and she called it cheapening herself.'

'Well, girls get fancy ideas,' I said cautiously. 'She did get a very good reception when I saw her. She might have been misled into thinking the act was better than it was.'

Denny nodded.

'That's exactly right,' he said. 'And I was dumb enough to tell her. Gee! Didn't she get mad at me! She said if I couldn't get her a New York engagement on the strength of the act I wasn't much of an agent. I guess I got a little mad myself. We had paid out good money to get those policies, and we couldn't afford to let them do down the drain. When I pointed that out to her, she said she would use them when she was established in New York.' He looked miserably at me. 'I was dumb enough to argue with her, and she really got mad. It's a funny thing but all the months I've known her I hadn't an idea she had such a temper. She walked out on me, saying she was going to stay with Conn, and we needn't meet again until I got her a New York engagement.'

'I'm sorry,' I said. 'I didn't know about that. So you didn't use the policies after all?'

He shook his head.

'No. It's so much waste of money. That's why I came to see you. I can't afford to go on spending money on them.'

'You don't have to. The premiums are automatically cancelled now.' I pushed my packet of cigarettes across the desk. 'Help yourself.'

He lit up.

'You said just now it was Miss Gellert who thought up the idea of insuring herself. I was under the impression the idea came from you.'

He blinked at me.

'Why, no. It was Susie's idea. I wasn't too keen on it at first, then when I got keen, she was the one to lose interest.'

'But it was you who approached Goodyear?'

'Oh, yes. I was her agent, and I looked after the business end of the act, but Susie made all the arrangements.'

'What arrangements?'

'She made the appointment with Mr. Goodyear for him to see me. It was she who picked your company.'

'I must have got my facts wrong,' I said. 'I was under the impression you ran across Goodyear accidentally.'

He looked surprised.

'Oh, no. Susie arranged for me to meet him.'

'Do you know how she met him?'

'No, I don't.'

'Well, it doesn't matter,' I said. 'I'm damned sorry it's ended this way.'

'Yes. Well, I won't keep you any longer. I thought I'd check up on those premiums. So I don't do anything about them?'

'Not a thing. We would like a copy of the death certificate. As soon as we get that the premium is automatically cancelled. If you like I'll handle the other companies for you.'

'I wish you would,' he said gratefully. He lifted into sight a worn brief-case he had brought in with him, opened it and took out the ten policies, neatly tied together with red tape. 'I guess you'll want these.' He laid them on the desk.

I nearly fell out of my chair. Without the policies he or anyone else hadn't a shred of evidence to support a claim. I was so startled it must have shown on my face.

'Is there anything wrong?' he asked.

'No, no.' I looked at Fanshaw who was staring at the policies, his eyes bolting out of his head. 'I was forgetting the policies.'

Denny pushed them across the desk to me.

'You'll let me know in writing that they're cancelled, won't you?'

'I'll do that,' I said, and felt sweat start out on my forehead.

If I took the policies and destroyed them, that would be the end of any chances of fraud. No one could make a claim against us without the policies to back it up. On the other hand, the policies belonged to Susan Gellert's estate, and I, as representative of the National Fidelity, had no right to take them. They represented a million dollars: whether or not the claim, if it was ever made, was a fraud. I reached out for them. My hand hovered over them, then slowly and painfully I withdrew my hand. Taking them would be gross dishonesty, and taking advantage of Denny's apparent ignorance. Also if it got out we had destroyed the policies, knowing a claim could be made with them, we would blast our reputation for all time. I couldn't be party to such an action.

Without looking at Fanshaw to see if he agreed with me, I shoved the policies back to Denny.

'You'll have to keep these until the inquest is over. In any case, they should be included in Miss Gellert's papers and sent to her solicitor.'

'Is that right?' He looked puzzled. 'But they're of no value. Is it necessary?'

I stared hard at him, trying to decide if he was putting on an act. It occurred to me he might be trying to get me to admit the policies were of value, but looking at his frank and bewildered face, I decided against the idea.

'You mustn't destroy any personal documents relating to a deceased person without the consent of the executors,' I said slowly. 'Has she a solicitor?'

'I don't know. I doubt it. Maybe I'd better talk to Conn.'

'Yeah, you'd better do that.'

He put the policies back into the brief-case and stood up.

'I must be getting along if I'm to get to Springville today. Thanks for everything, Mr. Harmas.'

When he had gone I stubbed my cigarette, pushed back my chair and drew in a deep breath.

'Go on,' I said, without looking at Fanshaw. 'Say it if that's the way you feel about it.'

'I would have done exactly the same,' Fanshaw said gloomily. 'I'm glad you did it and not me though. There was no other way to play it. Do you think he was genuine?'

'He was genuine all right,' Maddux said, coming in. 'I was listening outside.' He glared at me. 'Wouldn't it have been wiser if you had waited until I was consulted before you calmly handed him back those policies?'

'Why wait?' I said. 'Do you imagine you would have done it more gracefully than I did? You'd have probably broken a blood vessel.'

He started to say something, then grinned.

'I believe I would at that,' he said.

I was pretty certain that as soon as Denny had given the policies to Conn a claim would be made. Time was running out. I was certain too Maddux was making a mistake in not letting me identify the body of the girl Conn claimed to be Susan Gellert. If there had been a switch, and it had been Corrine who had been murdered, and I could prove it, the whole set-up would fall down. In spite of Maddux's orders, I decided I'd go up to Springville, break into the morgue and satisfy myself the girl was Susan. If I got there late enough, the risk of being spotted was negligible.

Telling Maddux I was going down to the South American shipping line to check if Corrine had sailed for Buenos Aires, I drove back to my hotel.

I went up to my room and settled down to do some telephoning. A five-minute conversation with a clerk at the shipping company convinced me a girl, calling herself Corrine Conn, was actually at sea, and had sailed on the evening of the day I had met Corrine at the airport. Whether or not the girl was actually Corrine I didn't know, nor did the clerk at the shipping line, but it was the kind of evidence that'd stand up in court.

I then put through a call to Helen's hotel at San Bernadino to be told she was out, but had been trying to get me. I left a long message, telling her of Susan's death that intrigued the girl at the other end. It was only her good training that stopped her asking questions.

I hung up and went over to my suitcase and dug out the bottle of Scotch I carried around with me in case of emergencies. This wasn't exactly an emergency, but I had a long drive ahead of me and I thought I might just as well fortify myself. I had finished one slug and was about to embark on another when the telephone bell rang.

Hoping it was Helen, I grabbed the receiver and said, 'This is Steve Harmas,' in an impressively loud voice, hoping to impress Helen if it should be Helen. It wasn't. It was Alan Goodyear.

'Have you seen the paper?' he demanded, his voice high pitched. 'That damned Gellert girl's got herself killed!'

'Yeah, I know,' I said. 'I was just going to call you,' which was a lie. I had forgotten all about him. 'I've been over to the office. Maddux is laying square-shaped eggs.'

'Well, don't take it so calmly,' he said, his words falling over themselves. 'What are we going to do? What's Maddux say?'

'Take it easy, Alan. You're breaking my ear-drums.'

'It's all right for you to joke about it!' he said. 'What about me? How do you think I'm feeling about it? What are we going to do?'

'We're doing nothing. Why should we?'

There was a short, sharp pause.

'Did Maddux say that?' His voice was more controlled now.

'Yeah.'

'You mean we're not going to honour the claim?'

'They haven't made one yet. What makes you think they will?'

'Of course they will! She bled to death! I didn't cover that in the policy. As soon as some smart lawyer gets hold of that policy, he'll see we're wide open for a claim.'

'Oh, I don't know,' I said. 'Denny knows the policies were only issued for publicity purposes. If Conn is persuaded to make a claim it'll be a fraud.'

Again there was a pause. I could hear him breathing heavily over the line.

'Are you trying to kid me?' he asked at length. 'You and Maddux were right, and I was wrong. This can't be on the level. That girl couldn't have died like that unless it was fixed!'

'Do you think she was murdered?' I asked, looking blankly at the opposite wall.

'She must have been. This is driving me crazy! What did Maddux say about me? He's blaming me, isn't he?'

'He didn't even mention you.'

'That's just as bad,' Goodyear said feverishly. 'I've cost the company half a million already. Now this has happened. It was my fault to have accepted that damned policy. I'm quitting before Maddux throws me out. I'll never sell another policy as long as I live!'

'For Pete's sake!' I said impatiently. 'Pull yourself together, Alan. Maddux won't throw you out. You're the best salesman we've got. You're not the first agent who's been taken for a ride. Besides, they haven't made a claim yet, so there's no need to get so worked up. Buy yourself a drink. That's what you want.'

'I don't want a drink!' His voice sounded hysterical. 'My reputation is shot to hell. I'm finished! I'm getting out before I'm tossed out.'

'You're crazy,' I said, realizing he was in a bad way. 'If you feel that way about it, go and talk to Maddux. He'll convince you fast enough you're making a fool of yourself. If he hears you're thinking of quitting he'll bust his truss. Go and talk to him.'

'I'm going down there right now with my resignation.'

'Aw, forget it. Maddux won't let you go.'

'Where can I see you?'

'Not now. I'm just going out. I'll see you tomorrow morning.'

'Can't I see you tonight?'

'I'm sorry, Alan, I'm going out of town. I don't reckon to get back until tomorrow morning. Tell you what. Suppose you look me up here tomorrow after eleven?'

'Well, all right. I'll go down and talk to Maddux now.'

'Do that, and take it easy. So long for now,' and I hung up.

I reached for my drink, polished it off and sat wondering if I should call Maddux and warn him Goodyear was flipping his lid. I decided to leave well alone. I wanted to get off to Springville. If I called Maddux he might give me a job that'd prevent me going.

I went downstairs and got the Buick out of the garage. Ten

minutes later, with a full tank, and a gun under my coat, I drove out of Los Angeles and headed for Springville.

IV

The dusty road leading into Springville was white in the harsh light of the moon.

When I was about a quarter of a mile from the town, I pulled off the road and drove the car into a thicket.

I had to play this very close to my chest. If I were seen and Maddux heard I had disobeyed orders I'd be looking for a new job. I locked the car, and set off towards the town, walking on the grass verge in the shadows.

Most of the buildings were in darkness. The hotel, the saloon and a couple of shacks showed lights, but the rest of the place had gone to bed.

The sheriff's office and the mortuary were towards the end of the main street. I had noticed the building when Helen and I were driving to Dead Lake on our last visit.

The forest began to thin out. I stopped behind a tree where I had a good view of the street. A half a dozen men were still sitting on the steps leading to the saloon, enjoying the warm night and talking together. There was no way past them without being seen, so I sat down, out of sight, and waited.

I had a long wait. It wasn't until well after eleven o'clock that the last straggler decided to go home. Even then I waited until the lights of the saloon went out before venturing from cover. The long, main street was deserted now, and I decided it was safe to make a start.

I walked quietly, keeping in the shadows of the buildings, my eyes and ears alert for any movement or sound.

Half-way down the street, a dog suddenly began to bark. Hurriedly, I ducked down in the shadows of the saloon. The dog continued to bark, and I could hear it throwing itself against its chain. It sounded savage enough to scare a lion-tamer, and I hoped the chain would hold.

To avoid passing the dog, I sneaked around the back of the

saloon where I found a narrow alley that appeared to run parallel with the main street. Two or three minutes' quick walking brought me to the back of the sheriff's office.

A solitary light burned in one of the windows. I moved up silently and peered in.

The sheriff, a giant of a man, sat at his desk, the blue smoke of his pipe curling above his head, a mass of printed forms spread out before him. He looked set for the night.

I moved on. At the far end of the building was the jail, and beyond that a low, wooden cabin. As I drew nearer I saw the word *Mortuary* painted in white letters across the door.

I walked around the building. The only window was heavily shuttered. I could see no light, and after listening at the shutter I convinced myself there was no one in the building. I returned to the door and examined the lock. It didn't appear to present any difficulty, and I set to work on it with a pick I had brought with me. After a little fiddling I got it to turn. I felt in my hip-pocket for my electric torch, then very slowly I pushed open the door. It creaked sharply as it moved, and I looked hurriedly over my shoulder at the lighted window, expecting to see the sheriff poking his head out. Nothing happened. I stepped inside and flashed my light around what appeared to be the receiving room. A wheeled stretcher stood against the wall. The only other furniture consisted of a desk, a chair and a telephone. Opposite me was a door bearing a white enamelled plate on which was printed 'Post-mortem Room'.

I went over to the door, turned the handle and pushed it open. Again I swung the beam of my light into hot stuffy darkness that smelt of disinfectants and formaldehyde. The beam picked out a deep sink with white faucets, the operating-table under a battery of lamps, and two trestle tables, one of which contained a body under a sheet. I went over to it.

I was breathing fast, and I was as nervous as an old lady who knows there's a burglar under her bed. With a hand that was far from steady I lifted the corner of the sheet and lowered my light so I could see.

Susan Gellert lay there; her dead, unhappy face waxy, and

as white as a fresh fall of snow. It was Susan all right: the features were the same, the blonde wavy hair was the same. I pulled the sheet a little farther down. Above her right breast was a small birthmark, crescent shaped and darkish red. I stared at it for a moment or so, trying to remember if I had seen it before. I had been close enough to Corrine to have spotted this mark when I had first met her. The halter she had been wearing wouldn't have hidden it. Whereas I hadn't been close to Susan when she had been dancing on the stage, and such a small skin blemish could have been easily painted out not to show at long range. It seemed on the evidence of the birthmark alone that this dead girl lying before me was Susan.

I had brought a fingerprint outfit with me. Working fast I took a set of prints from the cold, dead hand. A quick examination of the result told me the thumb-print was the same as the one on the policies.

As I slipped the finger-print outfit back into my pocket I was aware of a feeling of disappointment. I had hoped to have been able to prove the dead girl wasn't Susan, but there seemed no doubt about it.

I adjusted the sheet over the dead face, took silent steps to the door. Then as I turned the handle I heard a slight creaking sound on the other side of the door.

I stiffened, listening, and my heart began to jump against my ribs like a freshly landed trout. I heard nothing, but I had now a very strong presentment of danger. I was certain I was no longer alone in the building.

I snapped off my torch and slid it into my pocket. Then I opened the door slowly until it stood wide open. I remained motionless, listening.

Nothing happened. A wall of solid darkness faced me. I tried to convince myself I was imagining things, but the feeling of danger persisted. I thought of Susan Gellert's dead body on the table behind me. A cold chill chased up and down my spine like a car on a roller-coaster. Very cautiously I took two silent steps forward into the outer room.

Then things began to happen. I heard a movement to my

right, and threw myself sideways. Cold steel scraped down my arm, ripping open my coat. I heard a soft grunt that brought me out into a cold sweat. Hands brushed my face. I ducked, dived forward, my own hands reaching out into the darkness.

A body, hard and muscular, crashed into mine. Steel cut through my coat, passing against my ribs. As I went down I punched out wildly and my first thudded into a face. Someone cursed. I heard the knife drop on the floor. Then hands reached out, pawed at my chest, groped, and slid up to my throat. I kicked out as steel fingers sank into my neck. My foot encountered space, and I rolled over on my back. A knee rammed into my chest, driving the breath out of my body. I caught at thick, hairy wrists, and tried frantically to break the hold on my throat, but the fingers were like a vice. I couldn't shift them. Blood began to sing in my ears. I felt my senses leaving me. The pressure on my throat was awful. Whoever it was strangling me was as strong as a bull.

I hit out. My fists brushed against a face like snowflakes against a window. The darkness was turning into a roaring red ball before my eyes. I tried to lift my arms to strike again, but they were now as heavy as lead. I tried to yell. Then the red ball seemed to explode inside my head and my world became dark and silent.

v

The sheriff pushed the bottle of whisky towards me. His mild blue eyes never left my face.

'Have a snort,' he said. 'You look like you could use it.'

I had a snort. It was like drinking milk.

'Lucky for you I arrived when I did,' he said. 'That sticker looks business-like to me.'

He nodded to the thin-bladed knife that lay on the desk.

'It does,' I croaked, and stroked my swollen throat. 'Did you see him?'

'He heard me coming and scrammed. I came over so fast I forgot my gun.'

I poured myself another snort. I knew in a moment or so the questions would begin. I was still too shaken to think up a convincing story. I knew I had not only cooked my goose, but Maddux's goose as well. This mild-eyed sheriff wasn't going to let me go until he had got an explanation that'd satisfy him, and he looked as if he would need a lot of satisfying.

He had been through my pockets before I had come to the surface. My wallet, licence and business cards were spread out on the desk before him. He knew who I was and who I represented.

'Look, son,' he said mildly, 'you could land in jail for breaking in here, but I guess you had a reason. Came up here to identify the girl?'

'Yeah,' I said.

'She was insured with your people?'

'Look, sheriff, I'm in a jam. She was insured with us, but we suspect fraud. We figure she was murdered. I came up here to make certain she was Susan Gellert and not her twin sister, Corrine Conn. If it gets out I've been here, it'll cost my company and nine others a million bucks.'

He pursed his lips and whistled softly.

'Better tell me the tale, son,' he said, settling down in his chair. 'Maybe I can help.'

His politeness didn't kid me. I had to tell him or I'd be in even worse trouble. I told him. It took a little time, but he got the whole story, including Joyce Sherman's kidnapping.

'Yeah, I admit it looks a little off-colour,' he said when I was through. 'But you're on the wrong track. That girl died accidentally. There's no question of foul play. I took a lot of trouble checking up. As soon as Conn reported he had found her dead, I wondered if he had killed her. I didn't like that guy. He's a bad hat, and I went out to the island as suspicious as hell. I checked very carefully. I checked the ladder: it was rotten as he said it was, and one of its legs had snapped off. There was a broken window-pane, and what remained of the glass was bloodstained. The only footprints in the dust outside the cabin were Conn's and the girl's.

'But this is what makes it accidental. She was alone on the island when she died. The doc reckoned she died around three o'clock in the afternoon. Okay, let's give him a three-hour margin of error. Conn left the island and came down to the hotel at ten o'clock in the morning. There was a fella named Jake Oakley who does a little poaching up at Dead Lake when Conn's out of the way. He was concealed on the mainland, waiting for Conn to go. He saw him leave. He remained fishing until past four in the afternoon. No one visited the island between ten o'clock and half past four when Conn returned. Oakley ducked out of sight when he heard Conn start up his motor-boat. He watched him land. He saw him come running down to the jetty two minutes later, and come over to the mainland again. That was when Conn had found the girl's body, and was coming for me. Oakley was still watching the island, wondering what it was all about, when I and my men and Conn took the motor-boat over to the island and began our search. There was no one on the island when I got there except the dead girl. I went over the cabin and the island with a tooth-comb. I'll swear no one was there. It was an accident. You can get the idea of murder right out of your mind.'

'Sorry,' I said. 'I don't believe it. It was murder, but how it was worked beats me.',

He shrugged.

'Well, son, if you can prove it, good luck to you, but no jury will believe it's anything but an accident after they hear Oakley's evidence.'

'Suppose Conn's squared Oakley to tell that yarn?' I said.

The sheriff grinned.

'No. I've known Oakley since we were kids. He hates Conn, and he's as straight as a yard-stick. Sorry, that dog won't bark.'

'Do you have to report that I've been out here?' I asked. 'You can see the jam I'm in. We plan to let Conn sue. If he can prove I've been here to identify the girl, he'll have us.'

The sheriff grinned sympathetically.

'I mind my own business, but if I'm subpeona'd and I'm asked under oath, I'll have to tell them.'

I nodded I was sure it had been Conn who had attacked me in the post-mortem room. He must have recognized me, and was certain to rope in the sheriff to witness I had been up there. I was sunk, and there was nothing I could do about it.

'I'll have to cross my fingers and hope,' I said. 'I'd better get back to Los Angeles before I cause any more trouble. I'm sorry I acted as I did.'

'Don't do it again, son, or you'll be here for a long stay. Want to look at the body again before you go?'

I shook my head.

'I guess not. You got a picture of her?'

'I'll have one by tomorrow. I'll send it to you.'

'I want that birthmark to show. Can you fix that for me?'

'Sure.'

I walked up the main street, hoping Conn would start more trouble for me. I was mad with myself for what I had done, and I was ripe for trouble.

But no one paid the slightest attention to me.

IV

Around eleven o'clock the next morning I arrived at Fanshaw's office.

Maddux and Fanshaw were working on the Sherman kidnapping. Maddux scowled at me as I closed the office door behind me and walked up to his desk.

'Where have you been?' he barked. 'I've been trying to get you. Where were you yesterday?'

'Sorry,' I said. 'I went up to Springville. I hoped to find something that'd crack this case, but I didn't. Instead, I've given the show away.'

I expected him to blow up, but he didn't. He sat very still, his eyes suddenly like granite, and a faint flush mounting to his face, but he kept control of himself.

'How bad?' he asked, a rasp in his voice.

'As bad as it can be.'

'Sit down and give me the details.'

I sat down and gave him the details.

'Well, I hope you're pleased with yourself,' he said when I had finished. 'It looks to me as if they set a trap for you and you walked into it. God damn it! You've played right into their hands.'

'I guess that's right,' I said, sweating. There was no point apologizing. Maddux wasn't interested in apologies: he never had been.

He reached for a cigar, bit off the end, said, 'You heard Goodyear has resigned?'

'He said he was going to.'

'Frankly, I'm not sorry to see him go. He was a good sales-man up to a point, but he allowed outside influences to ball up his judgment. You're another.'

'I guess I'd better resign too then.'

I waited hopefully for him to disagree, but he didn't. He lit the cigar and brooded off into space for the longest two minutes I've ever lived through.

'This act of yours,' he said at last, 'could cost us a hundred thousand dollars. It could cost nine other companies the same amount. It wasn't an honest mistake. It was sheer pig-headed, irresponsible sabotage. You were told to leave it alone. You were told why. You were told more than once, and yet you went straight up there and walked into a trap without finding a damned thing to offset your blunder. I'm justified in firing you right now. In any case I'll have to report this to the other companies as I'm responsible to them for conducting this investigation. The odds are they'll tell me to fire you. When one of my men stops taking orders from me, he's out on a limb. What are you going to do about it, Harmas?'

'Quit, I guess,' I said, pretty sick with myself. 'Not much else I can do.'

He studied me.

'Are you sure there's nothing else you can do?' he asked evenly. 'You've landed us in this mess, wouldn't it be an idea for you to get us out of it?'

'If I thought there was a chance I'd say so. They haven't

even made a claim yet. Every move I make I come up against a blank wall. I guess we want someone a lot smarter than I to crack this case.'

'You've worked for me for seven years now, Harmas,' Maddux said. 'You've never been licked up to now. I tell you what I'll do. I'll give you a month's salary and a month's vacation. I don't want to know where you're going or what you're going to do, but if you come back with the case tied up you carry on with your job as if nothing has happened. If you don't tie up the case, then you needn't bother to come back.' He scribbled something on a slip of paper and tossed it across the desk. 'Take that to the cashier and get your money. In the meantime I'm going to turn Olley Jackson on the case and let him see if he can crack it.'

Olley Jackson was another of our investigators: a guy who thought he was much smarter than I, and who I had been up to now damned sure wasn't.

'You mean you're putting Jackson on in my place?' I said, staring at him.

'Jackson obeys orders, Harmas. He's going to be given the job. If you can crack the case on your own, good luck to you, but I've got to have a reliable investigator working on this, and Jackson's reliable.

I flicked the slip of paper across the desk.

'Make that into a fancy doiley and blow your nose on it,' I said, trying not to shout, 'I've quit!'

I walked out of the office and slammed the door after me.

CHAPTER TEN

I

I GOT down to San Bernadino in time for lunch. I found Helen eating a solitary meal in the restaurant, and I sneaked up on her.

'Enjoy yourself,' I said in her ear, 'that may well be the last expensive meal you'll eat.'

She jumped as if I had let a firecracker off under her chair, and promptly threw her arms around my neck. The rest of the diners watched with evident enjoyment.

'Hey, take it easy,' I said, 'or you'll give the hotel a bad name.'

'Steve! Where did you spring from?'

'I've just arrived,' I said, disentangling myself and sitting down. 'How's that expense account of yours looking? Think it could support me as well as you?'

She looked at me sharply.

'Is there anything wrong, darling?'

'Just let me attend to my inner man, and I'll tell you the sorry story,' I said.

After I had ordered the most expensive dish on the menu, and the waiter had gone away, I went on, 'I've dropped a cart-load of bricks, and Maddux has replaced me. He has given me a month's salary and a month's vacation, and if I don't crack the case by then, I needn't return. Olley Jackson has taken over.'

Helen's eyes sparkled fire.

'How dare he?' she said. 'He can't do that to my husband! I'll get him on the phone . . .'

'Thank you, darling, but it won't be necessary. I've quit. Do you think you'll be able to earn enough to keep us both in comfort?'

'You mean you've really quit?' Helen said, her eyes opening wide.

'I had to. The Harmas's family pride had been dealt a mortal blow. And what's more I threw next month's salary check right back in his face. I even told him to blow his nose on it.'

'Was that very wise, pet?'

I shook my head.

'I'm afraid it wasn't. When I got back to the hotel, I overhauled my finances and find I have exactly thirty-five dollars in the world. But I must say it gave me a lot of satisfaction.'

'Y – es,' Helen said doubtfully. 'Oh, well, we'll have to manage. Tell me all about it, Steve. What was the brick you dropped?'

'There were a lot of them. I'm not blaming Maddux.'

The waiter served my meal and while I ate it, I told Helen what had happened.

She forgot her own meal and sat listening, her face tense.

'I would have done exactly the same,' she said when I had finished. 'We had to make certain it was Susan. Couldn't Maddux see that?'

'You know what he is. All he's thinking about now is to block off the claim and make a legal fight of it. The more I think about it, the more I realize how smart they've been. How they killed that girl foxes me. The sheriff swears no one was on the island when she died. His evidence alone gives them a cast-iron alibi. Unless we can prove she was murdered, we're sunk. Maddux may kid himself he's going to fight the claim, but with the set-up as it is, he hasn't a hope of beating it.'

'It couldn't have been an arranged accident? I mean it's too much to suppose. Conn let her use the rotten ladder in the hope she would cut herself on the window glass?'

I shook my head.

'No. She might have jumped clear. She might not have touched the window. Oh no, I'm positive someone deliberately slashed her wrists after first setting the stage. But how he or she got off the island before the sheriff arrived beats me.'

'Couldn't he have swum across?'

'If it happened at night, but not in broad daylight. This guy Oakley says he was there all the time. He would have spotted anyone swimming across that stretch of water: it's nearly a quarter of a mile wide and without a scrap of cover.'

'Then whoever it was must have hidden on the island.'

'The sheriff says no. According to him he thought Conn might have killed her, and he practically took the cabin apart in his search.'

'Do you think Denny had anything to do with this, Steve?'

I shook my head.

'I'm sure he hasn't. He was in New York at the time, and I'm positive he was sincere when he brought those policies back to me. He couldn't have acted the part. He wasn't to know I wouldn't have taken them, and if I had taken them, that would have been the end of it. He's been used as a cat's paw, and I'm sure hasn't an idea what's going on.' I pushed back my chair. 'Let's go into the lounge and have some coffee. I want to hear your news. How have you been getting on?'

'As soon as I got here I made a list of all the hotels and called on them,' she told me. 'You have no idea how many there are. I walked and talked until I was dizzy, and with no results. None of the hotels ever had a receptionist named Joyce Sherman working for them. I decided she must have changed her name when she went into the movies, so I started all over again, checking back on every receptionist who had worked at the hotels during the past five years. Once again I drew blank. Most of them were still working at the hotels, and those who had left, I accounted for. Oh, Steve! What a job it's been, and all for nothing. I am quite sure Joyce Sherman never worked here as a receptionist.'

'Well, that's something, isn't it? You haven't worked for nothing. Did you find the hotel at which Rice stayed?'

'I found that,' she said, accepting the cigarette I gave her. 'It's the Regent. He stayed there two weeks, an then left without settling his account. The hotel detective told me he caught Rice with a girl in his room, and from the description it could have been Corrine.'

'Was Corrine in San Bernadino at that time?'

Helen nodded.

'Yes, both Susan and Corrine were here. They were playing at a night club, doing a strip-tease act. I found the night club and had a talk to the manager. He remembered them very well. He also remembered Rice. According to him, Rice was interested in Corrine, and often went backstage to see her.'

'And you didn't find out if Susan and Joyce Sherman ever stayed together?'

Helen shook her head.

'They didn't: at least, not here.'

'You're sure?'

'Yes. The manager of the night club gave me the address of the apartment house where Susan and Corrine stayed. I went around there this morning. It's changed hands, but I have the address of the woman who ran it when the girls were there. I was going out there this afternoon. Her name's Mrs. Paisley, and she lives in Barsdale. It's a tiny town about a hundred miles from here. Shall we go together?'

While she had been talking I had been watching her.

'What's on your mind, Helen?' I asked. 'You're not looking your usual bright self. Been working too hard?'

She hesitated, then said, 'I guess I'm letting my imagination run away with me. For the past two days I've had a feeling I've been followed wherever I go, and last night I imagined someone was trying to unlock my bedroom door.'

'Was someone?' I asked, not letting her see I was startled.

'I don't know. I called out, but nothing happened and I heard nothing. I didn't go and look.'

'What makes you think you've been followed?'

'Just a feeling. I haven't seen anyone, and I've kept a sharp look-out but the feeling has persisted. It's made me a little nervous.'

I patted her hand.

'You don't have to be nervous any more,' I said. 'Yeah, we'll go and call on Mrs. Paisley. You're not going to worry any more, are you?'

'Of course not, but don't let's run into any trouble, Steve.'

I could see she was a lot more jumpy than she made out.

'Look, suppose you leave this to me and go home? It's time someone went back to see if the place is still there.'

She shook her head.

'I'm not leaving you, Steve. I'm all right so long as you're with me. I've had to do quite a lot of night work, and it's been creepy feeling someone's just behind you all the time.'

'You're sure you're not imagining it?'

'I don't know, but let's watch out. I keep thinking of that brute Conn. I can see him now sitting in that boat and telling us he shot first and apologized after. He wasn't bluffing. He's dangerous.'

'So am I,' I said, 'when I'm protecting my wife. You just watch me and see. Let's fix up a double room. I'll take up my bag, and then we may as well get off. I'd like to get back here to-night. Then if we haven't found anything to keep us here, I guess we'd better get back to Los Angeles. I want to be on the spot when the claim is made.'

'But, darling, aren't you forgetting you've quit?'

'I've quit Maddux, but I haven't quit this case,' I said. 'Do you think I'm going to let Jackson wipe my eye? I'm going to work on this case independently, and if I break it, it is going to cost Maddux plenty. As an independent investigator I am entitled to one percent of the insurance coverage if I can prove fraud. You figure out what one per cent is on a million and a half, and start thinking about that mink coat.'

'I'll think about it when you've cracked the case, Steve,' she said, smiling at me. 'We're a long way from doing that.'

'You never know,' I said, getting to my feet. 'One little slip and it'll fall to pieces. You mark my words.'

Barsdale turned out to be even smaller than Willington: a general store, a couple of filling stations, a saloon and a bus depot seemed to be all it could boast of.

'Not exactly Macy's,' I said, as I swung the car over to the general store and pulled up, 'but maybe they'll know where Mrs. Paisley's place is.'

Helen followed me in. At one end of the big store, cluttered up with everything from a cake of soap to a broom was a bar.

'Seems we've happened on the right place,' I said, heading for the bar. 'What'll you have?'

'Beer,' Helen said, 'and lots of it.'

The storekeeper, a fat little man with a red cheerful face, came from behind a counter stocked with canned food, and got behind the bar.

'My help's off this afternoon,' he explained. 'What can I get you?'

We said beer.

While he was drawing it, he said. 'We don't often see new faces here. Passing or thinking of stopping?'

'Coming and going,' I told him. 'I bet not many people stop here. What's there to stop for?'

'Fine agricultural country,' he said. 'You want to go on for another five miles. You'll see the farms then. Come in here tonight and you'll be surprised. I get as many as fifty people in here of a night. We have dancing three times a week.'

'I guess you'd have to have something. It's a little too quiet for me. I'm looking for Mrs. Paisley's place. Can you put me on to it?'

'Sure, it's about five miles from here.' He glanced curiously at me. 'I didn't know the old lady had any friends.'

'This is a business call. How do I get there?'

'Follow the main road out of town, and take the third dirt road on your left. The house is at the top of the road. You can't miss it. It's all by itself.'

'Thanks. Do you know Mrs. Paisley yourself?'

'She comes in every so often,' the storekeeper said, and shook his head. 'Maybe I should warn you. She's a little eccentric. She lost her husband about two years ago. They came out here to farm. Bought a nice little place; ten acres of ground; put in orange trees, got the place ship-shape, then the old man suddenly went out like a light. It turned out his heart was on the blink, and he should never have taken on the farm. The old lady blamed herself. It was her idea, and it kind of upset her mind.'

Helen and I exchanged glances.

'Is she bad?'

He shook his head.

'Oh, no. Gets a bit queer now and then. Imagines her husband is still alive. Nothing to worry about.'

I finished my beer and slid off the stool.

'Well, I guess we'll call on her. Think she'll be in?'

'She never goes anywhere now.'

As Helen and I walked to the car I said, 'Let's hope her memory hasn't suffered. I'm glad I came with you.'

'So am I,' Helen said with feeling.

We continued up the dusty main road. The storekeeper was right. As soon as we got beyond the town, if you could call it a town, we could see the farms in the distance, and the acres of citrus groves. Barsdale may have been quiet and small, but it was also tidy and efficient.

At the dirt road, I slowed down and swung the Buick into it. We climbed for ten minutes. On either side of us were peach orchards, heavy with fruit. It was getting on for half past eight now, and the sun was dipping below the hills.

After driving a couple of miles, leaving the peach orchards behind us, we came up a stretch of land that hadn't been cultivated in years. Standing in an overgrown garden was a wooden bungalow that looked as if the first puff would flatten it.

'I guess this is it,' I said, and pulled up outside the big farm gates that led to the bungalow.

We got out. A dim light showed through one of the un-curtained windows, and as we walked up the weed-covered path, I saw a figure come to the window, and then move back out of sight.

'Well, she's in,' I said under my breath, and stepped up to the front door. There was no bell or knocker; I rapped on the split panel with my knuckles.

We stood for some moments, staring back at the garden and the flat uncared-for orchard of barren orange trees. Then the door swung open and a tall woman stood before us. Around seventy-five, her thin pinched face was wrinkled and dirty. Her white hair escaped from under a big straw hat and hung in wisps across her face. Her eyes were deep set and vague. Her dark green velvet dress had been patched again and again.

'You wanted something?' she said, looking at Helen, eyeing Helen's smart linen dress with the unembarrassed stare of curiosity you'd expect from a child.

'My name's Harmas, and this is my wife,' I said. 'I believe you kept an apartment house a few years ago in San Bernadino.'

She frowned.

'Did I? I don't care to remember. What business is it of yours?'

'I'm making inquiries about Susan Gellert. I believe she stayed with you at one time.'

The vague eyes showed interest.

'Is she in trouble?'

I had an idea that she'd be pleased if I said she was. I decided to give her both barrels.

'I think she has been murdered.'

'She has?' She stared at me. 'My husband warned her she would come to a bad end. You'd better come in. He'd like to hear about it. Many a time he's said to me she'd get herself murdered. He is very clever about such things. I always listen to him. He's never been wrong yet.'

She turned and walked down a dark passage to a room at the back of the bungalow.

'Here it comes,' I said under my breath to Helen.

The room was half kitchen, half sitting-room, and lit by an oil lamp. A big armchair was drawn up to the empty fireplace: a pair of worn carpet slippers stood before it. Mrs. Paisley was standing over the chair, talking as we came in.

'Wake up, Horace,' she was saying, 'here's a gentleman to see you. That Gellert girl's been murdered. Just as you said she'd be.' She turned to me. 'You'll excuse my husband not getting up. He's been very ill. He nearly died.' She leaned towards me, her eyes bright, and whispered, 'He has a bad heart, only he doesn't know. I have to be very careful of him.'

'I'm sorry,' I said, aware I was beginning to sweat gently. 'I don't want to disturb him.'

'Sit down. He'll listen. He'll want to hear what you have to say, but don't bother him with questions. I'll answer your questions.'

'Thank you,' I said, and sat down on a straight-backed chair. 'Miss Gellert is supposed to have died from an accident. The story goes she was cleaning a window, the ladder slipped and she cut the arteries in her wrists. I am an insurance investigator. She was insured with us, and we feel pretty sure she was murdered. We're looking for information; any information that might help.'

'Did you hear that, Horace?' the old woman said, turning to the empty chair. She gave a loud, crackling laughter that made my hair stand on ends. 'Cleaning windows! That little chippy, cleaning windows! That's something I'll never believe. She wouldn't raise a hand to clean anything. Both of them were bone lazy. They lived in dirt. Time after time Mr. Paisley had to speak to them about the way they kept their rooms.'

'She was staying with Jack Conn at the time of the accident,' I said. 'He recently married Corrine Gellert. Did you know him?'

'Recently married? They've been married for years. Do I know him? I'm not likely to forget him: the lousy jailbird! I remember him coming to the house before they nabbed him. Walked in and caught Corrine with that agent fella. I forget his name.' Again she turned to the empty chair. 'What was the name of that fella who was always hanging around Corrine? The one who dressed so well and ran a big Cadillac?'

'Perry Rice?' I said.

She turned to stare at me.

'That's him. Mr. Paisley would have told me. He has a very good memory for names. Yes, that was the one. I'll never forget that scene. Mr. Paisley went up and told them to stop making so much noise. That fella Conn threw him out. I was watching. Corrine hadn't a stitch on. Rice was backed up against the wall, as white as a ghost. Conn had a gun in his hand. I never could understand how Mr. Paisley had the courage to go in there. Then the cops arrived, and grabbed Conn. There was shooting. The cops broke Conn's arm. Even at that, he fought all the way downstairs. I'll never forget that night.'

I was drinking this in, and so was Helen.

'Conn was married to Corrine then at that time?'

'Of course he was. He was a stick-up man. Went round robbing service stations and lonely stores. The cops had been after him for weeks. As he was being taken away he yelled out that Corrine had given him away to the police. I shouldn't be surprised. He was always after her money, and when this Rice fella took up with her, she would be glad to be rid of Conn.'

'Was it ever proved she gave him away?'

'I don't know about proved, but I heard Susan quarrelling with her about it. That's when they parted. I thought Susan was going to kill her, and I had to send Mr. Paisley up to stop them from fighting.'

'Why were they fighting?' I asked, feeling I was learning something for the first time since I started to investigate this case.

'Why, Susan had been carrying on with this fella, Conn. She'd carry on with anyone in trousers. Corrine didn't know, but I did. I know Conn used to come to the apartment when Corrine wasn't there. He and that little chippy spent hours together.'

'Then she knew her sister had given Conn away to the police?'

'That's what she said. She said she would kill Corrine. I could hear her screaming at the top of her voice. Mr. Paisley went up and told them to stop. About an hour after, Corrine came down with her bags packed, and went off. I never saw her again. Susan stayed on for another couple of weeks, and then she went. A good riddance of bad rubbish!'

'What happened to them?'

'I don't know what happened to Corrine. I heard she went to Buenos Aires. Susan went to Los Angeles. Someone told me she was doing a strip-tease or something. I was glad to get them out of my house.'

'They were identical twins,' I said. 'Except one was blonde and the other dark. At one time I believe Susan wore a dark wig, and no one could tell them apart. When she was wearing a wig, was there any way you could tell them apart?'

'I'd know any time,' Mrs. Paisley said and grinned, showing a mouthful of gums. 'Those two hadn't any shame. They walked about without a stitch on. Many a time Mr. Paisley ran into them. It wasn't right, and I complained, but it made no difference. Corrine had a birthmirk. I could always tell her from her sister by that. A little crescent-shaped mark just here,' and she put a bony finger on her flat chest.

'You mean Susan had this birthmark?' I said.

'It was Corrine. What do you know about it?'

'I heard it was Susan who had the birthmark.'

'Well, you've heard wrong. I've seen it a dozen times. A little crescent-shaped mark, and for some reason or other she was proud of it. She pointed it out to me herself; not that it needed any pointing out. It was as plain as the nose on your face.'

III

We were both seething with excitement as Helen drove from the bungalow. I had kept at Mrs. Paisley for the best part of an hour, trying to shake her conviction that it was Corrine and not Susan who had the birthmark, but she was unshakable. If she knew what she was talking about, and the more I questioned her the more sure I was she was telling the truth, then the first big crack in the case had appeared.

If the dead girl was Corrine Conn the claim was void, and we could prosecute for fraud.

'We've got to find a more reliable witness than that poor old thing,' I said as Helen sent the car shooting down the dirt road. 'It'd be a waste of time to put her in the witness-box. Any defending counsel would rip her to bits. There must be some-one beside her who knows Corrine had that birthmark.'

'We've still got to get around the thumb-print on the policy,' Helen reminded me. 'We got Corrine's print, and it didn't match.'

'Let's work on that angle for a moment,' I said. 'We've thought all along there was something phoney about those prints.

'Suppose Susan had been impersonating Corrine? That makes sense to me. When we saw her at Willington she didn't have to be persuaded to give us Corrine's address. She must have known we intended to call on Corrine. What could be simpler for her than to drive to Dead Lake that night, while we were sleeping at Willington, put on a dark wig and a coat of sun-tan and welcome us as Corrine Conn when we arrived so trustingly the following morning. Remember how easily I got her prints? You said at the time it was almost as if she wanted us to have them.'

'But we also got Susan's prints,' Helen said. 'I took that mirror I found on her dressing-table, and the prints matched those on the policies.'

'You didn't actually see her handle the mirror, did you? It could have been a plant. Suppose it was Corrine's mirror, and Susan put it on the dressing-table for you to take?'

'You could be right, Steve,' Helen said excitedly. 'But where has Corrine been all this time?'

'Maybe in Buenos Aires. Then when the stage was set, Susan or Conn persuaded her to come back, trapped her on the island and murdered her. Then Susan disguised herself as Cor-rine and returned to Buenos Aires to establish an alibi in case anyone out there missed Corrine.' I had a sudden idea. 'I tell you who might be able to support Mrs. Paisley's evidence: Mossy Phillips! He photographed both Susan and Corrine. He might remember the birthmark. Feel like an all-night drive? The sooner we get back to Los Angeles and see Phillips the sooner we'll crack this case.'

'All right. Look, you get some sleep now, and half-way we'll change over. We should be back by one o'clock if we keep at it.'

'Sure you wouldn't like first turn?'

'I'm all right now, but I won't be in another couple of hours. Want to get in the back and stretch out?'

'You must have read my thoughts.' As she stopped the car, I went on, 'Most wives would have made their husbands drive all the way. You must admit I know how to pick my women.'

'I'm glad you're satisfied, darling,' and she sounded glad.

I hadn't intended to go to sleep. I started off by carefully considering the new facts we had discovered.

It seemed Corrine had been married to Jack Conn for five or six years. At that time she and Susan had been in some kind of night-club act, while Conn had made a living robbing filling stations: a small-time heist man. He had ceased to live with Corrine about a year after they had married, but he kept following her around, and whenever he was short of money, he demanded it from her. It was while the two girls were at San Bernadino that Susan and Conn had an affair together. Corrine knew nothing of this, and it was unlikely she would have cared, as she was having an affair with Perry Rice. But she was sick of having Conn turn up unexpectedly, and also scared he would find out about Rice, so she told the police where they could find him. Susan had found out what she had done, and had tried to warn Conn, but she was too late. Conn walked into a trap, and was arrested. He drew four years' imprisonment. Furious at losing her lover, Susan threatened to kill Corrine, who took safety in flight. She went to Buenos Aires and, at my guess, remained there during the four years Conn was in jail.

Putting two and two together, it seemed likely that Susan hit on the idea of insuring herself for a million dollars. She saw how she could get the million and revenge herself on Corrine. When Conn came out of jail, she hooked up with him, and told him of her plan. He moved to the island at Dead Lake, and Susan, wearing a dark wig, appeared now and then at Springville and created the impression Corrine was living on the island. In such an out-of-the-way place it was easy and safe enough to do. Somehow she managed to persuade Corrine to return when the stage was set, and Corrine was kept on the island as a prisoner.

I got that far when I began to doze off. The steady bouncing of the car, the warm night air and the fact I had been driving all the afternoon became too much for me. I slid off into a deep sleep.

Maybe I slept for an hour, when I was awakened by Helen shaking my arm.

'Time for me to take over?' I asked, yawning fit to dislocate my jaw. 'Where are we?'

'I don't know where we are, but we are out of gas.'

'We can't be,' I said, sitting up and staring at her. 'The tank was half full when we left Barsdale.'

'But we are. Look at the dial.'

I peered over her shoulder.

'Well, I'll be damned. Must be a leak. I was fully awake now. 'Any idea where we are?'

'I'd say about twenty miles from San Bernadino.'

I got out of the car, turned on my torch and lifted the hood. There was a leak all right. Someone had punctured the feed-pipe to the carburettor.

'Look at this,' I said. 'It's been done deliberately.'

Helen joined me to look at the damage.

'But when and why?'

'Could have been done when we stopped in Barsdale. I don't know why.'

She looked uneasily over her shoulder along the dark road.

'There's a car not far behind,' she said. 'I spotted its headlights just before we stopped.'

We looked at each other.

'I think we'll get under cover,' I said. 'This looks rather like a trap to me.'

I had scarcely finished speaking when out of the darkness, coasting soundlessly with a dead engine, a long black car swept down on us.

'Look out!' Helen screamed, and gave me a quick push away from our headlights. I caught the back of my knee against the fender and went sprawling.

The car was on us now, and as it passed, a flash of flame came from the driver's window, and the bang of a shotgun nearly deafened me. Shot hammered against the body of our car and churned up the road, inches from me. I heard Helen give a sharp cry as the car's engine woke into life and the car stormed away into the darkness.

I looked at Helen, my heart turning cold. She took two tottering steps towards me, and then crumpled on the ground.

IV

'Helen!'

My voice rocketed up into a yell as I rushed to her. I was in the worst panic I'd ever been in in my life.

'It's all right, darling,' she gasped as I knelt beside her. 'In the back of my shoulder. It's not too bad, but it's bleeding.'

For a moment I couldn't think or move. I was scared to touch her in case I hurt her.

'Steve,' she said urgently, leaning against me, 'That car's stopped. Watch out he doesn't come back.'

That jolted me to my senses. It was more than likely he would come back. He must have seen he had missed me as he went past. The puncture feed-pipe, the pursuit and the attempt to kill us showed his desperate determination to stop us from getting back to Los Angeles. He would return all right.

'I'll get you under cover,' I said. As I lifted her she gave a gasp of pain. 'Sorry, darling. I'll try not to hurt you.'

'It's all right. Only let's get off the road.'

Carrying her as carefully as I could, I moved into the pitch-black forest that ran by the roadside. I hadn't taken more than ten steps before I cannoned into a tree.

'I can't see a damn thing!' I gasped, stopping.

The glare of our headlights lit up the road, lighting the edge of the forest. Instead of entering the forest I began to move along in the shadows, keeping close enough to the reflected light to see where I was going. I hoped to come upon a path that would take me to cover.

I could feel Helen's blood seeping through my coat, and it scared me. She was breathing lightly, and now and then, when I took a false step and jarred her, she stifled a gasp of pain.

Twenty yards or so beyond our car I came upon a path that led into the forest. As I began to walk slowly along it, peering into the darkness ahead, I heard the sound of a car engine. I looked back over my shoulder. The car sounded close, but I couldn't see it. It was creeping back up the road without lights.

I began to hurry, and that was fatal. I ran slap into the trunk of a fallen tree and went sprawling; throwing Helen violently to the ground.

I scrambled to my feet, sweating and furious with myself. Pulling out my torch I turned it on. Helen was lying a few yards from me; her face was white and her eyes closed; she seemed to have fainted. Her right arm and shoulder were saturated in blood, and the sight of her lying there sent a chill up my spine.

As I moved towards her there came a flash and a crack of an automatic. A slug whipped past my face, missing me by inches. I snapped off the light and threw myself flat. More gunfire sent echoes crashing through the silent forest, and another slug whined overhead.

I had my gun out now, and I fired in the direction of the flash, then I climbed over the fallen tree and groped for Helen. My hand touched hers as the blinding light from car headlights lit up the forest.

As luck would have it both of us were close enough to the fallen tree to be screened from the light. I had to put those headlamps out of action right away. If this gunman circled around he could wipe us out with two shots.

Cautiously I raised my head and aimed carefully. My hand was steady. My first shot missed; as I fired again, a gun cracked some yards from the car and a bullet thudded into the tree trunk not six inches from my face, but my second shot shattered one of the headlights. I ducked down, waited a moment, then crawled along the length of the fallen trunk to take up another position. Once again I aimed at the remaining light. He must have spotted me as I was firing. His slug literally parted my hair, knocking me flat and scaring me out of my wits, but the second light went out. In the comforting darkness, my head singing, I crawled back to Helen.

I picked her up and started off along the path. I had to feel my way like a blind man, aware my feet were kicking up the dead leaves and advertising my progress in a way that made me sweat. My one hope was to get somewhere under cover so I could give Helen some attention. As I moved I was acutely aware I had only four bullets left in my gun, and no spare clip.

After I had been walking a few minutes, I stopped to listen. I caught the sound of rustling leaves somewhere in my rear, but the sound stopped almost immediately as if the gunman, following me, had guessed what I was doing.

Helen was a dead weight in my arms, and I was getting pretty tired carrying her, but I had to go on. I started off again, encouraged by seeing far ahead of me a faint light from the moon coming through the thinning tops of the trees. It looked as if I were reaching a clearing.

I went on, the way becoming easier as the light became more certain, but at the same time I wondered if I could be seen, and was careful not to walk in the middle of the path.

Suddenly a gun banged somewhere behind me and a bullet zipped overhead. I hastily stepped off the path and laid Helen down behind a tree. I hauled out my gun and faced about, peering along the shadowy path. I saw nothing and heard nothing, but I knew he couldn't be very far away.

I waited a few minutes, while I rested and got my breath back. Still nothing happened. I had to get on. I was worried sick about Helen. I had to do something about her wound. I put my hand on her shoulder. She seemed to have stopped bleeding, although I couldn't be absolutely sure of this.

By now my eyes were getting used to the darkness, and I could make out an opening between the trees that went away from the path. I decided to move on, leaving the path and trying my luck in the forest.

I picked Helen up and moved off. It was impossible to tread quietly. Dry twigs broke under my feet with the noise of exploding fire-crackers. The mass of dead leaves that covered the ground rustled alarmingly. But I kept on, zigzagging where I could, conscious all the time that at any moment I was going to be shot in the back.

A hundred yards of this kind of walking brought me suddenly to the clearing. The moon lit up a small wooden shack that stood in the middle of the clearing. The sagging roof and broken window told me it was empty and derelict, but I didn't care. At least it afforded some kind of shelter for Helen if I could only reach it.

I stood at the edge of the clearing, in the darkness, and listened. Away to my right I could hear an occasional rustle of leaves and the crack of snapping twigs. The gunman was now some way away, possibly he was still following the path, under the impression that was the way I had gone. If the shack door was locked I should be in trouble, but I was relying on being able to force it open before the gunman had time to get my range.

I lifted Helen over my shoulder, got my gun in my right fist, and taking a deep breath, blundered out into the open.

The twenty-yard run seemed endless, but I finally reached the shack without being shot at. I scarcely paused in my stride, and gave the door a violent kick as I reached it. The rotten fastening flew apart and the door sagged open. I stumbled forward into darkness and the shelter of four walls.

Once in, I laid Helen on the floor, swung around and propped the door shut. I put on my torch and took a quick look around.

The shack consisted of only one large room with a window facing the way I had come. In spite of its dilapidation the walls seemed solid enough, and after looking out of the window to assure myself I wasn't going to be attacked, I bent over Helen.

She was still unconscious, but a quick examination showed she was no longer bleeding. Again I went to the window, then fairly sure I wouldn't be surprised for a minute or so I took out my pocket-knife and hurriedly cut away the blood-soaked sleeve of her dress.

She had been hit on the shoulder by about half a dozen shot. No bones had been broken, but for all that she had lost a lot of blood. There was nothing I could do about it now, and I returned to the window in time to catch a glimpse of a shadowy figure, standing half hidden behind a tree, facing the shack. I brought up my gun and took a pot-shot at him. It wasn't a bad shot, and I saw bark fly off the tree behind which he was sheltering. He returned my fire, and I took another shot at him. Then he slid away back into the forest and disappeared from sight.

I stood waiting, trying to remember exactly how many slugs I had in my gun. I thought I had two left, but I wasn't sure.

'Steve.'

I turned quickly and went to her.

'What's happening?' she said. 'Did I faint?'

'Yeah. I dropped you,' I said, kneeling at her side. 'How do you feel?'

'A bit groggy, but I'm all right. What's happening?'

'He's out there. I managed to get you into this shanty. It's not much of a place, but if we can keep him off until daylight, we should be all right.'

When I looked out again there was still no sign of him. If I had been in his place I would have circled the shack and come up behind it. There was only this one window, and the back was blind, and that's what he did.

As I checked the gun and found I had only one slug left, Helen whispered, 'I think he's around the back. I can hear something.'

I didn't leave the window. If he was coming in he'd have to come in by the door or window. He couldn't get in the back.

'Listen,' I said.

He was at the back all right. We could hear him as his feet stirred the dry leaves.

I held the gun ready and waited. Minutes ticked by. Then the backboards of the shack creaked. Feet kicked against the wall. There came a scuffling noise that made me swing around, my heart pounding.

'He's on the roof,' Helen whispered.

I went to her and knelt at her side.

'He can't get at us.'

I wished I believed that, but I didn't want to scare her. Something dropped in the darkness and landed with a flop on the floor.

'What's that?' Helen said, clutching my arm.

I snapped on my torch and swung the beam around the shack. There was nothing to see. I sent the beam up to the roof. There was no opening up there.

'It came down the chimney,' Helen whispered. 'Oh, Steve! Do you think . . .?'

I stood up and slowly walked across the room to the rusty stove. I threw the beam of light on it. For a moment or so all I could see was cobwebs and dust, then out of the dust slid a six-foot rattlesnake. As the light hit it, it gave a conclusive twist and squirmed behind a pile of rotting sacks.

I felt sweat running down my back as I stepped hurriedly away.

'Where's it gone?' Helen asked, terrified.

I joined her.

'Behind those sacks. I've only one bullet left.'

'Wait then. Don't do anything. It – it might go away.'

My first impulse was to snatch her up and bolt outside, but I knew Conn was out there, waiting for me to do just that thing. I kept the light moving, the gun pushed forward, my eyes going continually from the pile of sacks to the window. I knew Conn might take a chance and sneak up to the window, hoping I was watching the snake. I had to be ready for both of them.

'There it goes!' Helen said, and stifled a scream.

The long scaly body came sliding across the room towards us. I focused the light on it, and it shied away. I didn't dare shoot. My hand was shaking, and if I missed it, we were sunk.

'Can you hold the light?' I said between locked teeth.

She took it out of my hand.

I slipped off my coat.

'Keep the light steady if you can. I'm going to trap it in this.'

'No, Steve! Don't go near it!'

'It's okay. Take it easy.'

I stood up, shoved the gun in my hip-pocket and, holding the coat in both hands like a bullfighter playing a bull, I began a very slow creep towards the snake.

Helen was shaking so badly she could scarcely hold the light steady. The snake snapped into a coil, and reared its spade-shaped head.

Okay, I was scared. I tried to take another step, but the sight of that brute paralysed me. I stood there, holding the coat, my knees knocking together as it swayed away from me to strike. As it came forward I slashed at it with the coat, knocking its head away, then I jumped back, pulled my gun and tried to sight on its head as it again coiled itself for a spring, but my hand was unsteady. I dropped the gun with a curse and grabbed hold of the coat again.

As I did so a shadow darkened the window, and a gun banged. For a moment I wasn't sure if I were shot or not. I flung myself on my gun, grabbed it and twisted around.

'Hold it . . . Hold it!' a voice bawled.

'Don't shoot, Steve!' Helen cried. 'It's the police!'

I let go of the gun like it was red hot, and sat up slowly. Standing in the doorway, covering me with a gun, was a State Trooper.

'Get your hands up!'

I got my hands up, and looked for the snake. It was lying coiled up, its head shot off.

'Nice shooting,' I said, aware of the sound of a car starting up on the main road, but not caring. 'Brother, that was damned nice shooting!'

CHAPTER ELEVEN

I

THREE days later I drove into Los Angeles, leaving Helen in San Bernadino hospital. I hated leaving her, but she wasn't fit to be moved, and as the doctor had assured me there would be no complications, I had to get back on the job.

The San Bernadino police had asked a lot of questions, but I didn't give them the whole story. I wasn't ready yet to blow the lid off the case, and I didn't want them rushing in before I was set. I told them we had been attacked by a gunman and had taken shelter in the shack. I let them believe the snake had been in the shack when we got in there. The State Trooper told me he had heard the shooting, and had investigated. He hadn't seen the gunman, but he had heard him drive away. I had no doubt the gunman was Conn. The rattlesnake clinched it, but I kept quiet about his identity. As soon as I had got through answering questions and had taken leave of Helen, I set off for Los Angeles.

I called first at my hotel and collected my mail. Sheriff Peters had been as good as his word. He had sent me a quarter-plate photograph of the girl I now believed to be Corrine Conn. It was a good photograph and clearly showed the birthmark. I studied the photograph for some minutes, trying to convince myself the girl was Corrine, but she still looked like Susan to me.

I had to find out if a claim had been made yet. I went over to Fanshaw's office.

Maddux was with Fanshaw, and he glared at me when I came in.

'What do you want?' he demanded. 'You've no business to come in here. You've quit!'

'I was under the impression this office belonged to Fanshaw,' I said, shutting the door. 'If he wants me to go, I'll go.'

Fanshaw grinned.

'Come on in, Steve. How have you been getting on?'

'All right. How's that cluck Jackson making out?'

'Nothing yet,' Fanshaw said, while Maddux gave a snort that lifted papers off the desk.

'I've come along to offer my services,' I said. 'Of course you'll have to pay for them much more substantially than you have in the past, but I'm making the offer.'

'I wouldn't hire you if you were the last investigator left alive,' Maddux snorted. 'Now, get out!'

I turned to Fanshaw who was eyeing me expectantly.

'What's the latest news?' I asked. 'Has a claim been made?'

'Yes. Mrs. Conn arrived yesterday morning. The claim was made yesterday afternoon. She's hired Ed Ryan, the smartest shyster in the business, to handle it, and I think they've got us cold.'

'You're letting them sue, aren't you?'

'Thanks to you,' Maddux exclaimed, banging his fist on the desk, 'we haven't a case to take into court. Whatever case we might have had is washed out because you've given proof we're liable.'

'Too bad,' I said, and shook my head. 'Well, never mind. I've a proposition to put to you. If I can crack this case, what's it worth?'

Both Fanshaw and Maddux stared at me.

'What do you mean?' Maddux snapped.

'I should have thought it was plain enough. You didn't like the way I handled the case so I've quit. That makes me an independent investigator. I'm still prepared to work on it if it's made worth my while.'

'I don't want you!' Maddux roared. 'You can get out!'

'Okay, if that's the way you feel.' I got up. 'Have it your own way.'

'Wait a minute,' Fanshaw said quickly. 'Can you crack it, Steve?'

'I can tie it up in six hours.'

'Are you bluffing,' Maddux demanded, leaning across the desk, like a bull about to charge.

'No. I can crack this case if you and the nine other companies make it worth my while,' I said, smiling at him. 'There's a million involved. You've just admitted you're sunk. I can save that million if you're ready to pay me the same as any independent investigator.'

Maddux made a hurried calculation.

'Now, wait a minute,' he said, 'you don't want to be hasty about this. All right, if we hire you as an independent investigator you'll make a little money. I admit that, but how long will it last you? I'm willing to let by-gones be by-gones. You come back to us, Harmas, and I'll see you right. You have your future to think of.'

'That's pretty nice of you. Remind me to break down and sob on your shoulder when you have your diver's suit on. The little money you mentioned just now works out at ten grand. I've been hankering for a long time to set up on my own. I'm tired of taking orders from you: crummy orders at that. You either treat me as an independent investigator or I'll walk out of here and leave you holding the bag.'

Maddux started to explode, but Fanshaw chipped it.

'If you crack this case, Steve,' he said, 'I'll see you get paid one per cent and you can have your job back too if you want it. If Maddux doesn't play, I'll go direct to the old man.'

Maddux suddenly gave me a wolfish grin.

'Okay,' he said, 'get going. You're hired. I don't promise you your job back, but if you prove fraud, I'll see you get paid off.'

'One per cent?'

'Yeah – damn it! One per cent.'

'Right,' I said. 'Block Ryan off for today, and tomorrow with any luck I'll have it tied up for you.'

'If I can prove the dead girl's Corrine Conn and not Susan Gellert the thing's in the bag.'

Maddux blew out his cheeks.

'Are you still working on that angle? If that's all you've got, you're not going to crack the case.'

'That's what you think,' I said, gave Fanshaw a wink and slid out of the office.

I paid a call on Miss Faversham, Fanshaw's secretary, on my way out.

'Do you keep a personal file here?' I asked. 'I want to check up some details about our staff.'

She produced the file.

'I don't know if I should let you see this, Mr. Harmas,' she said doubtfully. 'It's confidential.'

'To set your mind at rest,' I said, 'take your own file out. You're not the one I'm interested in, and that's only because I'm a respectably married man.'

She took her own file out, blushing.

'Well, I wouldn't want everyone to know my private life,' she said archly. 'Not that I have anything to be ashamed of.'

'If you think I don't know about your five husbands,' I said, taking the rest of the file from her, 'you're making a grave tactical error.'

'Why, Mr. Harmas!' she exclaimed. 'I'll have you know I've never been married in my life.'

'There's plenty of time,' I said mysteriously. 'I'm clairvoyant.'

II

A half an hour later I pulled up outside Mossy Phillips's Camera Studio. The time was a few minutes after ten o'clock, and I noticed the iron grill, guarding the entrance to the shop was still in place.

Across the street a cop aired himself and stared at me without interest. From behind the garbage bin standing outside the camera studio a sleek black cat appeared and began to wash in the bright sunlight.

I got out of the car, crossed the sidewalk and stood in front of the shop, staring at the iron grill. I had an uneasy feeling something was wrong. In spite of slack trade, Mossy Phillips hadn't struck me as the kind of man to oversleep or take a vacation without putting a notice on the door.

Away to my right was an alley that probably led to the back of the shop. I looked over my shoulder at the cop who was now taking a little interest in me. I beckoned to him.

He came over reluctantly, swinging his night-stick, and joined me.

'Can't leave that car there all day,' he said, planting himself before me.

'I don't intend to,' I said, took out one of my cards and pushed it under his red, thick nose.

He read it carefully, his lips moving soundlessly, squinted at me, said, 'So what do I do? Drop a curtsey or fall dead?'

'I'm establishing my authority to break into this shop,' I said mildly. 'I would like you to pinch me.'

'To – what!' His thick neck thickened and his red face reddened.

'Relax, brother,' I said. 'I want you and me to go around the back of this shop and see what's happened to Phillips.'

'What should have happened to him?'

'He hasn't opened this morning. I have a business date with him. I want to make sure he hasn't overslept.'

Without waiting for him to reply I set off down the alley. He came after me slowly, not sure if I was pulling his leg or not.

A door at the back of the shop stood ajar. The woodwork by the lock was splintered.

'Take a look at this,' I said as the cop caught up with me. He eyed the broken lock, exchanged his night-stick for a gun, shoved out his jaw aggressively and pushed open the door.

I followed him down a short passage and into the studio. The place looked as if a cyclone had hit it. Thousands of photographs and all Mossy Phillips's carefully arranged files were scattered over the floor. Drawers had been wrenched open and left sagging from the steel cabinets. In the fireplace was a big pile of ashes. I went over and looked at the ashes: someone had been burning a number of photographs.

The cop said, 'What the hell did they expect to find here? The dinge never had any dough.'

'Let's look for him,' I said, and walked across the studio into the shop.

We found him lying by the counter, struck down from behind, the back of his head battered in.

'Holy smoke!' the cop said, drawing in a sharp breath. 'This would happen to me.'

I bent and touched the old Negro's hand. It was still warm.

'He hasn't been dead more than a quarter of an hour.'

'That puts me right outside the shop when it happened,' the cop said, blowing out his cheeks. 'You stick around,' and he went over to the telephone.

Twenty minutes later the Homicide Squad rolled up: with them was Police-Captain Hackett.

While the boys were going to work, Hackett drew me aside.

'What brings you here?' he asked. 'Know anything about this?'

I told him I had hoped Phillips would be able to establish that the dead girl was Corrine Conn and not Susan. I told him about the birthmark.

'It's my bet Conn guessed I'd come here and got here first,' I concluded.

Hackett was doubtful.

'Could be an ordinary sneak thief. Let's see what the boys turn up.'

We lit cigarettes and stood around for a while, watching. The boys didn't seem to be making any progress.

'Any trace yet of Joyce Sherman?' I asked.

He shook his head.

'We keep hunting, but she could be anywhere. I have an idea we're not going to find her.'

'I've heard Conn has a record. You might like to check on him. He was arrested in San Bernadino about five or six years ago, and served a four-year stretch. I'm still betting he killed Phillips.'

'I'll check on him,' Hackett said. 'We'll pick him up and find out what he was doing at the time Phillips was knocked off.'

'Do that,' I said, stubbed out my cigarette, went on, 'If you don't want me, I'll get moving. I've things to do.'

'Okay,' Hackett said. 'Don't go far. I may want you.'

I left the boys still hunting for clues and not finding them, and went out into the street. I climbed into the Buick. Already there was a large crowd grouped outside Phillips's shop. The news he had been murdered had gone down the street like a forest fire.

I drove to a drug-store at the end of the street, and called the hospital at San Bernadino. I was told Helen had passed a comfortable night, and no complications had set in. I left a message to say I hoped to see her sometime tomorrow evening.

I came out of the drug-store and sat in the car. I lit a cigarette and stared thoughtfully along the street without seeing anything, my mind busy. I was certain Mossy Phillips had been killed to stop him from talking. That meant it was almost certain the dead girl was Corrine. The whole plan to get the million would blow up once I could prove Susan Gellert was still alive. Phillips's killer knew that. From the burned photographs it looked as if Phillips had had pictures of Corrine, showing the birthmark. Well, I hadn't got them, so I had to try something else.

It suddenly occurred to me, and I don't know why it hadn't occurred to me before, that as Corrine was dark and Susan fair, if the dead girl was Corrine her hair would be dyed.

I was furious with myself for not having thought of this before when I was examining the body up at Springville. Jumping out of the car, I went back into the drug-store and called up Sheriff Peters.

He sounded glad to hear me.

'Sheriff,' I said, 'I have reason to believe that dead girl is Corrine Conn. It's simple to prove. Will you take a look at her hair and see if it has dark roots?'

'You don't think I've still got the body, son?' he asked surprised. 'Jack Conn claimed it. The cremation ceremony took place two days after the inquest.'

'They cremated her?' I bawled. 'You're sure of that?'

'Sure. There was nothing I could do about it once the coroner had brought in a verdict of death by misadventure. Conn had every right to claim the body. But I have got her fingerprints. He asked me to take them and file them as he said there'd be a claim against insurance companies, and he didn't want any trouble about identity.'

'The prints are no use to me,' I said in disgust. 'I've got those myself. Well, thanks, Sheriff. Be seeing you sometime,' and I hung up.

I opened the booth door and took in a couple of lungfuls of drug-store air while I considered my next move. If I couldn't prove Susan was Corrine, I must try to prove Corrine was Susan.

I shut myself in the booth again and called Fanshaw.

'This is Harmas,' I said, when he came on the line. 'Do you happen to know where Mrs. Conn is staying?'

'I don't, but I guess I could ask Ryan. He might tell me,' Fanshaw said, 'but he'd want to know why.'

'I guess he would. No. I can't do it that way. Think she'd be at a hotel?'

'No idea, and look, Steve, I hope you're getting somewhere; Ryan's been on to us a half an hour ago, yelling for action. He's not going to leave us alone for a day now.'

'I'm getting somewhere,' I lied. 'I'll have this tied up by tonight or bust.'

When he had got off the line I phoned police headquarters and asked to be connected with Hackett.

'Any news of Phillips's killer?' I asked.

'Could be Conn,' he told me. 'We have a witness who saw a man leave the shop by the back entrance around ten o'clock. The description fits Conn. We're hunting for him now.'

'How about Dead Lake? He may have gone back there.'

'I've been through to Sheriff Peters. He's taking some men out there right now.'

'I want to find Mrs. Conn fast. Any ideas?'

'What do you want her for?'

'Too involved to go into on the phone, but it could crack the Sherman kidnapping if I get the breaks.'

'You kidding?'

'If I can find Mrs. Conn it's my bet I'll bust the whole thing wide open, and that goes for the Sherman kidnapping too.'

'What do you want me to do?'

'Find Mrs. Conn for me. You can do it faster than I can, and it's got to be fast. Suppose you put three men on three telephones and get them to call every hotel and apartment house in town? She'll be staying somewhere close in case Ryan wants to consult her about the claim. Will you do that?'

He said he would.

'I'll call you back in an hour. And listen, Captain, don't go after her until I've talked to her.'

'Conn may be with her.'

'Not a chance.' I hung up before he could argue.

I opened the booth door and let some fresher air in, mopped my face, and shut the door again. I dialled Alan Goodyear's number.

He answered almost at once.

'Steve here,' I said. 'I'm about three minutes from your place. Want me to come up for that talk of ours?'

'I wish you would,' Goodyear said. 'You heard I quit?'

'I heard,' I said. 'I've quit too.'

'You have? When?'

'Right after you. I'll tell you about it. I'll be right round.'

'Fine.'

Goodyear had an apartment off Sunset Boulevard. It was on the top floor, and the entrance was imposing enough to satisfy a millionaire.

I was conveyed up ten floors in a smartly appointed automatic elevator.

Goodyear was waiting for me just outside his front door.

'Quite a joint you have here,' I said, as I closed the elevator doors.

'It's all right,' he said. 'Too expensive for me now. I'm pulling out at the end of the week. Where have you been, Steve? I've been trying to find you for the past three days.'

'I'm sorry. I had a bust-up with Maddux and I quit. Helen was in San Bernadino so I went down to see her. I clean forgot you wanted to talk to me until just now.'

He led me into a large sitting-room.

'Say, this really is living well,' I said, looking around. 'Jeepers! You're going to miss this.'

Goodyear shut the door.

'I guess I am. So you've quit, Steve?'

I picked a lounging chair, built to sleep in, and sat down.

'Maddux wanted to put Olley Jackson on the case, so I walked out on him,' I said.

'Well, can you imagine?' Goodyear looked shocked. 'So what are you going to do, Steve? Go to another company?'

I shook my head.

'I'm going to make myself a little dough. If I crack this case, Alan, I stand to pick up the usual terms: one per cent, and one per cent of a million is a little dough.'

He moved about the room, his hands in his pockets, a frown on his pale face.

'But can you crack it?'

'Sure,' I said, taking out a cigarette. I pasted it carefully on my lower lip. 'I've cracked it already.'

'But how?' He stood still, staring at me. 'You mean you can prove it's fraud? That the girl was murdered?'

'I guess so. I've cracked the Sherman kidnapping too.'

He came over and sat down near me.

'Well, come on! Tell me.'

'Ever since Hoffman died, I began to wonder about you, Alan,' I said seriously. 'You and I were the only two who knew I was going to see him. After I left you, you phoned Conn and told him to silence Hoffman, didn't you?'

He stared blankly at me.

'What are you talking about, Steve?'

'Aw, come off it. It won't work. You're at the back of both

the kidnapping and Corrine's murder. It stands out like a neon light. Besides, you told Maddux you met Denny accidentlly, but you didn't. Susan Gellert arranged for you to meet him. That's a minor point, but it helped me to make up my mind about you. You were always turning up unexpectedly, asking for information. I told you about the short-wave radio set, and nearly got myself killed because you passed on the information. It was you who said Susan accidentally put her print on the policy. It wasn't her print. It was her sister's.'

'I hope you're joking, Steve,' Goodyear said, looking at me, his eyes angry. 'You're either joking or you're crazy.'

'I also happen to know how the girl on the island was murdered. You know, Alan, you might have got away with if it you had pulled one fraud, but pulling two was a little too much. You could have got away with Joyce Sherman's kidnapping, but the other one was just a little too fancy.'

'I guess I don't want to listen to any more of this,' Goodyear said quietly.

'Suit yourself,' I said, getting to my feet. 'I thought you might appreciate me coming here and telling you. I haven't told anyone else. Well, I'll be running along. Don't think you're going to get away with this, Alan. You can't. It's come apart at the seams.'

He didn't say anything, and I walked to the door. As I opened it, he said, 'Wait.'

I turned and looked at him.

'Okay, the set-up's a little out of hand,' he said evenly, 'but it still could be fixed. There's a million and a half in it. That's a lot of money. You're talking about one per cent. I'd give you a third.'

'What's the matter with a half?' I said, wandering back to my chair.

'A third. There's you, the girl and me to be taken care of.'

'How about Conn?'

'We'd have to get rid of him. He's too dangerous. I have an idea as soon as the money's paid out, he'll try to get rid of me. He's too fond of murder.'

'You're forgetting Rice,' I said. 'Isn't he in the pay off?'

'I don't reckon to bother with him. The police have got him tied up so he can't make a move. He daren't do anything. As soon as the claim is settled, the girl and I and you – if you'll come in with us – plan to skip. Rice can't give us away without giving himself away.'

'You have the half-million from the Sherman kid-napping?'

He nodded.

'I've got that all right. Ryan will force the claim through in a week's time at the latest. I'm offering you a third of the total to keep your mouth shut, Steve.'

'Is that all you want me to do?'

He hesitated.

'And help me get rid of Conn. None of us is safe so long as he's alive.'

'He was seen leaving Phillips's shop. The police are search-ing for him.'

'They' won't find him. He's been on the run before.'

'Know where he is?'

Goodyear nodded.

I reached forward and stubbed out my cigarette.

'You must be nuts, Alan,' I said. 'What put the idea into your head? You were doing all right as an agent. What made you pull a fast one like this?'

'Who said I was doing all right?' he returned. 'I've been spending twice as much as I earn. I'm up to my eyes in debt. I had to do something. A million and a half seemed too good to be true, but I didn't know about Conn then. I don't stand for murder.'

I looked steadily at him.

'Don't you? It was you who killed Corrine Conn.'

His face went white.

'That's a damned lie! Conn killed her,' he said, leaning for-ward to glare at me.

'Conn was at Springville collecting his mail when she died. You killed her, Alan.'

He pulled himself together with an effort.

'Oakley was watching the island all the time,' he said. 'He didn't see me come or go. I'd like to know how you'd prove I killed her.'

'I had no idea until I looked at your confidential file this morning,' I said. 'But as soon as I learned you had served in the special services, submarines, during the war, I saw how you did it, I bet I'll find a frog-man's suit hidden somewhere along the lakeside. It would be easy for you to swim under water to the island, kill the girl and swim back again without being seen. Nice idea, Alan, but you forgot your personal file.'

He stood up, his face now granite hard.

'Are you coming in with me?' he asked. 'I'll give you a third of the take when the claim succeeds.'

'It's not going to succeed,' I said. 'You're washed up, Alan. If you hadn't killed that girl I'd have given you time to get clear, but you'll have to take what's coming to you now. I'm sorry. You must have been nuts to have done such a thing, but you've done it, and you'll have to pay for it.'

He walked over to the desk that stood in the window recess, pulled open a drawer and took out a gun. He turned and pointed it at me.

'I'm going through with this,' he said, his voice hoarse and unsteady. 'I have half a million. If I can't get the rest I'll go without it. You and nobody else will stop me!'

'Don't play the fool,' I said. 'Killing me won't get you anywhere. You can't fire off a gun in a joint like this without starting trouble. You'd never get away.' I stood up. 'I'm going to the police, Alan. You have twenty minutes. It's up to you to do what you think best. Whatever you do, you're sunk.'

I turned my back on him and walked to the door.

'Stop!' he said, and I heard the safety-catch click back.

I looked over my shoulder at him.

'So long, Alan, and good luck,' I said, opened the door and stepped into the passage.

He just stood there, his face going to pieces, the gun sinking in his hand.

'So long, Steve,' he said.

I closed the door and walked to the elevator. I had been friends with him ever since he had joined the company. I liked him. I felt pretty bad as I opened the door of the elevator.

The sudden sound of a shot was as if someone had kicked me under the heart.

III

It wasn't until five o'clock the same evening that the final pieces of the jig-saw fell into place. It would have taken even longer if I hadn't had the inspiration to go along and talk to Myra Lantis, Perry Rice's girl friend.

As soon as I had told her the set-up, she lost her nerve and talked.

She convinced me she had had nothing to do with Joyce Sherman's kidnapping nor with the plot to soak the insurance companies for a million and a half dollars.

When she realized that Rice would be facing a murder charge, she became co-operative, answered my questions and allowed me to look over Joyce Sherman's bedroom again.

With the information I got from her, I felt ready to break the case. I drove over to police headquarters and spent a half an hour explaining the set-up to Hackett. After I had convinced him I phoned Maddux and asked him to come over.

He was over in under ten minutes, and came marching into Hackett's office where Hackett and I were waiting. While I had been talking to Goodyear, Hackett's men had found Corrine Conn. She was staying at an apartment house on Canyon Drive.

'You owe me fifteen grand,' I said as Maddux planted himself in front of me. 'I've bust the case, and we're ready to make a pinch.'

'Is that on the level?' Maddux demanded. 'If it is, I won't mind shelling out. Ryan has been driving me crazy all day.'

'Shall we go?' Hackett asked impatiently.

'Right,' I said. 'We're calling on Mrs. Conn,' I told Maddux.

'The three of us, and a couple of dicks in case she turns rough.'

'Gimme the story,' Maddux said, following us out of the office. 'How did you bust it?'

'By disobeying orders,' I said, grinning at him. 'If I'd stayed away from Springville as you told me to this case would never have been cracked. That's why it's going to cost you fifteen grand.'

'Don't be so damned smug,' Maddux snarled. 'Who's behind this racket?'

I stood aside to let him get into the car first. I got in front with one of the dicks.

'Goodyear,' I said.

The long, stunned silence lasted until we reached the apartment house on Canyon Drive.

We pulled up a few yards from the house, got out and walked quickly up the steps. The landlady, already warned, had the front door open for us.

'Second floor. The door facing the stairs,' she whispered, her eyes popping with excitement. 'She hasn't been out all day.'

Hackett told one of the dicks to stay in the hall, and the other to go around and watch the back of the building.

He looked at me.

'You handle it,' he said. 'I'll take over when you're ready.'

'I wish to hell I knew what this was all about,' Maddux snorted. 'Why couldn't you have told me before we left headquarters?'

'No time, besides I wanted it to be properly stage managed. You want value for your money, don't you?'

I went up the stairs first, paused outside the door, rapped and waited.

After a moment's delay the door opened and a woman who looked like Corrine Conn stood looking up at me, her blue eyes startled.

'Why, Mr. Harmas . . .'

'Hello,' I said, 'can we come in?'

'Well, I – I rather you didn't. The place's untidy. Who are these gentlemen?'

'Reading from left to right: Mr. Maddux, head of the Claim Department, National Fidelity, and Police-Captain Hackett,' I said. 'We want to talk to you about this claim you're making.'

She shook her head.

'I'm sorry, but you must talk to Mr. Ryan. He's my attorney.'

'We've already talked to him. He's withdrawn from your case, Mrs. Conn, or should I call you Miss Gellert?' I said, and walked forward, riding her back into a big, well-furnished sitting-room.

Hackett and Maddux followed me in, and Maddux closed the door.

She backed away, her face going white.

We all sat down.

'I'll make this short,' I said. 'It's only fair to you for me to tell you how much I know. Mr. Maddux isn't in the picture yet, so you'll bear with me if I go into details.'

'I don't want to listen,' she said. 'I want my attorney.'

'I don't think your attorney would be able to help you even if he wanted to mix himself up in this, which he doesn't,' I said. 'Goodyear's dead. Before he died, he talked.'

She froze into white-faced, motionless silence.

'The story starts five years ago in San Bernadino,' I said, lighting a cigarette, and making myself comfortable. 'You and your sister, Corrine, were working in a night club. Corrine was married to Jack Conn, a small-time heist man. By chance, Corrine met Perry Rice who was desperately trying to find a girl whom he could build into a star. Corrine had had dramatic training before she turned stripper. She convinced Rice she was the girl he was looking for. She had talent and looks and the right figure, but her background damned her. She was married to a crook who had already served ten years in jail. She was a stripper in a cheap night club. She herself had been in jail for indecent performances. Not the kind of background for a famous movie star, and a background the Press were certain to ferret out. But Rice wanted a star. If he went back to the studios without one, he was sunk. He was up to his ears in debt,

214

and he knew he would get tossed out if he didn't produce a girl to justify his salary. He decided to give Corrine a new name, new looks and a new background. The first move was to get rid of Conn. Corrine was sick of him anyway, and she was easily persuaded to tip the police where they could find Conn, but she didn't know you and he were having an affair, and she unwisely told you what she had done.' I paused to ask, 'How are you liking this? It gets better as it goes on.'

She didn't say anything, but sat motionless, staring at me, her face as hard as stone.

'You tried to warn Conn,' I continued, 'but you were too late. Conn was arrested, and Corrine ducked out of sight after you had threatened to murder her. She started a rumour she had gone to Buenos Aires. Instead, she put herself into Rice's hands, and he set to work to change her identity and appearance. He did a fine job of it. He had her hair dyed red. He took her to a plastic surgeon who gave her a pair of almond-shaped eyes. Two very simple alterations, but which effectively changed her appearance. Then he took her to Hollywood with the story he had found her working as a receptionist at a hotel in San Bernadino. And that's how Joyce Sherman was born.'

'You mean Joyce Sherman is Corrine Conn?' Maddux said, his eyes popping.

'Yeah, although you should use the past tense. Joyce Sherman or Corrine Conn is dead. That's her sister, Susan,' I went on, nodding to the white-faced girl who glared at me. 'At the start of this business Helen warned me to watch out for a conjuring trick. She was right, and you'll see why in a moment. Rice hadn't anticipated that Corrine would be such a sensational success, and when she became one of the highest paid stars almost overnight, he decided to make sure of his discovery. He persuaded her that Conn would never find her, and she could forget he existed.

'He pointed out the conveniences of marriage, and married her. For the next two years all went well for them both. But Corrine wasn't made of the right stuff to cope with riches. She began to drink. Rice did his best to stop it, but he didn't succeed. Soon she was drinking to excess, and it began to affect her work. Then Conn, released from jail, appeared on the scene.' I pointed a finger at Susan Gellert. 'He and you hooked up together. Both of you were determined to fix Corrine for giving Conn away to the police. You had a vague suspicion that Joyce Sherman was your sister, and Conn went to Hollywood to investigate. He recognized Corrine. He found out she had married Rice: a perfect set-up for blackmail. He called on Rice, and demanded money to keep quiet. But by this time Rice had other ideas about Corrine. He could see the writing on the wall. He knew she would be washed up in movies within a few months. More often than not she was hopelessly drunk. She couldn't learn her parts. At times she went to the studio scarcely able to walk. Howard Lloyd was just waiting for her contract to run out to get rid of her.

'At this time an insurance salesman was trying to persuade Rice to take out an accident policy. Rice had an idea this salesman could be bought: the salesman was Alan Goodyear.

'Rice told Conn what he was planning to do. He asked Conn if he'd help him. Conn liked the idea Rice put up to him. Once the plan had succeeded it would be simple to wipe Rice out, and grab the whole of the proceeds for himself. He agreed to drop his blackmail and work with Rice.

'Luck was on Rice's side. Goodyear was in debt, and living above his income. He listened to Rice's proposition, saw the possibilities and agreed to go in with them.

'The plan was an ambitious one. It was also a convenient one. If it succeeded it made for the four of you a million and half dollars. It got rid of Corrine. It freed Rice to marry Myra Lantis. It settled accounts so far as you and Conn were concerned.

'The idea was this: you should take out ten accident policies at the lowest possible premium and with a coverage for a million. Goodyear was to sell Corrine a policy that covered her against kidnapping in the sum of half a million. As soon as the policies were accepted, Corrine was to be kidnapped by Conn and taken to the island. Her hair was to be bleached, and she was to be murdered in such a way that a claim could be made against the insurance companies. You would then dye your hair dark and appear as Corrine and collect the money.

'Goodyear started the ball rolling by selling Corrine the policy that'd cover her against kidnapping. He was a first-rate salesman, and hadn't any difficulty in persuading Corrine to take out the policy. Then he persuaded the boss of my company to accept the accident insurance policy in your name, waiting until friend Maddux was out of the way, before swinging it.

'As it was to be Corrine who was to die in your place, it was necessary to guard against any of the companies raising doubt about indentification. The fool-proof check was to get Corrine's finger-prints on all the policies. This Rice undertook to do. He waited until Corrine was drunk, and then put her print on the policies. But Corrine wasn't as drunk as Rice imagined. She got a glimpse of the policies. She began to wonder what was going on. She hired Hoffman to watch Rice. Hoffman spotted him with you and Conn. Corrine realized you three were up to something. She told Hoffman to hunt for the policies, which he tracked down in Denny's office. Corrine and Hoffman went to the office, and she discovered you had taken out accident policies worth a million.

'As she was leaving the building Mason, the janitor, surprised her, and recognized her as the famous movie star, Joyce Sherman. She had to shut his mouth. She was drunk and scared. She knifed him.

'In the meantime Goodyear was keeping track of me. He learned I was going to see you, and he warned you to be ready for me. You got a mirror from Rice with Corrine's prints on it and planted it for me to take. You knew I would want to see your twin sister and you were ready for me.

'Conn had rented an island sometime before the policies were taken out. You – wearing a wig and a coat of suntan – used to go to the island every so often to establish the fact that Corrine lived there.

'While my wife and I were spending the night at Willington,

you drove to Dead Lake, put on your wig and suntan and were there to meet us when we arrived the next day – as Corrine.' I paused to light another cigarette, asked her, 'How am I making out?'

'You can't prove any of it,' she said viciously. 'You're lying!'

'I can prove it,' I assured her. 'But let's get back to Corrine. After she had killed Mason she decided to get out. She was sure Rice was going to get rid of her, and her one thought was flight. Then Hoffman started to blackmail her. The night she fixed to see him and pay him happened to be the night Rice and you had arranged to kidnap her. Hoffman saw the kidnapping, which was handled by Conn. He decided to hold his tongue until he could see if he could get anything out of the kidnapping himself.

'Conn and you took Corrine to the island and kept her there until you had collected the ransom. She was actually on the island when we called on you. It was she who screamed and not a paroquet as you said. I've checked that you never had a paroquet. Later you disguised yourself as Corrine and made it your business to meet me and tell me you were off to Buenos Aires. It was necessary for you to be well out of the way when the supposed body of Susan was discovered.

'It was left to Goodyear to murder Corrine. He had served as a frog-man during the war, and all he had to do was to put on his underwater apparatus and swim under the water to the island, murder Corrine and swim back without Oakley being any the wiser.

'The set-up looked perfect, but there was one snag. Corrine had a distinctive birthmark. Two people knew about it: Mrs. Paisley whom you didn't bother about as she wouldn't stand up in court as a witness, and Mossy Phillips who had taken photographs of Corrine for the strip act. When I went to Springville to check your sister's identity. I was seen by Conn who had a shot at wringing my neck, but luckily for me he was interrupted. He had another shot at wiping my wife and me out after we had talked to Mrs. Paisley, but again he was interrupted. He murdered Phillips and destroyed the set of photos Phillips had in his file that showed Corrine's birthmark. Goodyear tried to bribe me to throw in with him, and when I turned him down, he committed suicide.

'There was yet another person who knew about the birthmark: Myra Lantis. She is ready to go into the box and swear to it. I've been over Joyce Sherman's room, and have collected specimens of her finger-prints: the same prints that are on the policy. It now remains to prove your hair is dyed to clinch the case, and that won't be difficult to do.' I glanced at Hackett. 'I guess this is where you take over, Captain. Go ahead and make a meal of it.'

Before Hackett could get to his feet, a door behind Susan jerked open and Conn slid into the room: a .38 in his hand.

'Make a move, and I'll blast the lot of you!' he said viciously.

Susan got up. Her eyes glittered as she looked at me. None of us moved.

'Get their guns,' Conn said to her.

She went over to Maddux.

'Get up!' she said.

Looking dazed and a little shaken, Maddux got to his feet. She ran her hands over him, then, satisfied he wasn't carrying a gun, she turned to me.

'And you!'

I let her frisk me, watching Conn out of the corner of my eye. His gun pointed between Hackett and myself. Susan found my gun in its shoulder holster. She fished it out, standing behind me.

Then she crossed over to Hackett. He watched her come, his hat in his lap, his hand under the hat, his face expressionless.

He stood up when she told him to. Then as she reached to open his coat, he smashed my gun out of her hand, took a quick step sideways, putting her between himself and Conn, dropped his hat, and showed the .45 he had been holding.

The two guns boomed simultaneously.

Hackett's heavy slug smashed into Conn's forehead, throwing him across the room. He crashed against the wall and slid to the floor.

Hit by Conn's bullet, Susan bent forward as if she had a hinge in her back, her hands clutching her stomach. She gave a long, sobbing sigh as she sagged down on her knees, then she spread out at Hackett's feet.

IV

An hour later Maddux and I walked into Fanshaw's office where he was impatiently waiting for us. One look at Maddux's beaming face told him the case was cracked.

'Yeah,' Maddux said, rubbing his hands, 'we beat them to it. Boy! Was I pleased to see that little bitch get hers. She's given me sleepless nights for weeks. I knew right from the start that was a phoney policy, and I knew that rat Goodyear was no good.' He sat down at the desk and beamed around expansively. 'That's the best job we've done yet, Harmas.'

I looked over at Fanshaw who was grinning behind his hand.

'But I don't work for this company. I've quit – remember?' I said. 'And I'm damn well going to take some individual credit. You owe me fifteen grand, and if you don't keep your word, I'll go to the old man.'

Maddux selected a cigar, lit it and blew smoke at me.

'You'll get your money if that's the way you want it,' he said, 'but if you know what's good for you, you'll forget you resignation and continue to work with me. There's a big future here for you, Steve. I'm going to get you a hundred dollar raise. How do you like that?'

I sat down.

'I want my fifteen grand!'

'Do you really mean you don't want to work with me any more?' Maddux asked, his eyes popping.

'I might think about it after I've had a month's vacation,' I said, weakening. 'That's what I'm going to have: a month's glorious vacation, throwing money around like a drunken marine. Helen and I and a fistful of dough. What could be nicer? Give me your cheque and make it snappy. I want to get to San Bernadino tonight and break the news to Helen.'

'I tell you what I'll do. I'll give you five grand, six weeks' holiday with pay, your job back and a hundred buck raise,' Maddux said coaxingly. 'Can't be fairer than that.'

'You're a crook,' I said heatedly, 'but if you'll give me a chit to the cashier for five grand right now, and promise me free educational policies for my children to the value of another five grand, I'll take you.'

'Done!' he said, and leaning across the desk, offered me his hand.

I watched him write out the chit to the cashier. Then as he handed it to me, he said, 'Hey, wait a minute! What's that again about educational policies? You haven't any children.'

'But I will have,' I said, easing myself out of my chair. 'Up to now I couldn't afford children. Now is the time to perpetuate the Harmas tradition. I'm going to raise a smart boy who'll keep me in my old age.'

As I reached the door, Fanshaw said with a wide grin. 'Watch out you don't have twins.'

LAY HER AMONG THE LILIES BY JAMES HADLEY CHASE

It was odd that a healthy young heiress like Janet Crosby should die of heart failure. Odder still, that on the day she died she sent a note and $500 to Vic Malloy, private investigator, asking him to trace the person who was blackmailing her sister.

Intrigued by the note, Malloy tried to see Maureen Crosby but only got as far as her nurse – a curvaceous blonde with an engaging bedside manner. Next he tried to see Janet's personal maid, but found that somebody else had reached her first and made sure that she wouldn't talk to anyone – ever again . . .

552 09551 6   35p

I WOULD RATHER STAY POOR

BY JAMES HADLEY CHASE

Like most bank managers, Dave Calvin had acquired an irresistible charm that he could switch on whenever he felt the necessity. Underneath it he was cold, calculating, brutal – a perfect murderer . . .

For years he waited – watching an endless stream of money pass through his hands – knowing that a risk was only worth taking if the reward was justified. And a three hundred thousand dollar payroll was justification enough – even for murder . . .

552 09491 9   35p

THE PATRIOT BY CHARLES DURBIN

The exiled king of the international Mafia – killer, sadist, heroin millionaire. But first of all, an American . . .

THE PATRIOT

A raw, revealing 'insider's' novel about the methods, murders and men of the mob . . . 'Spares nothing in the way of violent brutality and sexual depravity . . . Destined to be a highly popular success!'

552 09486 2   50p

THE DESTROYER: DEATH THERAPY

BY RICHARD SAPIR AND WARREN MURPHY

The security systems of America had failed. Every government agent was being systematically wiped-out by an organization whose aim it was to control the most powerful nation in the world – and then sell it to the highest bidder! There was only one man who could save Congress from becoming the sole item in the biggest auction of all-time – one man who could not be tortured physically or mentally – REMO WILLIAMS, the man who called himself THE DESTROYER . . .

552 09595 8   35p

A SELECTED LIST OF CRIME STORIES FOR YOUR READING PLEASURE